PUPPY
PURSUIT

Other Kate Killoy Mysteries

Fashion Goes to the Dogs

Other Books by Peggy Gaffney

The Crafty Samoyed Knits

The Crafty Labrador Retriever Knits

The Crafty Golden Retriever Knits

The Crafty Bernese Mt. Dog Knits

The Crafty Newfoundland Knits

The Crafty Welsh Corgi Knits

The Crafty Poodle Knits

The Crafty Cat Knits

The Crafty Llama and Alpaca Knits

Knit a Kitten, Purl a Puppy

Do It Yourself Publishing Nonfiction in Your Spare Time

PUPPY
PURSUIT

a kate killoy mystery

Suspense for the Dog Lover

PEGGY GAFFNEY

KANINE BOOKS

Kanine Books is a division of Kanine Knits Books & Patterns
877 Marion Rd, Cheshire, CT 06410

This book is a work of fiction. Names, characters, places, and incidents are products of the author's imagination or are use fictitiously. Any resemblance to actual events or locales or persons, living or dead, is entirely coincidental.

http://www.peggygaffney.com/

Cover design by the author

ISBN   978-0-9964531-2-7

ACKNOWLEDGMENTS

I would like to express my thanks to friends in the world of Samoyed dogs who have made my life full and happy, especially three very special ladies: Lisa Peterson, Cheri Hollenback and Judy Mears, who helped me gather the material for this story, encouraged me throughout its writing and made it possible for me to bring the wonderful Dillon into my life.

I also want to thank my editor Kate Richards and Wizards in Publishing for their help in creating the best book possible for my readers.

I want to thank my son Sean for his support and encouragement, as well as my fellow members of Sisters in Crime and The Connecticut Authors and Publishers Association.

DEDICATION

For Dillon and all my Samoyeds down through the years.

CHAPTER ONE

"Kate, I don't understand how you manage to live in the twenty-first century and travel all over the country showing dogs when you've never flown." Sal Mondigliani, Kate Killoy's kennel manager, settled deeper into the second of the two kitchen chairs as yet another fear-of-flying lecture descended.

"We drove. Gramps, Dad, and I took a bunch of dogs, loaded up the van, and hit the road. That way we got to see the country."

"Wait, are you afraid of flying?"

Bam. Right on schedule. "Sal, I'm not having this discussion. In the last twenty-four hours, every Killoy possessed of a Y chromosome has weighed in on the subject. Seamus has been inundating me with statistical information on car vs. plane crashes, Tim with the aeronautical data on lift forces, Tom on time vs. cost ratios, and Will has forwarded me forty

-one online articles about overcoming the fear of flying. In spite of—or maybe because of—this, I will admit I'm not anticipating flying to Denver alone this afternoon."

"Wait, didn't Foyle say he had to be in Denver tomorrow? Aren't you two going together?"

"Apparently not." The hurt she struggled to keep out of her voice crept in. Harry Foyle, her fiancé, and she had planned weeks ago to take this flight together. They'd been so busy lately, a day spent together, even flying, would be a treat. He'd hold her hands so she wouldn't be afraid. He'd referred to himself as her security blanket. It only took a ten-world text message this morning to yank the blanket away.

"I still think I should drive to Texas to get the puppy, rather than bringing it back on the plane," Kate proposed once more in her struggle to stay on terra firma.

"You don't have time. You have to be back by Tuesday to cover for my vacation. You do remember I'm taking Pete, Sarah, and little Emma to spend the rest of the month at the Cape."

"How'd you manage to score a beach rental on Cape Cod this time of the year?"

"We'll be using a friend's cabin while he's in California for his first grandchild's birth. Imagine, three weeks on the beach, avoiding the August heat. It's perfect. Plus, I'll get to spend some time with my new granddaughter."

He's right, Kate thought. *I'm a selfish bitch, and I've got a T-*

shirt to prove it, and all because I don't want to strap on metal wings, defy gravity, and take to the sky. She would not only be depriving Sal of his first time off in a year, but also of spending time with his son, back from serving in Afghanistan, his daughter-in-law, a brand-new mother, and their three-month-old daughter. This would be their perfect vacation together.

Kate finished packing, stepping carefully around a block of guilt the size of an elephant he'd dropped right in the middle of her kitchen.

"Kate," he began, "being afraid to fly is nothing to be ashamed of if you've never done it before. I was scared stiff the first time I flew."

"Where were you going?"

"Nam."

The guilt in the room took on blue whale proportions. Leaning her whole weight on the suitcase, Kate managed to zip it closed and roll it over to the space by the door already holding her oversized purse, ticket, and Kindle.

She sighed at the thick belt left on the counter and began shoving it through the loops in her jeans.

"What's the problem with the belt?"

"It's Gram's. I love her dearly, but there are times when she wants to wrap me in cotton wool. She insists she never traveled without a money belt filled with cash and I shouldn't either. She doesn't realize those little pieces of plastic do a fine job. But, if I don't use this, she'll know."

"Well, I tend to agree with her. Maybe it's my generation, but a little extra cash can't hurt."

Fastening the buckle, Kate reached for her phone. She picked it up to check for texts again and then set it down. The purple funk dogging her since the last text grew. Kate switched on the kettle to heat water for tea. The thought of lunch didn't hold any appeal, but Seamus had bugged her to eat because airlines no longer fed you and to take the airsickness pills he'd left on the counter. Kate was going down for the third time, drowning in brotherly love. The tea helped her down the pills. A minute later, she jumped up and grabbed an apple off the counter, dropping it into her purse. Circling the table again, she slid into the other chair.

"Okay, I know you, girl. You're nervous as a cat. What's going on? As much fun as it is to tease you, this jumpiness is not a fear of flying."

Kate stared out the window overlooking the dogs in the exercise yard, avoiding the question. She noticed each of her sweet Samoyeds had claimed his preferred shady spot and slept. Dillon, on the other hand, slept at her feet. She hated going to a strange place without him. Sal's stare finally got to her. She needed him to laugh at her suspicions and tell her she was overreacting.

"Last night, Harry called to talk, as he does every night." Kate smiled at the thought. "Before he hung up, he sang 'I Want to Hold Your Hand,' telling me he'd hold it all the way to Denver. I slept like a log, reassured he would be there. However, at ten thirty this morning, I got a text saying, *Flying out of Boston. See you when I get back. H."*

"So Harry won't be meeting you at the airport? A text you say, not a call," he mused, a frown settling on his face. "He didn't tell you why? It doesn't sound like him."

"I tried calling him when I got it, but the call went to voice mail." Kate pulled out her phone and opened the text, holding it for Sal to see. "He signed the message, H."

"Yeah? I would imagine Harry wouldn't bother writing out his name."

"Except, since February, he's signed all his texts with F for fiancé." She flipped though earlier texts, showing him. "Of course, something could have come up, or he could have gotten an emergency job, but it doesn't feel right. Sal, do you have Sadie's number?"

Kate had never spoken to the wondrous Sadie, the other love of Harry's life. She remembered being jealous hearing about her the first time. She'd then discovered this amazing woman who managed Harry's business was a former FBI agent and a brilliant cyber-tech plus a grandmother five times over. "Something feels off to me. For my peace of mind, I need to know I'm wrong, just bummed and frightened of flying."

Sal pushed up the brim of his Red Sox cap and stared at her. Reaching into his back pocket, he pulled out his phone, took hers, and loaded the number. Dropping it back where she'd left it, he then reeled in his lanky timeworn six foot four inch frame and pressed dial.

"Sadie, how are you doing? It's Sal. I'm trying to get ahold of our boy, and it keeps going to voice mail. Do you know where he is? Right, they are. I must have forgotten. Yeah. No, I'll wait and talk to him later. Thanks, Sadie." He slowly shoved the phone back into his pocket and pulled out his keys. Then he stood.

"It's time to hit the road, girl. You have a puppy to get."

Dillon stood, licking Kate's face as she hugged her new-daddy dog. Telling him she'd be bringing his kid back, Kate let him out into the yard with the others. Silently, she followed Sal out to the van. The quiet between them lasted until the turn onto I-84, heading toward Hartford.

"She'd talked to him at eight this morning, and he was all packed. He couldn't wait to head out to meet you. She thought he might have turned off his phone so you two could have some alone time without interruption. She said she'd let him know I want him when he calls in. But she told me since you two have so little time together, not to bother you. Kate, why do you suppose he would change his mind between eight this morning and—when did you get the text?"

"Ten thirty but I'm not sure he did change his mind." Kate stared through the windshield, her head playing with the possibilities that kept bouncing up, like a game of whack-a-mole. This early in the day, the descent through the tunnel and the climb up the flyover through Hartford moved easily. They transitioned onto I-91, heading north. Her brain tried to play hide-and-seek with possible answers but came up with zilch. "I'm worried he's in trouble. What I want to do is drive to Boston and find him, but I haven't any idea where he is. So I've got no choice but to get on a plane and fly to Denver. Sal, it'll be late here when my flight gets in so I won't call you, but if I don't hear from him, I'm calling Sadie tomorrow. At least she'll know who he's meeting and where he's staying. Maybe she can call those places and see if he's there." Kate glanced again at her phone then, sighing, jammed it into her pocket. She turned toward Sal. "I'll be staying with Joyce Marks tonight, and traveling with her and Cathy Harrison, whose numbers are by the phone. We're scheduled to hit the road by five tomorrow morning for the drive to Lubbock. I'll call and let you know if I find anything out."

"Why are these women driving you all the way to Texas on this puppy pursuit?"

"Well, Joyce is thinking about using Dillon at stud with her new champion bitch who is a half-sister of Katja, the puppies' dam. She and Cathy, who bred Katja, already planned to go see the litter, so when she heard I'd be coming out to choose my stud puppy, she suggested I join them. Since it's a direct flight between Hartford and Denver and I can take the puppy in the cabin as carry-on luggage, it worked out well for me. This way, I won't have to change planes with the puppy on the way home, and it will be a much shorter flight."

"How do you know these people?"

"Joyce is an old friend who began showing and breeding a few years after Gramps did. Cathy wanted to see what her next generation is producing. Both Joyce and Cathy are judges, as well as breeders, and have judged at the Samoyed National Specialty Show. Since this is Lily Peters' first litter, she wanted them to use their expertise to critique the puppies. Lily's bringing the litter up to Lubbock, a couple of hours north of her home, to make the drive shorter."

"Shorter? What is it, about ten hours?"

"Yeah. Since Cathy and I have never met, she's flying down to Denver from Idaho, so we can visit on the drive. She's got a judging assignment to get to next week so she won't have any spare time. Joyce works for the Denver sheriff's office. She's got to be at work on Monday and, of course, I've got to be back here. This way, we won't waste time. We'll drive down tomorrow then spend all day Saturday with the puppies. On Sunday, we'll drive back to Denver with my stud puppy, and Cathy can make her connection home Sunday night. Then, on Monday, I'll get my direct flight back with the puppy. Except for the flying, this trip is a 'piece o' cake.'"

The highway had begun to get congested with people heading north out of Hartford, homeward bound after the early shift. Kate rejoiced when they pulled onto the connecting road heading directly to Bradley International Airport. As the terminal came into view, her stomach clenched. Ready or not, she was going. With only a carry-on, she didn't need to check luggage. Hopping out at the Southwest entrance, she waved good-bye to Sal and strode quickly through the automatic doors before she could change her mind.

Tim, her younger brother and the bigger pain in the butt

of the twins, had made her put up with a gallon of mockery in exchange for guiding her through the steps to get her boarding pass online and to double check the return reservation said she'd be traveling with a puppy in the cabin. Not to be standing in the long line at the ticket counter made it worth the grief.

Turning left, Kate followed the signs to security. Automatically, she reached with her hand for the dog always at her side. She felt naked without Dillon. She put her carry-on suitcase on the conveyor then, taking one of the blue plastic bins, loaded it with shoes, phone, keys, and her purse. Kate watched it slide out of sight into the x-ray machine. Next, she stepped into the little cubicle for the TSA combination x-ray and MRI.

"You need to stand with your feet on the marks on the floor, miss, and extend your arms over your head."

Kate heard a beep and assumed she was done, but, no, the noise indicated she had set off their alarm, labeling her a threat to the country. Except for her watch, earrings, and the ring on her finger, she had nothing metal on her. The agent waved a wand over her, front and back then between the legs and over each arm. Her watch set it off. Kate had forgotten the steel band. She'd gotten it after countless generations of Shannon Samoyeds had dined on a menu of leather bands. In the end, the TSA agent decided Kate Killoy was not a danger to her country, only stupid. Trying to hide her embarrassment, Kate slipped on her shoes and asked directions to the gate.

The flight had seemed an ideal time to be alone with Harry, the man she'd fallen in love with at first sight. Their unusual engagement remained a work in progress. However, this trip felt more like the first level of Hell, with flunking her first-ever security check qualifying as Limbo. Ten minutes later, the trip reached the second level when the announcement came that the flight, scheduled to take off in twenty minutes, remained in Baltimore, causing a delay of at least an hour.

Kate's stomach, rapidly twisted itself into a knot. If she had another hour, she should eat. Her feet instinctively took her to Dunkin' Donuts. Five minutes later, she emerged with toasted croissants, marmalade, and cocoa—a Killoy tranquilizer. She settled into a seat near the gate's check-in area, satisfying her now-real hunger and prepared to wait. The fact tons of people, even small children, happily waited to do the thing she most dreaded impressed her. Standing to discard the empty cup in the bin by the check-in desk, she noticed the boarding attendant, somewhat tight-lipped, being harangued by an irate would-be passenger.

"Make the page, lady," the man snarled.

Kate move to her seat as the attendant picked up the microphone and announced, "Would passenger Harry Foyle please report to the Southwest check-in at gate eight?"

Kate froze. Harry? Here? This guy didn't appear to be one of Harry's corporate clients. Turning back toward the desk as he made the woman repeat the call, she got an insane idea.

Pulling the phone from her pocket and waving it as though unable to get a signal, she snapped two photos of the man's face. Then, casually, she returned to her seat. Before she could talk herself out of it, she sent the photos to Sadie, telling her Harry hadn't made it. She asked whether she knew the man, since he was angry and hunting Harry.

A minute later, Kate's pocket buzzed. Reaching for the phone, she read the text from Sadie.

Don't worry about Harry. Continue your trip. Stay away from this man. He's dangerous.

CHAPTER TWO

Earlier, in Boston, Harry had set the phone on the kitchen counter, sipped his coffee, and smiled. He hadn't been able to stop smiling since he got up this morning. He needed to get Kate alone, even on a crowded airplane.

They'd had so little time together since their rather unconventional engagement that had almost cost them their lives. He had planned to use this trip to get her to set the date for the wedding. If he'd had his way, it would have been yesterday. He hated every minute away from her. They talked for hours on the phone, but he wanted her to sleep in his arms each night. He wanted to wake each morning to those enchanting sky-blue eyes staring up at him, her rumpled golden curls resting on his shoulder, and her sweet body spread across his. He'd need a cold shower if his mind kept wandering down this track. He'd started to go upstairs and finish packing when his phone rang. Caller ID showed Rufus.

"Rufus, what's up? I'll be leaving for the airport soon."

"I've got a couple of favors to ask. I know you like to

work when you fly, but Jordy's coming home from summer school, and I need you to pick him up and bring him with you. I know he likes to talk a lot, but tell him to read and he'll stop."

Harry closed his eyes and groaned inwardly. Just what he needed, a twelve-year-old chaperon. The urge to say no overwhelmed him, but he wouldn't. Rufus' family had given him a home when, in fourth grade, he'd been sent across the country to Caltech to be part of a program for young math geniuses. They'd kept those years from being a lonely nightmare. So much for the chance to snuggle Kate for hours as they flew west.

"I'm flying out of Hartford, nonstop. It leaves at two fifteen. He needs to be ready soon."

"Why aren't you flying out of Logan?"

Harry ignored the question. "What's the other favor you need?"

"Remember Stubbs, the professor you blew away at age ten?"

"Yeah, he sends me a Christmas card every year." Harry smiled, remembering the day he'd won the stuffy professor over."

"Well he's in trouble, as in go-to-jail-for-a-long-time trouble."

"What did he do?"

"He didn't do anything. He's being set up by someone.

They're accusing him of embezzlement."

"Stubbs! Never."

"Someone's stealing millions and making it appear like the old man's doing it. He needs you to figure out what's going on and stop it."

Harry sat on a stool and asked, "Isn't he somewhere in Texas now?"

"Lubbock. He's head of the math department at Texas Poly."

Harry's smile returned. A certain sweet blond dog nut was headed to Lubbock. This might not be all bad. "Okay. I'll see you tonight."

He disconnected the call and, after setting his phone down, finished his coffee, rinsed the cup and then headed upstairs. He'd better get going if he needed to pick up Jordy and still be on time for their plane. He wondered how Kate would react to his bringing a friend along. Catching his refection in the mirror as he reached to close the closet door, he wondered also how Kate would react to this cowboy style when she was used to his sartorial splendor of vintage double-breasted suits. He'd wanted her to see his playful side, but she had a tight schedule to get Dillon's puppy and be back in time for Sal's vacation. And now, damn it, this had become a work trip.

If he hadn't been standing still musing, he would have missed the click. Swiveling on the balls of his feet, he moved silently to the top of the stairs in time to see the front door being eased open by a silencer attached to a Sig Sauer nine millimeter. His focus drew back to include the man behind the gun who could easily have stepped off the pages of GQ magazine. The well-built, white haired figure in the charcoal-gray slim designer suit, lavender shirt, silk tie, and Italian shoes would have been at home in any Fortune 500 board room, not housebreaking.

Harry cursed silently. He had a plane to catch. He didn't have time for this. He reached for his phone then remembered he'd left it on the kitchen counter and he'd already locked his guns in the den safe because he couldn't take them on the plane. Stepping silently back into his room, automatically avoiding all the squeaky boards, he picked up his bag, opened the door to the balcony and then latching it, pulled it shut as he eased over the railing and onto the porch roof. His worked his way to a spot where his condo met his neighbor's. Staying out of view, Harry continued across the next two condo roofs and then dropped his bag to the ground and followed, rolling to cushion his drop.

He ran to the garage where he and two other residents rented space, slid into his SUV, tossing his bag in the rear, and backed out onto the side street. Turning the corner, he drove past his home. The man, appearing relaxed as though visiting, had opened the door and climbed into a light-blue Chrysler. Harry kept moving, turning in the direction of the MIT campus to pick up Jordy.

Last February, he'd seen a man who had most wanted him dead end up behind bars. This could be a backlash from what happened to him, but he doubted it. He had no idea what this guy wanted. However, if someone here wanted him dead, he needed to "get out of Dodge" as well as find a way to keep Jordy and Kate safe. As he sped west on the Mass Pike, Harry used Jordy's phone to call Sadie and fill her in. She'd take care of contacting the police about the break-in. If this guy could get past his phone's security and had checked his calendar, he'd know about the trip to Denver this weekend, but not where or with whom he'd be staying or out of which airport he was flying. Harry warned her he'd be without a phone until he picked one up. For now, she had Jordy's number. Handing the phone back to Jordy, he concentrated on getting to Bradley fast. Then he must come up with a plan to keep Kate safe. Jordy, for once, sat silent.

Though time seemed to drag, they actually made it to the airport before Kate and settled into seats in the back of the waiting area. Jordy disappeared to buy food while Harry kept an eye out for Kate. By the time he spotted her, he'd decided she'd be safer on her own in spite of her fear of flying. But he had an idea. Slumped in his seat, he watched her fidget, nerves showing in every move. When they announced the flight's delay, she headed for Duncan Donuts, returning with classic Killoy comfort food—croissants and cocoa.

He leaned toward Jordy and put forth his plan. Hopefully, it would work.

"What?" Jordy's shocked reaction to learning of his engagement had him now staring hard at Kate. "She's hot. Maybe you're smarter than I thought."

As he finished going over the details with Jordy, Harry heard his name paged. He glanced from the attendant to the man making the demand. It wasn't the gunman. This guy could pass for an accountant on welfare. In his sixties, the guy had dark hair and eyes and wore a suit as wrinkled as though he'd slept in it for a week. He saw Kate freeze when she heard his name then take out her phone a minute later, wave it around to get a signal and, if he guessed right, photograph the man creating the fuss. She then sat and seemed to be sending the photo to someone. The response came a few seconds later and had her heading for the ladies room. Whatever it had been, she looked upset.

Harry turned his focus back to the man still bugging the attendant. The stranger held a newspaper clipping with a photo up to compare to the face of every guy who went by. After a few minutes, he saw Kate return and survey the room. Her gaze first slid past him, and then it whipped back in his direction. He thought she'd spotted him but, luckily, the announcement came for the first group to board. He told Jordy to get behind her while he moved into line a few people back.

The old guy still compared faces against his newspaper photo, but Mr. GQ from Boston was a no-show. Stepping onto the plane, he saw Jordy grab a middle seat with a grandmotherly type on one side and Kate next to him on the aisle. She struggled to lift her bag into the overhead, and Harry couldn't resist giving her bag a shove in as he pushed by to slip into the aisle seat in the next row across from them, pulling down his hat to hide his face.

The plane filled quickly. As the flight attendant started to close the door, the old man pushed his way onto the flight. The attendant pointed out the only available seat in the rear. He started down the aisle but stopped when he spotted Kate. She'd ducked her head, but not in time. He smiled, holding the newspaper photo near her face. Then, at the impatient urging of the attendant, he headed to the back of the plane. Harry saw Jordy tell Kate she'd been spotted and watched as the color drained from her face. What the hell was going on? How had their romantic trip turned into such a nightmare?

CHAPTER THREE

"Good try, but he made you." The small voice beside her had glibly asserted.

"What…"

"He spotted you. Nice dog, by the way."

Kate asked confused, "What dog?"

"The one sitting next to you in the newspaper clipping he had. You are Kate Killoy." She stared at him. "I read upside down. The article talked about some fashion show with dogs. I'd say it took place in New York because the *Times* doesn't cover society stories from other places in the country. It showed you, some stuffy guy, and a beautiful white dog. What's his name?"

"The guy or the dog?"

Jordy snorted, "The dog."

"His name is Dillon. He's a Samoyed."

"He's a white fuzzball."

"He is. He's a white fuzzball with teeth. And attitude!"

"So don't mess with him."

"Damn straight." Kate heard a snort from the cowboy. She turned and her breath caught as she spotted a dimple and cockeyed smile that disappeared almost instantly beneath the hat. It seemed her favorite Boston cyber detective had shed his normal dapper style for a John Wayne disguise and that emphasized his broad shoulders and narrow hips. She stared at the face below the Stetson. Green eyes peered over his reflective sunglasses as he flashed his familiar half smile. I loved his smile, Kate thought, and she grinned back. Dillon may not be with her, but she had her human guard dog on duty.

"Hi, I'm Jordy Blackburn." Her young seatmate pulled Kate's attention from her happy thoughts.

"Kate Killoy, as you already know. Nice to meet you, Jordy." She returned the greeting and shook the small hand. As he bent to rummage around in his knapsack and retrieve his creature comforts: a kindle, ear-buds, a tablet, and computer pen that doubled as a ballpoint, plus a small pad, Kate glanced back over her shoulder again. She couldn't see the man who spotted her. Cowboy Harry's body, stretching out as much as the cramped quarters allowed, seemed to be relaxed in sleep.

The stewardess began her safety talk, and suddenly Kate's mind was wrenched back to the fact she sat in a metal box about to be thrown into the air. Kate grabbed the plastic card from the seat pocket, needing to learn how she could keep from dying. The panic, which began as a buzzing in her ears and shivering, and the shaking in her hands now spread throughout her body. Kate, fighting the terror, needed to breathe.

Harry watched her panic set in and wanted to jump up, ditch the seat belt, and reach out to hold her. Seeing this girl who could face down killers without turning a hair, suffering fear beyond her control killed him and he couldn't do a damn thing. Then he saw a small hand snatch the card from her and jam it back into the seat pocket and grab her hands. "Kate," he heard Jordy shout. "Everyone is terrified of flying the first time but the odds are eleven million to one against crashing so don't sweat it. Any bookmaker would tell you, those are great odds and I should know because I'm at the top of my class in statistics."

"Statistics?" Harry watched as she was diverted by the comment, her head jerking in the boy's direction.

"I'm working toward a degree in Quantitative Analysis, but this summer I've been taking extra classes in number theory and logic. My goal is to work in cryptography and cyber-security," Jordy told her.

Harry, his attention focused on Kate's every breath, heard her voice change as Jordy distracted her from panic. For a minute, he felt a raging jealousy for his twelve-year-old wingman. Then, as he saw her lean back and her shoulders ease, he grudgingly thanked him.

"Umm…where do you go to school?" Kate asked.

"MIT." His voice hinted that he expected her to contradict him.

"How old are you?" She asked, now curious about her seatmate.

"I'm—umm twenty-one."

Kate stared for a second then broke out laughing. "So you're telling me MIT exists in a world with a base eight numerical system?"

Jordy flushed.

Kate smiled to herself as memories came flooding in. Both her dad and granddad had played this game with her growing up. In fact, discussions about the what-ifs in a non-decimal world became one of their favorite ways to pass the time on long drives to dog shows. Meeting a kid who used base eight to freak people out while on her first plane flight felt like a blessing. "I assume, since you attend a school that uses base ten numbering, your age of twelve will keep you in graduate school and out of the workforce for a while." She grinned at him.

He returned her smile. "I like you, Kate Killoy. Do you date younger men?"

Kate grinned as a snort came from the other side of the aisle. "Sorry, but I think my fiancé would object to me dating other young men."

Jordy shrugged but then smiled so she knew his heart remained undented.

Changing the subject, Kate asked him about his studies. The detailed outline of Jordy's courses followed; which he liked or didn't, his favorite professors and what he did for fun filled the time between take-off and climbing through the clouds.

"I still need to take a bunch of classes in psychology and social engineering. You see, hacking is not all math. It's about finding the anomaly in a system. It's fun because you are constantly trying to find the answer to 'what if?' If I'm going to work at stopping hackers, then I need to understand the psychology behind those who do it."

Kate smiled as she listened to Jordy going off on his obviously favorite topic. What followed was a forty-minute lecture on the scientific approaches to stopping the criminal hacker by being a better hacker than the criminal. She wondered if Harry had been like this at approximately the same age. Knowing him now, she doubted he ever had been that confident.

Kate yawned, her ears popping. Jordy must have heard her since he turned his attention to his Kindle. Kate settled deeper into the cushions of her seat and relaxed. This steel box may be thousands of feet up in the air, but Jordy's chatter had transported her back to the comforting familiarity of the many arguments that flew daily across the breakfast table as she grew up. The boy's resolute tone and the quiet certainty of his statements plus his "I dare you to contradict me" gaze showed an attitude that had ruled every discussion in the Killoy household. Their house rule had been, arguments could go on as long as necessary so long as the math worked. If you got called on your proposed hypothesis, you'd better be able to defend it.

Harry had spent his youth as such a prodigy at Caltech. Her geeky young friend's prattle helped her understand the man she loved a little more. The lesson in what it might have been like for Harry caused her to relax much more than all his statistical data on the lack of crashes.

She glanced over her shoulder at the cowboy's green eyes still peeking over the sunglasses at her. Kate stared into those eyes and smiled.

Harry caught Kate's gaze, which came at him like a heat-seeking missile, stealing his breath and knocking him sideways. Her smile could bring him to his knees. Not moving, he locked eyes with her, staring until her eyes shifted and her smile turned into a scowl. Harry knew, at once, who was approaching down the aisle.

Kate flinched as the man Sadie had told her to avoid approached her row and stopped. He bowed slightly in her direction, his face splitting into a caricature of a grin. "Miss Kate Killoy?" He waved the clipping in front of her face. "It is you. I'm so glad I found you, Miss Kate Killoy. I need you to help me to find your friend, Mr. Harry Foyle. It's very important. I need to speak with him. He must help me."

Before Kate could answer, karma interceded in the form of the *fasten your seat belt* sign lighting up and the stewardess chasing him back to his seat.

"Please, it's very important." His words floated back to her.

Kate peered across the aisle at Harry. She knew he had heard every word the man said. Confused, she watched the old man disappear into his seat. Sadie had marked the man dangerous, but Kate classified him desperate. He seemed to be crying out for help. She began to ask herself if he searched for Harry as a lifeline rather than threatening to do him harm. Sadie hadn't said what danger he posed. Kate needed to ask her. Then the question arose of how he had known Harry would be at Bradley to take this flight. Harry lived in Boston. He flew out of Logan. No, this couldn't be classed as a simple case of being pursued by a so-called dangerous man.

She turned back to ask Harry about the man and noticed worry cross his face. He turned his gaze, avoiding her. The Stetson began to bug her. She wanted to talk to him, but if she couldn't, she at least wanted at least to see his face. Kate squelched the urge to lean across the aisle and grab her fiancé's now annoying hat. Screw it. Sadie had said to stay away from the dangerous man, so she resolved to deal with Harry later. All she needed now was figure out how to escape her stalker.

Trying to find a distraction, she got out her laptop where the designs for the February show took form. She plugged away for a few minutes refining the designs, but work that usually enthralled her didn't seem to be working as a distraction here, nor the photos and descriptions of the puppies Lily had sent. She closed the laptop lid and gazed out the window. Denver's Airport seemed to hang like fairy lights halfway into the sky. They were about to arrive. Racking her brain, she tried to figure the best way to get through the airport and at the same time avoid this guy who wanted to use her to get to Harry. Kate hadn't come up with much of a plan except using speed. She should be able to outrun a man of his age and condition.

She lifted her oversized purse, slid the laptop inside, and slipped the strap over her head, to settle it behind her back. However, she still had to worry about bag in the overhead compartment.

Jordy had been watching her. As they got ready to land, he leaned in to whisper in her ear. "Don't worry about your suitcase. I'll bring it to you in the terminal. Where are your friends meeting you?"

Kate remembered she'd explained to the boy about her trip. He thought traveling across country and then driving ten hours to get a puppy rocked. She told him where she would be met.

"Good," he said. "When they open the plane's door, go."

Breathing slowly to force her body to relax, she only jumped a little as the wheels touched the runway and the plane braked for approach to the terminal.

"Please remain in your seats with your seat belts in place until the plane has come to a complete stop." The flight attendant made the announcement with a scowl aimed toward someone at the back of the plane. The crawl to the gate seemed to take forever.

When the lights came up, the plane's door opened and the overhead bin doors popped up. Harry half dragged her into the aisle, his size blocking the other passengers. He turned her toward the door. "Go. I've got your back." he said into her ear over the noise of the passengers and, with a kiss on her cheek, he shoved her forward as Jordy cried out, "Run, Kate. Run!"

CHAPTER FOUR

Kate ran. Luckily, the sight of someone running at top speed through an airport was viewed as perfectly normal, as someone trying to make a connection to another flight. She burst out onto a vast, seemingly endless concourse at top speed. Years of running around the show ring and teaching agility paid off. Here, though, the obstacles became people to be avoided. Silently cursing the distinction of being the largest airport in the country, she tried to gauge the distance to the escalators that would take her to the terminal shuttles and increased her speed. Reaching the turn to go down a level, Kate glanced back at the passengers moving into the concourse. Her pursuer shoved past Harry and Jordy, running as though determined to catch her. She descended the moving staircase with her feet barely touching the steps and, in a final burst of speed, managed to catch one of the shuttles starting to close its doors. Kate dove inside, grateful to be without a suitcase. She gripped the pole as the cars slid toward a tunnel heading for the main terminal. Glancing back, she spotted her stalker arrive at the top of the escalator. She was surprised he was so close behind her.

When the train stopped at the terminal, Kate realized she would have to do almost the same run in reverse. As soon as the door opened, she fled up the escalator only to be slowed when the buzz of an incoming text distracted her. *Missed connecting with you at loading. Going around again. Red SUV. We'll meet U in 15.*

She noticed upon reaching her level that the terminal rose like a series of white tents in the desert. Unfortunately, similar to the desert, it had few places to hide out for fifteen minutes. Spotting a boutique kiosk, Kate positioned herself where both the exit door and the escalators could be seen but where she hid out of sight.

A quick glance at the contents of the kiosk told her she'd struck gold. Kate found a cowgirl hat and denim jacket to act as disguise. She chatted with the pretty, dark-haired girl with a killer sense of humor as her credit card processed, telling her she wanted to hide from an older guy who had gotten too friendly on the plane. The girl, named Rita, nodded. "I understand, honey. You hide here as long as you need." Kate quickly put on the hat, tilting the brim so it shaded her face, and slipped the jacket over her bright-red shirt. She finished the disguise by looping a turquoise scarf around her neck so nothing of the red silk showed.

Kate spotted Harry reach the top of the escalator, and noticed when he spotted the frustrated man looking around. The man was watching Jordy move from booth to booth, seeming to browse and finally heading toward one with Western clothing. Appearing to give up on the boy being a way to find his quarry, her stalker finally moved toward the exit. She looked about for Harry but didn't see him.

Kate checked her watch. Six minutes to go. She inched around the booth to stay out of the man's line of sight then spotted Jordy moving in her direction, pulling her suitcase. He stopped for a few seconds at each of the other kiosks before coming up to stand next to her checking out the belts.

"When is your ride coming and describe it?" he asked, seeming to be interested in the booth. Pulling out her phone, she held it so he could read the text. He nodded and headed for the loading zone. Kate held her breath, hoping the man wouldn't grab him because he'd been sitting by her. Jordy showed nerves of steel by strolling right by him without even a blink.

Kate studied her stalker by the exit. His eyes swept the area of the kiosks as she watched but slid right by her. At last, he turned all his attention toward the loading zone. A hand landed on her shoulder. Kate's scream, muffled when a mouth covered hers in a kiss, faded as she curled her toes.

Harry lifted his head and smiled down at her, dimples flashing. She put a hand on his chest to steady herself. Finally getting control of her breathing, she hissed, "Harry, what the hell is going on? It's like February all over again."

"Kate, I'm so sorry you've been pulled into this."

"This what? You disappear, leaving me worried, then

pop up in disguise. Are you hiding from this joker? I haven't a clue what's happening except I seem to be training for the Olympics in the Denver Airport. And, what's in the world is Jordy's role in this cat and mouse game?"

"Actually, this guy isn't the one I'm hiding from. I don't know who he is. Jordy's father is my best friend. Hopefully, your friend Joyce can drop us off at his place in her town. Rufus called this morning, asking me to bring Jordy home. And to answer your other question, no, this guy isn't the reason for my disguise. Someone broke into my condo as I left and tried to kill me. I arranged Jordy's ticket so he can go back with you and the puppy on Monday because I don't know how long this new problem will keep me here or rather in Lubbock."

"Lubbock? Harry—"

"There's the signal." He threw his arm around her shoulder and pulled down the brim of her Stetson so her vision included her knees and shoes. Dragging his case, they dashed for the exit, passing right by her stalker.

Kate saw Jordy already in the van, chatting over the seat with Cathy. Harry tossed in his bag and then climbed into the middle seat, pulling Kate up onto his lap. A shout, "Miss Kate Killoy, I must talk to you," came from close by the open van door, making Kate yell "Drive." The automatic door slid shut as Joyce pulled out into traffic. Kate turned back to see a very frustrated stalker staring after them from the curb.

"Way to go," Jordy bounced in his seat. "Wait 'til I tell the guys about this getaway."

"We aim to please." Joyce's cool reply sailed back to them as she maneuvered through the heavy traffic. "I take it, Kate, the man holding you in his lap is your fiancé?"

"Harry Foyle, I want you to meet Joyce Marks."

Harry smiled at her. "Thanks for giving us a lift, Joyce. Did Jordy explain?"

"Your stop is on the way, so I'm happy to drop you two off. It's nice to meet you at last. Lily told us something about you. She met you last February at the Westerland show."

"Yes, I got to see her pretty bitch finish her championship," Harry told her.

"Among other things equally exciting, I heard."

"The week tended to be a little crowded with non-dog show activities." He chuckled as his arms tightened around Kate and his head rested against her shoulder. "And I take it," he said as his smile turned its focus on the pretty woman with the auburn hair in the passenger seat, "you are Cathy Harrison."

"It seems Lily's assessment of danger following wherever you go is right on the mark." Cathy turned with a grin. "This getaway, as Jordy put it, became a perfect introduction."

"For myself," Kate said as she lifted her head to stare hard at Harry, "I could have used a bit less excitement, thank you very much."

"Honestly, Kate, I have no idea who the man following you on the plane was. I've never seen him before," Harry said frowning. "The reason for my disguise happened this morning. As I packed the last stuff in my suitcase, I heard someone working the lock on my front door. I peered over the banister and saw a SIG Sauer with a silencer pushing through the door. Since I had to pick up Jordy and catch a plane, I decided to leave by way of my bedroom window and roof. After getting Jordy, I headed for the airport. Since I'd left my phone downstairs with the gunman, I decided to go without it and couldn't call you. By the way, I picked up a new one at the airport." He pulled Kate's phone from the pocket of her jacket and entered his new number.

"So do you know him? Did you see him on the plane? I knew someone else had sent me the text about your not coming."

"A text from my phone? How could you tell it didn't come from me?"

"The signature was H." She grinned.

He smiled back, tightening his arms around her.

"You have no idea what your shooter wanted? Did you get a good enough look at him to recognize him again?" Joyce put on her blinker and moved into the right lane for the exit.

"I suspect killing me might have been near the top of his

list, but why is beyond me. And, yes, I would easily recognize him if I saw him again. I didn't spot him at the airport. I suspected he'd think I flew out of Logan. But, to be on the safe side, I decided to avoid my usual business suit. I knew he wouldn't focus on a cowboy with a kid."

"So the guy with the gun wasn't the man on the plane?" Kate said.

"No. A silver-haired fox, dressed as though he stepped off the cover of GQ, broke into my place. Definitely not your stalker who had all the sartorial style of an accountant on a three-day binge."

"Good thing you kept your hat down, hotshot," Kate told him. "My stalker had the *Times* photo of us, taken following the fashion show last February. It's how he nailed me. He wants to talk to you desperately, but Sadie says he's dangerous."

They exited the freeway, and Jody leaned forward, directing Joyce to a street lined with big, older homes. They slowed before a building surrounded by a high wall. At the wrought iron gate between brick columns blocking their entrance, Joyce stopped and rolled down her window. Jordy stuck his head out her window, waving at the security camera. "Hey, Raymond, it's me and Harry." The gate slowly opened, and Joyce drove up the driveway circling a beautiful, but, unfortunately, dry, fountain. The front door opened as the van stopped. Grabbing his backpack, Jordy yelled his thanks to Joyce and pushed past Kate and Harry, hopping out and running into the arms of an older man in a wheelchair.

Harry's hands circled Kate's waist and lifted her gently to the ground. He grabbed his bag and joined her, his arms once again around her. Kate gazed up into those green eyes she loved. She had five thousand questions to ask him, but they must wait. He leaned his head against hers. "We're heading to Lubbock tomorrow early to help out an old friend, so if I don't meet you on the road, I'll see you there." Harry lifted her hat and kissed her hard. Then, the Stetson properly seated back on her head, he leaned in to talk to Joyce. "Kate's stalker may have made your license number so be very careful." Stroking Kate's cheek, he said, "I'll need more information in order to figure if these two men are working together. I haven't a clue what the hell is going on, so please keep your head down and find a puppy like Dillon to bring home." He lifted her back into the SUV and, thanking Joyce, waved as the door closed. The SUV headed back down the driveway and stood watching 'til they cleared the gate.

"Well, Kate, you've managed an interesting way to inject dose of excitement into a normally calm day, but it's late and we need sleep. Tomorrow, we're going to be on the road by five. You haven't eaten. Will eggs and toast do?" Joyce asked.

"Sounds wonderful." Kate leaned back, startled it could still be Thursday. When they got to Joyce's house, Kate ate and then crawled into bed, her tired body still operating on Eastern Time.

Harry set his bag down and eyed the men sitting across the table. Ewen Blackburn had aged considerably since his stroke. Being confined to a wheelchair must be frustrating for someone'd who'd been so active, but he seemed to be managing. Rufus had his laptop open next to a stack of printouts covered with code. Raising an eyebrow, Harry asked, "Does this have something to do with Professor Stubbs' problems?

"Maybe." Rufus frowned and closed the laptop. "To give you the fifty cent tour of the mess, I'll start with the fact Stubbs headed the math department at Texas Poly for the past eight years. He's a year away from retirement and, up until three weeks ago, his life was right on track. Everything derailed when Baxter, Kline and Baxter did an audit and found three million dollars missing from the college retirement fund. A committee from the math department oversees investing the monies and Stubbs, as head of that committee, was blamed."

Harry pulled out a chair, poured himself a cup of coffee, and, since he wasn't going to be getting much sleep tonight, started asking questions. "Who discovered the discrepancies?"

"The auditors found them during their annual audit. It seems the recorded deposits to the account did not match the actual deposits."

"How did they connect it to Stubbs?"

"His committee supervised the transfer of funds, but Stubbs' computer made the actual transfers. What his group recorded as being added to the account differed by millions. Baxter, Kline and Baxter, the brokerage handling the actual investments, has accused him of embezzlement and reported the shortfall to the SEC. When I talked to the professor two days ago, he insisted it was all a big mistake. Being Stubbs, he's convinced an error in their math will turn up as soon as they check their numbers. He's doing nothing to save himself. He hasn't even hired a lawyer."

Ewen snorted. "Lyndon's spent his whole life with his head in the clouds. If he doesn't watch out, he'll be using the walls of his cell as a blackboard for the next thirty years."

"Okay." Harry eyed the five inch stack of paper in the middle of the table. "What's this?"

"Those are the records of the actual transactions for the last six months. Prior to then, everything seemed normal."

Harry stared at the pile of papers. "Please tell me you have the information in some form other than as a printout."

"I was lucky to get this. A former student of mine, Kevin Connelly, is working on his PhD in the department. He printed out a copy for me when he prepared the one to be sent to the SEC."

"It sounds like what is needed is a good forensic accountant. I can recommend one."

"We need more than a bean counter," Rufus growled. "The situation requires someone who Stubbs respects to convince him to defend himself and help him find out what's going on. It needs Harry Foyle. You're the only one he respects enough to convince him to fight back. Whoever is doing this is not going to be easy to catch and stop. They have laid a crystal clear trail to Stubbs. No one else on the committee, in the brokerage house or working at the university is being considered. It's a perfect frame-up."

"No frame-up is perfect."

"I know you're not with the bureau anymore, but whoever is doing this must have had practice before taking on something this size. Your former colleagues at the FBI might have some suggestions."

"Possibly. However, it's late, and I need sleep if we're leaving for Texas in the morning. Heading out about five?"

"Yeah, and Jordy is coming with us. My Aunt Emily called yesterday to inform us she is visiting a specialist in Denver for a series of test tomorrow and Monday. She'll be staying here. Since she's incapable of being in the same room with Jordy for two minutes without criticizing him, we're taking him with us."

"Getting on the road early will help, since it's a long drive. I'd like to be there by supper time. I'll see you in the morning." Harry rose, picked up his bag, and headed up the stairs. He wanted to be in Lubbock in time to see Kate before he got swallowed up in this mess.

Rufus had followed him upstairs, but stopped him outside the door to the guest room he used when he visited, keeping his voice down. "What's this Jordy tells me about you being engaged? Is he kidding?"

"Not in the least. You'll get a chance to meet her. She'll be in Lubbock, too." Avoiding any more questions, he stepped inside and closed the door.

CHAPTER FIVE

Kate thought she wouldn't sleep with unanswered questions doing gerbil circuits in her brain, but even those gerbils must have been pooped because the next thing she knew, Joyce called them to get up.

Kate had a lightning-fast shower, said hi to Joyce's Samoyed bitches, giving them all hugs, and then loaded her bag back into the car as Joyce kenneled most of the Sams who'd been exercised and given a snack, until her kennel help arrived. Lexi, Joyce's latest Samoyed champion bitch, would travel with them, to be company for the puppy on the trip back.

First stop, the local Starbucks. Cathy took their orders and headed inside while Joyce walked Lexi. The cool bite of early morning made Kate glad for the jacket she'd bought yesterday. Pulling her phone out of her pocket, she decided it would be too early to call Harry, but Sal would be up and cleaning the kennel runs. She hit speed dial three, and he answered on the first ring.

"Kate, are you okay? Someone broke into Harry's condo yesterday. Though Sadie said the police found no prints, they did find Harry's phone with the text you got."

"Sal, I'm fine, and so is Harry, but that's another story. Did Sadie get a name for the guy whose photo I sent her yesterday? Apparently, it's someone who is trying to find Harry. Neither of us have a clue about him. Sadie called him dangerous but, from what I saw, he seemed more sad and desperate. I need to find out what he wants with Harry."

"No way," he yelled. "You stay as far away from him as you can. You hear, Kate?"

"Okay. What's his name?"

"He's Anton Soucek, who's apparently managed to get out of a Texas prison, which was closing, on a provisional parole. The authorities are keeping track of him and, if he does anything, he'll be back inside. You say he's not the one who broke into Harry's place? Where is my boy, anyway?"

"He actually ended up sort of traveling with me, but in disguise, and he brought a boy named Jordy with him. Joyce dropped the two of them off at Jordy's home. Harry says Jordy's father is his best friend."

"I haven't seen Jordy in a year," Sal said with a chuckle. "How's the little genius? He probably loved working as an undercover agent on his way home. The kid wants to grow up to be Harry."

"Actually, it came in handy since this Soucek followed us onto the plane, Harry and I escaped, but he may have made Joyce's license number, so I'm keeping an eye out." Kate spotted Cathy coming toward the car. "I've got to go, Sal. I'll call later." She gave him Harry's new number then stowed the phone in her pocket and went to relieve Cathy of some of the food. Once everyone settled, she checked to be sure they didn't have a tail then sat back and relaxed. "Ah," Kate sighed. "Tea and croissants is manna from Heaven."

Harry's day started early with the smell of coffee and bacon bringing him from a half-asleep state to full consciousness by the time he reached the bottom of the stairs. He followed his nose to the kitchen and spotted Antonia bustling around putting plates with stacks of pancakes in the middle of the table. She greeted Harry with a hug.

Harry remembers she had come to work for the Blackburns when he was fifteen. In fact, Stubbs got her the job. Mrs. Blackburn had been suffering from cancer, and hiring Antonia had eased her last years of life. Antonia married Raymond Duarte two years later, and they'd both been with the family ever since. Raymond served as gardener, chauffeur, and general man-of-all-trades in this household.

Antonia and Raymond now lived in the guest house, and Ewen, Rufus, and Jordy live here. Harry topped her list of favorite guests. He sat while she loaded his plate and then set it before him along with a cup of hot, fresh coffee. Harry re-

laxed. So long as pancakes existed in this world, life couldn't
be all bad.

CHAPTER SIX

Happily full of good food, the trio headed south out of Denver at sunrise, before traffic got too heavy. As Rufus drove, Harry settled with the stack of printouts and a pen, prepared to spend the next ten hours plowing through computer code, hunting the proverbial needle in the haystack. Jordy settled into the backseat to play a game he'd found online, but, when it got quiet, Harry glanced back and saw him sound asleep.

They'd been driving for a little over an hour when Rufus began yawning. "There's a place I usually stop when I'm headed south. Jordy will need another breakfast. He has his favorites on their menu. Stopping will give your eyes a rest from staring at code, as well. Have you found anything yet?"

"Actually, I've hit on a really familiar section. I remember writing something exactly like this the winter before I went back to Boston for an assignment in Stubbs' master's degree seminar on coding."

"Really, you still remember it after all these years?"

"The assignment dealt with an early approach to hacking. The five of us in the seminar had a ball. I got an A. In fact, what I learned in the seminar helped me when I worked for the bureau."

"I'm hungry." Jordy's sleepy voice came from the backseat. "We're going to stop, aren't we?" He struggled to sit up, rubbing his eyes.

Rufus laughed. "You haven't missed our second breakfast. We'll be there in about five minutes."

He grinned at Harry. "I swear he's got an automatic alarm that goes off whenever we're near this place."

A few minutes later, Rufus pulled into the parking lot of a large log cabin, explaining that it was half restaurant, half gift shop. He pointed out it has everything a traveler or souvenir hunter would need. They follow Jordy toward the front door.

The two men followed their bird dog as Jordy sniffed out all his favorite foods, following a familiar path through the aisles of clothing into the restaurant. Harry and Rufus catch up with Jordy inside the restaurant entrance. While they waited to be seated, Rufus caught his breath.

"I think I'm in love. She's beautiful." Rufus muttered, not taking his eyes from an area the other side of the restaurant.

Harry's gaze turned in the same direction and his own

heart jumped. Kate and her friends Joyce and Cathy sat at a table in the corner. Turning back to Rufus, Harry felt a jealous urge to step in and block the table from his sight. Kate belonged to him and, best friend or not, Rufus had better keep his distance. A whoop broke through his jealousy as Jordy rushed across the room toward the women's table.

Jordy waved and ran on ahead, calling to Joyce and Kate and giving Cathy a hug. The two men, who had stopped in the restaurant doorway to remove their hats and sunglasses, watched his retreating back. Harry glanced at Rufus only to see a deer-in-the-headlights expression on his face. Harry used his long legs to reach the table where the women sat first and, much to Kate's apparent surprise, he kissed her, staking his claim in front of everyone.

"And a very good morning to you, too." Kate grinned. "I could get used to this."

"I'm counting on it," he said, pulling out the chair next to hers.

When he glanced toward his friend, he saw Rufus had stopped next to Cathy, who chatted with his son. Rufus cleared his throat and asked Jordy to introduce him. Rufus shook Cathy's hand, holding it maybe a little longer than normal. There was a blush on Cathy's cheeks and a sparkle in her eyes

The men pulled a nearby table over and slid chairs in to make a cozy grouping with Jordy handling the introduction of Rufus to Kate and Joyce.

"Killoy," Rufus asked, "as in Claire Killoy? She is…?"

"My mother," Kate finished his sentence.

"I didn't know she had a daughter."

"Not surprising." Kate answered but didn't go on to explain. Rufus paused for a few seconds before turning to watch to the interplay between his son and the lovely Cathy Harrison.

Kate's attention moved between father and son, brow furrowed in concern. Harry leaned in to whisper the answer to her unasked question. "Rufus is a widower."

Nodding, Kate relaxed.

Harry settled his hand on her shoulder, lifting the scarf she'd bought. "This is a perfect color with your eyes."

She smiled and told him how she'd lost her heart to the lovely scarf, colored in gently shifting shades from midnight through turquoise to the faint blue of a misty sky, on the way in. How a small pewter antelope pin in a jewelry display at the cashier's station had caught her attention. "This place is set up perfectly to waylay tourists with temptations stop for food. I knew as soon as I stepped inside I wouldn't be leaving empty-handed."

He smiled. "Good for you. It's good to see you get something for yourself. You are always thinking of things for other people. You have excellent taste, for a dog nut." She swatted his hand but a grin brightened her face, and he smiled back at her.

Talk waned as the food arrived and enticing smells focused their attention on the massive breakfast. By the time Kate finished her second cup of tea, Rufus had happily begun sharing stories of when Harry arrived at Caltech at the ripe old age of nine, and Rufus found he'd been stuck with the responsibility of showing him the ropes. "He was so quiet and formal, he stuck out like a sore thumb in Southern California."

Harry grabbed his hat to cover his face.

"The first weeks, he sat in class, taking a few notes and staring around. Then came the now famous day in Lyndon Stubbs' good-sized lecture class. We'd spent most of the hour reasoning out a hypothesis and had finally reached a solution. Stubbs gave the next assignment to be done for the following class when Harry raised his hand. Now, so far, nine-year-old Harry got sort of lost in the crowd, so short his feet didn't even reach the floor. Not giving up, he climbed up onto his chair and called the professor an idiot."

"I did not," Harry said, laughing, and took over the story. "You see, the students in these classes were more than twice my age. The problem didn't come from them, though, but from the faculty who had agreed to accept kids from this program into their classes. Professors tended to treat us more as mascots than academics, Stubbs being the worst of the lot. He'd led the class through an equation covering two blackboards by the time he finished. With a flourish, he guided us to reach the solution. Stubbs told us he expected us to produce this kind of work every time. I'd had my hand up for what seemed like an hour, being completely ignored, as always. Only, this time, I didn't sit there. I climbed up onto the seat of my chair, stood as tall as I could, and said at the top of my voice, 'You're wrong.'"

"Wow you had guts," Jordy said.

"Not guts—frustration. Stubbs glanced around the room, smiling and gathering his audience, then said, 'Show us, my young scholar who knows more than all of these students and your professor, where is the flaw in the solution? So I simply pointed out he had forgotten to solve for one, three steps back, and the correct answer was cosine two minus three. Stubbs walked back to the board, studied it for several minutes, then me, and proceeded to pick up the chalk, enter the correct figures, and reach the solution I'd mentioned. He turned back to the class and scowled. Finally, he said, 'Mr. Foyle, apparently your time in my class hasn't been wasted.' After that, I got the same chance to participate as the other students. Word spread quickly, and not only the other teachers but the older students all accepted me. I suddenly belonged both academically and, thanks to Rufus and his parents, in my new family."

Rufus added, "I'm told Stubbs begins every semester with Harry's story, telling the students not to get cocky because you never can tell when you'll be shown up by a nine-year-old. We're heading down to visit Stubbs now. He's teaching at Texas Poly and sent me a note asking if I could contact Harry and bring him by. He has a problem that could use a Foyle approach. So we'll probably be seeing a lot more of you lovely ladies." He smiled at Cathy. Jordy rolled his eyes and made small gagging sounds.

Rufus and Cathy chatted about his work with PhD candidates in numerical analysis at UC Denver.

Harry, keeping his voice pitched so only she could hear, filled Kate in. "When Jordy's mother died, Rufus was a rising star in the math department at UC Denver. Having a full-time career and an infant to raise as a widower took its toll on him. At the same time, his father suffered a stroke that left him in a wheelchair and forced him into retirement from Caltech. Ewen Blackburn announced his decision to move into the Denver house his late wife had inherited from her parents and make a new home in Colorado. It was quite a change for a guy who used to surf in the morning and ski in the afternoon. But the move made it possible for the men to work together raising Jordy."

"So it's an all-male household?" Kate asked.

"Well, when Rufus' mother was dying, they took on a housekeeper. Antonia later married Raymond Duarte, head groundskeeper at Caltech. When Ewen moved to Colorado, they came along and live in the guest house on the property, so there has been a woman around as Jordy grew up."

Meanwhile, the conversation across the table had changed, and Rufus now talked about Jordy's education.

"Homeschooling worked for a few years with both my father and me teaching him," Rufus said. "But our specialties only covered certain fields of mathematics, and UC Denver didn't have any programs for gifted kids working on a college level. MIT had developed a program similar to the one Harry enrolled in when he came to live with us. Dad and I decided to send him east. With Harry living in Boston, he'd know someone local. So the kid is now at MIT."

Joyce said, "It's nice that it's all worked out and he's happy." She smiled when Jordy settled in to teach her a math trick she could use to stump her grandson.

Harry took Kate's hand under the table. She leaned on his shoulder and whispered, "This is more like the trip I pictured."

"Not what I pictured," Harry grumbled. "Too many people."

She grinned. "You know I love your suits and fedora, but I've got to tell you, Foyle, the Wild West you is really hot."

"Hmm, I'll have to keep it in mind when and if I ever get time alone with my fiancée." Since they were being watched, he changed the topic. "Have you decided which puppy you will be getting?"

"Well, the litter has only one boy with four girls. I'd like to get the male, but if he isn't show quality, I'll take one of the girls. I'm really hoping for another Dillon, though."

"Kate, face it, there is only one Dillon. He's my man. His kid might come in a close second, but he's a hard act to follow."

"I am really anxious to see them. Joyce is interested in using Dillon at stud with Lexi if she likes what comes of this litter.

Kate's phone buzzed with a text. She glanced down, sighed, typed her answer, hit send then cautiously turned to Harry and said, "It seems Lily isn't the only familiar face from last February now in Lubbock."

He stared at her for a minute then, as realization dawned, he groaned. "No, please no, Kate. She hates me."

"She doesn't hate you. She only thinks I should have dated about five hundred guys before I got engaged to you."

"Wrong, she really hates me. She is running a one woman campaign to break us up."

"Well, you may be in luck. Her fashion shoot is stressing her out, which could provide a distraction. Sean is with her as well. You can get even by teasing them about when they're going to get engaged. Anyway, I think something has her distracted. You don't seem to be on her radar at all."

"Impossible. Agnes Forester can't resist going after me like a bull to a red cape."

Cathy's head swiveled in their direction. "Did you say Agnes Forester? You mean the supermodel? The one who's always on magazine covers? She is so beautiful. She lives such an exciting life, traveling around the world. Do you know her, Harry?"

"Not by choice, since she hates me. She's Kate's cousin,

and apparently she's going to be in Lubbock, making my life miserable."

Jordy bounced in his seat. "Wait 'til I tell everybody Agnes Forester is Will Killoy's cousin. Kate's brother Will is at MIT with me."

"Hey, Scoop." Kate interrupted his enthusiasm. "You might want to check with Will before you broadcast that little nugget of news. Think about it. You might get more of his help if you tell him you're going to keep this a secret. Will doesn't need Agnes' help to get attention, and neither do you."

Jordy studied Kate for a few minutes. "You may be right." He turned to Harry. "You mean you know Agnes Forester and you didn't tell me?"

"She hates me," Harry grumbled again, and Kate burst out laughing.

Joyce interrupted their banter with a gasp. They all turned to follow her gaze out the window.

"If I'm not mistaken, he's the man from the airport," she said, pointing at a man walking away from a blue sedan and heading for the door.

Harry jumped into action. "Rufus, you and Jordy go with Joyce and Cathy." Holding out his hand, he said, "Keys. Kate and I will take your car." He slapped some cash for the meal onto the table, put Kate's hat on her head then grabbed his own hat. He managed to pull her out of sight behind a rack of clothing as the man entered the building.

Rufus and Jordy quickly shifted the tables, left the extra dishes piled up for the busboy on the empty table, and, by the time the man entered the restaurant, became a classic American family on vacation. They acted relaxed, ignoring Soucek who sat at a table facing the window.

Harry reached up to silence the bell as they slipped out the front door. Turning left, they moved in the opposite direction from the restaurant window and circled around toward the back of the building. All the cars stood in the front, in Soucek's line of sight, so they had to wait.

"Kate, I'm so sorry to put you through this. It seems like with every attempt to spend time together, we're running, and hiding or being chased by people wanting to hurt us."

Kate reached out and hugged him. "Technically, it's not true. I remember spending a whole day last June walking the Freedom Trail in Boston without a single musket shot fired."

"You know you're crazy, don't you?"

"Yes, but my dogs love me."

"They aren't the only ones." Harry pulled her close. "I want to find some quiet time to talk to you about our future."

"Considering what you said about us, you're a brave man to want a future with me."

"The only thing I'd be frightened of would be a future without you."

CHAPTER SEVEN

They found a hidden spot beyond the dumpsters that, luckily, had not yet received today's garbage. Kate settled on a large rock and stared out over the empty plain stretching behind the buildings to the horizon. The low clouds had kept her from seeing the very tops of the Front Range and Pike's Peak as they'd left Denver that morning, but Kate now got a taste of the great flat expanses of high prairie. She'd learned on their drive the deer and antelope were less likely to play and more likely to hold staring contests with tourists driving by.

This land seemed about as different from her familiar New England landscape as you could get in the US, aside from Death Valley, and it held her entranced with its stark vistas and minimalistic color palette. Occasionally, as they had driven south, she had seen a ranch house with a barn, or some cattle, but, for the most part, this barren land displayed Mother Nature's exercise in restraint. The drought had taken its toll over the last few years. The land before her, patterned in at least fifty shades of beige, held the muted, slightly softened appearance of a rotogravure photo. Harry sat on the rock behind her, his arms wrapped around her shoulders. They took in the stark beauty before them, at peace.

"Penny for your thoughts?" Harry asked, breaking the quiet.

"You might not like them." Kate took her eyes away from the peaceful scene to face him. Ever since the encounter with Soucek on the plane, something hadn't seemed right with this game of cat and mouse. She no longer thought the man the threat Sadie did. When she'd seen him on the plane, she hadn't felt threatened. He'd appeared to be someone who desperately needed help.

"Tell me anyway."

"I think we should go back inside and talk to Soucek."

"Kate, the man is a criminal."

"He was in prison and now he's out and, yes, I know he's on probation and could be sent back. However, we don't know why. Sadie never told us what crime he committed. Plus, why did he want you? You don't know him from Adam. Unlike the man with the gun who broke into your condo, who I definitely see as a threat, this man paged you at an airport while holding a newspaper photo of us. And another thing. There are only a few people who knew we'd be at Bradley Airport waiting to fly to Denver. Who told him where to find us? It had to be a friend because our enemies didn't know. I don't think he wants to hurt us, Harry. I think he wants your help."

"I think you're wrong, but I'll talk to Sadie and see what she can find. In the meantime, he's a criminal, and you will stay away from him."

Kate frowned but didn't argue.

At the sound of an engine starting, Kate leaned back against Harry. Peeking around the corner of the dumpster at the sound of a door slamming, they spotted Joyce's SUV, with Rufus driving, swing into sight, pause at the entrance to the highway, and then pick up speed, heading south. After a minute, a second door slammed, followed by quiet. They inched deeper into the cover of the big steel boxes that had begun to cook in the day's early sunshine, emitting the residual smell of rotting garbage. An engine started but idled, waiting. Finally, it backed over the gravel but, instead of heading for the exit, it circled the building, pausing while the driver surveyed the area behind the building, moving forward and then pausing again. Their bodies pressed against the dumpster's warm, rough metal, Kate buried her face in Harry's chest, inhaling the scent of evergreen, mountains, fresh air, and him. She caught her breath. His closeness made her pulse begin to race and her breathing grow short. And she was not alone in reacting to their position. After a few minutes, the blue sedan crept slowly by and picked up speed, entering the highway heading south.

Harry knew he should step back and head for the car, but the feel of Kate's body held tight against him offered too much temptation and, before he even thought, he had dragged her into a deep, searching kiss, making him want to know every inch of what lay beneath his hands. Hers slid up to pull his head closer, and she returned his kiss, inflaming him with a moan. The sound of a door opening and someone emptying garbage into the dumpster had them both jumping back and catching their breath. When the door clanged shut, Harry grasped her hand and ran for the car. It only took a minute for them to join the others on the highway, though it took considerably longer for them to get themselves back under control and breathing normally. Kate grabbed Harry's phone and dialed Sadie's number, putting it on speaker.

Harry nodded at her and said, "Hey, Sadie."

"Harry. What's going on? Sal said you are traveling in disguise."

"Sadie, why is Soucek out? More to the point, why did he go to prison in the first place?"

"He was in one of those private Texas prisons that closed down because of money problems and released him as part of a mass parole. I checked with the bureau. They hadn't been notified of the widespread egress, and the boys are pissed.

"Was Soucek important?"

"Him? No. He's a white collar little fish incarcerated on a small time embezzling charge. Unless he hooked up with someone while inside, I've got no idea why he is hunting for you. I've got a list of bureau names on the release, some from cases you did while with them, but you weren't lead. We're still working on your description of the guy who broke into your place. They've got a partial profile and three numbers of the license plate on his car, but, so far, no ID. Thank God he doesn't know about you and Kate. Sal would kill you if you put his girl in danger."

Harry's knuckles went white as he gripped the wheel. He stared straight ahead and didn't respond.

"I'll keep you posted, Harry," Sadie said. "Stay away from Soucek. He may not be bad on his own, but you never can tell who he might have made contact with while inside. Be careful."

Kate gazed out the window; thinking now might not be the best time to press her point about talking to Soucek. The silence in the car filled the space between them crowding them against the doors. She didn't speak. Her piece had been said. Now was the time to shut up. They drove for over half an out without a word, until her phone played a short Mozart air. She glanced at the screen. This would really make Harry's day, like adding gasoline to a fire. She glanced at his face, decided enough was enough, and put the call on speaker.

"What are you up to, Agnes, needing Lily and the puppies?" she asked.

Agnes' voice sounded rushed and excited. "You are going to love it. You remember Maddox Fox? His show came second from last in the bandstand at Fashion Week. Sean and I were staying with him when the mess happened last February. Anyway, he's doing his shoot for spreads in *Vogue* and *Paris Match*, and I talked him into using Lily's puppies. It will be fabulous. It's being shot at his home, tonight, and he's having a barbecue as well. They're very relaxed about such things in Texas. It's very strange. Anyway, I need you to do what Andy calls your magic, so the puppies, and therefore the whole shoot, will be perfect. It must be perfect. I heard Joyce's champion bitch is coming, too, which will be great. She can pretend to be the puppies' mom, as opposed to their real mom, who I'm sure is stark naked, having completely blown her coat following whelping. This absolutely, positively, must go off without a hitch and be fabulous. See you later." She hung up before Kate could say anything.

Putting away the phone, she glanced over at Harry. "You know, Agnes is getting more like your sister every day."

"You mean a pain in the butt?"

"No, she's always been a pain. It's the one-sided phone conversations, with no participation needed from the person on the other end."

He laughed, and Kate relaxed, some of their tension gone. They approached Raton, New Mexico. The idea of lunch appealed in spite of having put away a good breakfast. Since they'd change from I-25 to I-87 and I-27, it seemed as good a place as any to fuel up both the car and themselves.

They exited the highway and swung into a Phillips station to fill up the SUV. Next, they opted for McDonald's, after checking out the lack of blue sedans in the parking lot. Harry gave their order while she used the restroom. It felt good to stretch her legs for a minute. She then took Harry's place in line waiting for their food. When it came, she decided to settle into a booth rather than returning to the car. They were making good time and would be in Lubbock on schedule to take part in Agnes' three-ring circus.

Kate's eyes, used to green trees and grass, searched the palette of beiges before her to identify the subtle color change inspiring her designer's sense. Even the cloudless sky seemed a paler shade of blue, more in tone with the setting. Her mind conjured up a landscape knit from a variegated yarn running from off-white through dark-chocolate with every fluctuation between. What could have been bland would work beautifully under the direction of Mother Nature's paintbrush. She could picture a sweater designed with this palette as a backdrop for a pair of coursing Saluki or a Rhodesian Ridgeback poised on a rock gazing out at the merest suggestion of antelope in the distance. She mentally stored design ideas she'd work on next week.

Kate disappeared into one of her design states, sitting without moving and creating beauty in her head. Later, it would appear worked in yarn. It was something she'd done since childhood. She'd sit and let her mind take over.

Without a word, they did justice to their meal then, tucking the apple pies away for later, got back on the road. Turning from a southerly direction to south-easterly, they headed across the upper right corner of New Mexico and into the panhandle of Texas. Though they'd covered a lot of mileage, they still had almost five hours to go before they reached Lubbock.

This drive seemed to never end, and who knew how long the photo shoot would extend their waking hours. Kate began to feel the effect of having gotten up before five o'clock. "I'm full and ready for a nap, if you don't mind. I'll leave you to plan how we're going to handle Soucek and any other problems coming up because, from experience, I know he won't be the only thorn in your side over the next forty-eight hours."

Harry glance over at her, frowning. "Right, there's still Agnes."

Kate had opened her mouth to reassure him when he cracked a smile and the dimple she adored appeared for a few seconds. She laughed. A button by her right hand let the seat tilt back slightly, and though it seemed she'd barely dropped off, she woke to find Harry pulling into a rest stop in Amarillo. Kate made a quick dash to the restroom and when Harry reappeared with coffee and tea, croissants, and jelly donuts, she'd settled behind the wheel.

A half smile flashed, but he put up no argument as they got back on the highway. Kate went for a jelly donut first and gobbled it down with a speed having four brothers had instilled in her. She signed in satisfaction and settled into enjoying her tea as the miles rolled past. An occasional sorghum field stood out on the landscape like a single green square worked into the patchwork of a monochromatic beige quilt. Harry dozed for maybe half an hour then sat up to dig around in their bag of treats.

Determined to get him talking, Kate asked, "What's Professor Stubbs' problem, and why does it involve you?"

Harry faced her, drawing one knee up onto the seat, leaning against the door, and, after a moment, began. "You know what Rufus said about my being sent, at nine years old, to study at Caltech. My family had been unprepared to handle my being different from others my age. I'll admit I saw it as rejection. But after what happened in Stubbs' class, I fit in. I got the same feeling when I first came to visit your family." Kate did not mention he fit in better than she did. Now wasn't the time. "So I feel as though I owe him for changing my life and allowing me to be me. When he asked for help, I couldn't say no."

"So, once again, Professor Stubbs needs your help to solve a problem." She smiled, waiting for Harry's grin. Instead, she saw concern.

"Yes, but this time"—he paused as Kate riveted her eyes on him—"I need to keep him from going to prison."

CHAPTER EIGHT

"Let me get this list of possible problems straight," Kate said as they finally approached Lubbock. "You and I have got an ex-prisoner chasing us, a gunman is hunting you, and a professor who needs to be kept out of prison needs your help. Oh, and let us never forget Agnes. Did I miss anything?"

Harry smiled at her. "Nope, it's the score so far."

"So this must be Friday."

The silence following scared her for a minute until she heard the snort.

"Face it, Kate. In the world of trouble, we're a pair of overachievers."

She was glad the road lay straight because the tears brought on by her convulsing with laughter made the road blur. Harry reached for her hand and held it as the tension between them dissolved.

Though the end of summer, with Labor Day coming up next weekend, meant the approach of fall even at home, this far south the evenings fell quicker and twilight set in as they finally approached the city. The flatness of Lubbock revealed the glow of buildings like the Wells Fargo Bank from a great distance. They maneuvered the car onto the Martha Sharp Freeway, heading for the hotel where they'd be staying.

Kate's brain, up until a few minutes earlier filled with criminal worries, suddenly zeroed in on the reason she came to Texas. Dillon had sired his first litter, and she wanted to do nothing more for the rest of the day than sit, watch, assess, and compare these puppies to the litter from which Dillon had come. Her tablet, stuffed into the oversized bag at her feet, contained almost a hundred photos of that litter to use as reference.

The GPS told them to exit, and they began working their way through the city streets. Finally, after a series of left turns had her thinking she was going to be heading back the way they'd come, they reached the hotel. Kate spotted Joyce's SUV in the parking lot, and, as if conjured by the thought, the lady herself came around the corner of the building, walking Lexi.

Approaching the car, she called out, "You're late. We have to leave for this shindig in fifteen minutes. Your stuff is already in room 112, Kate. You and Lily are sleeping with the puppies. Harry, Rufus booked a room for the men. Everyone went inside to wrangle the pups. You'd better hustle your butts."

"Any sign of the blue sedan?" Harry asked.

"Nope. Does he know you're at this hotel?"

"No. Lily only sent me the address after we'd started south." Kate said as she headed inside to clean up and change into a less travel-worn outfit. Room 112 overflowed with bodies and squeaking white puppies. Resisting the urge to stop and focus on the pups, Kate picked up her suitcase, stepped into the bathroom, and began the process of turning from worn traveler into someone who could rub elbows with the likes of Maddox Fox. She put on one of the permanent press blouses Agnes had made her buy, donned clean slim-fitting jeans, a silver linked belt, and knee-high brown suede boots. Kate then added her silver and turquoise earrings and necklace. She checked her reflection in the mirror, fluffed her hair, applied lipstick, and finished off with a tiny bit of blush. She was good to go. Harry had arrived while she changed and now snuggled a puppy. Grinning, he raised an eyebrow making her smile at their private joke. She laughed. "Four minutes flat." Kate's lack of fuss with clothing had been one of the first things he'd complimented her on after they met. And she wasn't the only one with a burst of speed. He'd already changed his shirt and shaved.

Her designer attire caught the attention of the other women who burst into complaints of not having brought any fancy outfits to wear. Kate reached into the front pocket of her suitcase and pulled out the three gift-wrapped packages. Each scarf came from a different designer, but they all were beautiful. She showed them the little twists they could do to make the scarves appear as though they had been planned as the focal point of the evening's outfit. Kate's grandmother had taught her always to bring hostess gifts.

Finally, Kate zeroed in on the puppy pen, spotted the male from his resemblance to Dillon at eight weeks, and plucked him from the pile of squirming white fur balls clamoring for attention. "The perfect accessory." she announced, tucking him under her chin.

"Let's party." Her declaration led to a mad scramble to pick up puppies and leave. They deposited all the puppies in the back of Lily's station wagon, converted into a traveling puppy pen, and then sorted themselves into the three vehicles. Jordy claimed the right to ride with the puppies. Kate climbed in next to Harry and programmed the address they'd been given into the GPS.

"You're beautiful," Harry said. "Keeping your end up with Agnes?"

"More a case of meeting a highly respected designer and not wanting to resemble kennel help."

"I've got news for you. Even dressed as kennel help, you're gorgeous. I know you don't see it. Remember who you're engaged to when you're with Mr. Haute Couture tonight."

"Same for you, handsome. There are going to be a bunch of models at this bash." They had been driving through winding roads leading to a neighborhood of substantial homes on larger pieces of property. "There it is." Kate pointed as the GPS informed them they had reached their destination. Before them stood a Southwestern-style palace complete with high adobe walls broken only by a pair of elaborate wrought iron gates displaying the initials M.F. worked into an intricate, gilded design.

"Still think I'm overdressed?" Kate asked.

They pulled up under a portico. A valet stepped forward to open Kate's door as Harry, pulling on his sports jacket, rounded the front of the car and handed over the keys. The others arrived right behind them and, en masse, they moved toward the broad red brick steps leading to a pair of what must be twelve foot high solid oak doors featuring, a carved bas-relief, fox.

Kate, with a slight nervous reservation, slid her bag onto her shoulder as the girls joined her. They'd left the puppies asleep in the car while they got the lay of the land.

Both doors, responding to what must have been the breaking of an electric beam, suddenly opened of their own accord, revealing a cavernous two-story entry, complete with marble floor. An art deco mariner's compass, its center medallion bearing the initials M.F, as well, formed the center for the diamond tiles extending out for about twenty feet in all directions. The compass' true north led their eyes to follow a single diamond point and to focus on the grand marble staircase connecting the entry with the floor above. Railings on either side of the stairs, had been worked in the same intricate wrought-iron lace-work. A swooping banister of highly polished brass descended in a graceful arch. The wrought-iron chandelier above their heads repeated the use of lace-work and brass. Sconces in similar patterns interspersed along the room's robin's egg-blue and white paneled walls drew the eye. The only thing to mar the drama of this sight seemed to be the crowd of technicians, makeup people, and lighting grips, plus, of course, a photographer.

Always one to make an entrance, Agnes suddenly appeared. Kate's eyes focused on the top of the grand staircase where a Valkyrie descended from Valhalla. Her magnificent golden hair shone above a midnight-blue silk jacquard evening gown with a gold Chantilly lace halter embellished with tiny sequins and seed pearls. A train of organza and lace in the same blue floated behind and above her as she swooped down the stairs, mesmerizing everyone.

"Got it, thank you," the photographer yelled.

Everyone let out a collective sigh as reality came crashing in. The effect on those watching worked like pulling back the curtain on the Wizard of Oz. Here, the wizard had a huge commercial fan lifting the train to float behind her. The lights bounced off reflectors highlighting her perfect hair and skin. The photographer's assistants had moved portable spots to highlight specific areas as she descended. But these things, though distractions, did little to lessen the impact of Agnes Forester, in full-blown supermodel mode, as the photographer, along with the technical and lighting crews, worked to create sorcery and to capture magic in a single perfect shot.

"Impressive," Joyce said, moving to stand beside Kate.

So much really hard work went into creating such an illusion. "Now there is something I can add to and at the same time check off my bucket list," she whispered, chuckling.

Agnes reached the bottom of the steps only to be surrounded by dressers who lifted the gown and train and moved as one with her to change for the next shot.

"Kate," she shouted, stopping. "Thank God you made it. You need to do your thing to make the next shot perfect. We're going for the cover."

A man descending the same flight of stairs with as much confidence and style as Agnes must be Maddox Fox. He stood barely five foot six, with curly black hair, black eyes, round cheeks, and was built like a soccer player, slim but muscular. He wore a white silk dress shirt with the top four buttons undone to show an abundance of dark chest hair, black jeans, and stylish hand-tooled cowboy boots. The king at home in his castle. Reaching the bottom step, he leaned in to kiss Agnes on the cheek. "You were marvelous as always, sweetheart." Agnes took his arm and turned him in Kate's direction.

"Maddox, this is Kate Killoy, who is not only a new and rising star in the design world but my cousin. She will be able to make the shot we discussed happen. When it comes to dogs, she's magic. Introduce your friends to Maddox, Kate, while I go change." She swept off, surrounded by her entourage.

Familiar nerves tightened, as they did when she entered the ring for Best in Show. But she'd been taught well and pasted on her show ring smile. Remembering her father's instructions never to show fear, she moved forward, hand extended, to meet this giant in the world of haute couture. Kate introduced him to everyone, beginning with Joyce, Cathy, and Lily. He earned points with Joyce right away, saying he knew of her by reputation because she had apparently given the Siberian Husky owned by a friend of his a group one at the Tucson show last year. He told Lily he eagerly anticipated seeing these magnificent white puppies and paused for an extra minute over Cathy's hand, glad to meet another friend of Agnes' cousin. Then Kate introduced Harry, Rufus, and Jordy. Maddox sized each up, giving a smile only to Jordy.

Sean Connelly appeared out of the crowd and stepped up to swing Kate about in a hug. He shook Harry's hand and then met the others. He bent over to whisper to Kate, "Her royal highness is in full diva mode, so get your brass knuckles polished." The two greyhound bitches at his side shed their normal regal cool at the sight of a friend and bounced up on Kate, begging to be hugged. Both had lived with her while Agnes traveled abroad, and she'd trained them for protection as she had Dillon. Considering the passive personalities of the breed, she achieved a much lower level of success. They had, however, in spite of their natural couch potato natures, learned to do the protection exercise when signaled after Kate turned it into a game, with prizes. Never let it be said Agnes' bitches couldn't be bribed.

Lily, Cathy, Joyce, and Jordy headed back to Lily's car to get the puppies while Sean showed Kate where a pen had been rigged up. Agnes' greyhounds followed him. She saw the puppies react to these tall creatures with fascination. Both of Agnes' girls had whelped litters of their own over the years, so they had the patience to handle their popularity with the noisy, squirming pups.

"Wow, Kate, when did you get so hot?" She turned quickly and spotted a younger but equally as handsome clone of Sean emerge from the direction Agnes had gone. Kevin Donnelly had been her brother Will's best friend since they were both in diapers. At six foot four and in possession of the Donnelly muscular body, he must have attracted the attention every the model at this party.

"Hi, Kev," she answered. "I've always been hot. You guys needed your eyes examined." Kate hugged him and then asked gazing around, "Where is herself?"

"She's…"

"I'm right here. Let's get this over and done with so I can get back into my jeans and eat. Come on, we've got work to do." Kate turned around and, at the vision of Agnes entering with her parade of attendants, her breath caught. She wore the most beautiful wedding dress Kate had ever seen as she swept down toward them as if from Heaven.

The photographer called out, "Perfect, Agnes, sweetheart. Let the girls redo you and we'll set up for the doggy thing." He headed to a ballroom off the entrance, followed by his assistants carrying his gear. Agnes' forward momentum slowed to a crawl, surrounded by the people lifting her gown and veil, by those with makeup brushes and fists full of paints and powder, to say nothing of those working with combs, brushes, and sprays as she walked across the foyer and through the arched doorway. Agnes and the many planets orbiting her sun, moved past an equally large mass of humanity and into a space laid with rugs and pillows to create a scene reminiscent of a sheik's tent, but in colors more fitting to this Versailles-style room.

The word room didn't convey enough grandeur for what stretched out before them. It appeared to be about half the size of a football field, with gleaming parquet floors. Rows of floor-to-ceiling windows draped with golden silk were interspersed with huge gilded mirrors tilted to reflect both the room and the Michelangelo reproduction ceiling. This defined opulence. Every cornice, fixture, picture frame, and chair had been gilded as if awaiting the arrival of the empress. Kate stepped forward grinning. "Damn, Agnes, someone finally found a setting to fit you. Great dress, by the way. I hope no puppy pees on the hundred-dollar-a-yard silk."

Jordy ran up with the blue puppy on lead. "He's all set, Kate. He's peed and pooped."

She rotated her short friend to face Agnes. "This is Jordy Blackburn, who got me through my fear of flying. He thinks you're hot by the way."

Agnes smiled at him. "Well, thank you, Jordy. You're kind of cute yourself." He blushed, mumbled something, shoved the puppy into Kate's arms, and ran for the exit. Agnes smiled. "New boyfriend?"

"He's Harry's wing man and yet another math genius to make me feel out of step in my world. My mother should meet him. He and Harry worked together yesterday to help me avoid a thug at the airport."

"Why was a thug after you at the airport?"

"Long story. When I can share, I'll let you know. This trip is beginning to get some dangerous overtones. To paraphrase Bette Davis, 'we're in for a bumpy ride.'"

Agnes stared at her for a minute, raised her eyebrows, and said, "So, what else is new?"

Agnes turned to the women poking and fussing at her and said, "Thank you, ladies. Let's get this done because the barbecue smell coming through the door is making me hungry."

As Kate snuggled the puppy, she felt Harry's hand on her shoulder and leaned into him for a minute. She was tired. Today seemed like a year long, and she still had hours more to get through. His arm came around, pulling her into a quick hug. Then he spoke in hushed tones. "Rufus got a text saying there is some trouble going on at Dr. Stubbs' home. Kevin, Rufus, Sean, and I are going to go check what's going on. Are you alright here without me?"

Kate felt a quick stab of loss but reassured him. "No problem. Between puppy wrangling and dealing with my cousin, I won't have a spare minute. If I don't see you later, I'll see you in the morning." He kissed her quickly and headed out the door. She watched him join the men and leave.

If this matched the rest of the day, whatever was happening at the home of Harry's friend wouldn't be good.

CHAPTER NINE

Kate snuggled the boy puppy under her chin, breathing in his lovely puppy smell as she strolled over to where Jordy and the girls stood with the rest of the puppies. Kate responded to Cathy's questions by filling her in on where the men had gone. Since they could do nothing to help Harry's professor, they returned to the ballroom to watch the technicians set up.

Kate had spent four years doing endless fashion shows prior to receiving her degree in clothing design, and she'd had her own fashion show in New York City last February. The experience made all this seem like old hat. For the others, it was new, so keeping her voice low, she began giving them a running commentary on the action.

"What they are doing now is testing for the white balance so all the colors in the shot will be true. They don't want any direct light creating a shine or dark shadow, so all the lighting will be bounced off reflectors. Agnes must sit in the exact spot where they are doing test shots to check for levels of shadows, exposure, and how the light will play on the fabric. These tests used to be done with Polaroids, but everything is digital now. Once the photographer is satisfied with the lighting on Agnes and the dress, they'll introduce the puppies and Lexi then do one more quick check to make sure the lighting works with their white coats."

Kate next spelled out the rules for dog handlers at this fashion shoot. "You don't talk, which might distract the puppies, you freeze when told to, you don't create a shadow, and, the big one, you ignore what I'm doing and simply watch the puppies for any escape artists."

The photographer shot about two minutes of frames with Agnes moving slightly into poses obviously sure winners. Then the photographer bellowed, "Okay, let's get these puppies in here and get this fiasco over with."

They moved forward, gently placing the now very sleepy puppies where told. Joyce moved Lexi around to Agnes' right, had her step gently onto the skirt of the gown and then drop into a perfect down-stay. Joyce then positioned herself where the photographer wanted Lexi's attention. He shot half a dozen frames of Agnes, Lexi, and the sleeping puppies, and then Agnes interrupted the photographer, instructing him to have Kate direct the next few shots.

"I don't take orders on how to shoot from amateurs," he growled, waving Kate off with a flip of his hand.

Agnes raised an eyebrow, daring Kate to stand up for herself. She stepped up and stared the photographer in the eye. "Well, when I work with Sibowitz, he relies on me completely to get the best fashion dog shots."

"Sibowitz. Andy Sibowitz?"

"Yes, of course. He's the only photographer I use."

The photographer faced Agnes, who nodded. He scowled as he turned back to Kate, but, after a minute, shrugged and said, "It's your party."

First she had him lower his point of view to almost puppy level. Then she had Agnes lay a hand on Lexi's back and bend forward, curving her body, like a guardian angel, over the sleeping puppies. She nodded, and he shot some frames. Next, Kate pulled from her pocket the wind-up quacking duck mechanical toy she'd brought to test puppy reactions. Holding up the wound duck, Kate told him, "Get ready— shoot!" At the same time, she flicked the release, and the room filled with quacking.

The set came to life. The puppies, now awake, animated, and in motion, crawled all over the dress and Agnes.

"Blue boy," Kate yelled to Agnes. Agnes reached down into the pile of puppies in her lap who were pulling each other's tails and reaching for Lexi's muzzle. At the same time, the fan behind her sped up, making the bridal veil float like a cloud above Agnes' head. She swung the puppy high above her head so the floating veil backdrop set him off perfectly as he barked, while, at the same instant, all the puppies and Lexi stared up at Blue Boy far above them as a laughing Agnes created pure sunshine, becoming the quintessential bride filled with pure delight and alive with the joy of the moment. Knowing they'd gotten the money shot, Kate said, "It's a wrap. Everyone grab a puppy, and let's eat."

The photographer, whose name turned out to be Dominick Raffo, handed his camera to an assistant who transferred the shots to the computer. He then whipped out his phone while turning away from the crowd. Kate stepped around the miles of fabric and carefully gave Agnes a hug. Maddox Fox came up and air kissed Kate's cheeks, telling her he'd never seen anything like it in a shoot. She told him since her boutique line centered on fashions for the show dog crowd, it was what she did. Kate guaranteed he'd have any number of money shots to choose from. The thought of future owners of the puppies linking to Vogue and Paris Match on their Facebook pages when the photos came out made her laugh. Those last shots had definitely been cover worthy.

A phone got shoved into her face by the now slightly more polite photographer. "He wants to talk to you."

"Hello," Kate said, taking the phone. "Oh, Andy, yes, I finally got on a plane. Don't worry. I won't give him all your secrets. Yes, I'm still engaged to Harry. Love you, too." She handed the phone back and smiled to herself.

Over in the corner where they had set up the X-pen to hold the puppies, a crowd of admiring models and staff had gathered. Spotting a clipboard and marker on one of the side tables, Kate quickly made a sign. *ANYONE WHO FEEDS A PUPPY FOOD FROM THE BARBECUE MUST HOLD IT WHILE IT HAS PROJECTILE VOMITING AND DI-*

ARRHEA. She stepped through the gathering and posted the sign on the fence above the puppy pen.

"The puppies are adorable," she told the admiring crowd, "but when they beg for treats you've got to be strong. No matter how cute they are, you must refuse."

A chorus of, "Sorry, puppies," followed as the crowd headed for the tables laden with enough food to feed a small third-world nation.

Kate didn't blame the puppies. The smells from this Tex-Mex banquet were causing her stomach to grumble. She should take her own advice and be careful what she ate. Her stomach, raised on a New England diet, might suffer the same malady she predicted for the puppies. She'd taste the spicy foods, but she'd eat some bread to soften the blow.

Sliding her arm through Cathy's, she went to join Agnes, who descended the stairs wearing jeans, a T-shirt, and loafers. "Good. You're back to normal again. I always feel I need to treat you like a China doll when you're in supermodel mode." Kate linked her free arm through Agnes'.

"Where's Harry?" Agnes asked. "Is he off sniffing around all the young cuties?"

"What put you in bitch mode, princess?" Kate noticed her cousin's hunched shoulders and the stiff as a board arm linked through hers. "Hey, Cuz, what's going on? Is it Sean? You don't usually snipe at me in public."

"I'm sorry." Her body slumped, and she dropped her

head forward. "I apologize to both of you. I really need to talk to you, Kate, without Harry or Sean."

"All the guys except your devoted fan Jordy have left to try and help one of Harry's former professors. Give me a ride back to the hotel, and we'll talk. I've had two days of travel without even had a minute to play with puppies yet. Let's get some food and then play with the little fuzz butts."

They joined the crowd around the buffet table. The other models chatted with Agnes and teased Jordy. When the other models spoke to Agnes, she'd smile and answer cheerfully, but there was tension in her neck and shoulders. She was her usual charming self, but she didn't eat, only pushing food around her plate. Maybe she'd tell her what was wrong later.

Conversation flowed around her, but Kate fell silent, about to tip over from exhaustion. Agnes chatted to Joyce, Cathy, and Lily, explaining the both the good and the horrors of life as a fashion model. Though Agnes had an enthusiastic audience, when Kate spotted her glancing at her watch for the second time, she interrupted saying, "Let's round up these puppies and head back to the hotel. I don't know about you guys, but I'm wiped out."

Kate signaled to Jordy to head out and ran into her only objection. She let him know he was outvoted. They loaded Lily's van and split up for the trip. She told the others she and Agnes had some family business to discuss, so Agnes would drive her back. As soon as Lily and Joyce left, the valet brought up Henry, Agnes' Ford, and the greyhounds jumped in with them.

The lights of the city lit the car like daylight so Kate could see Agnes' face, which showed a troubled conversation she seemed to be having with herself. Ten minutes into what proved to be a silent tour of downtown Lubbock, Agnes turned onto the campus of Texas Poly and spoke. "I turn thirty tomorrow."

"Happy Birthday!" Kate had a birthday gift for Agnes in her luggage. Who knew the concept of reaching the big three -o should upset Agnes this much. She saw a shine of tears in her eyes. "Let's pull over and talk," Kate said.

Agnes parked, took a deep breath, and faced her. "It's not a happy birthday. Kate, I'm a dinosaur."

"T. rex or stegosaurus?" She smiled trying to lighten the mood.

"Not funny. I mean it. Do you realize I'm almost twice as old as most of the models there tonight? Modeling is a game for girls. Most are retired by their mid-twenties. This shoot is my last."

"Is it your choice to leave the business, or are you being pushed out?" Kate asked as gently as she could.

"Pushed out? Are you mad? I'm the top grossing model in the country, maybe the world today."

"Do you love the life of a model?"

"Hell, no. I haven't enjoyed it for years. I like doing something I'm good at, but the schedules are miserable. I don't get enough time with the dogs or Gram or Sean. I'm always running somewhere or other."

"Then, what's the difficulty? Am I missing something here? Agnes, you have a whole other career waiting for you. Hell, you own a bank. I fail to see a problem."

Agnes shifted and stared out the window as the real problem filled the car. Forester Savings and Trust had been in Agnes' family for three generations. Kate remembered going there as kids when they visited the city and loving it when Uncle Robert would nod to someone and a buzzer would sound and doors would open. He took them into the huge vault where there seemed to be a million locked drawers running up each wall. He made them feel like grownups, showing them how to dictate letters and letting them sit in his big leather chair behind his desk and whirl around. It had been a magical place for two little girls. Kate gazed at her cousin, picturing her sitting in the special chair again. She needed to stop being a smart-ass and be the family Agnes needed.

"So the problem is the bank," Kate said in a now quiet voice. "Agnes, do you remember when my dad would take us into the city and we'd stay with Maeve? When she had things to do, she'd drop us off at the bank. Your dad always made the place seem magical. He'd show us how everything worked from the vault to the coin-sorting machine. He'd made us feel like bankers, spinning around in his big leather chair."

"It was a lot of fun. Dad made the day seem like a trip to an amusement park."

"You're right. But I got a picture in my mind of you in the chair, not as a little kid waiting to go for ice cream, but as you are now, a bright, confident woman ready to take on the world."

"Kate, you've spotted the problem. I can't picture Agnes Forester in that role. All I see is someone who has spent her life prancing around in expensive clothes, sorting through endless documents and doing nothing of value. When Uncle Paul got murdered last month, I couldn't take over running the bank. I had contracts to fulfill and, to tell the truth, I wasn't ready. By the way, thanks again for having your friend Richard Carsley find someone to take over on a temporary basis."

"You're welcome." Richard, a dear friend who trained his dog with her back in Connecticut, owned the number one Chihuahua in the country and filled the role as president of his family's bank in New York. She had called him for help when Agnes went through the trauma of having her mother's brother murdered and almost getting killed herself by a man trying to use Forester's for his money laundering operation.

"I was only a kid when the car crash killed my parents. Everything in my world changed. Living with my grandparents turned out to be wonderful, but I think I wanted to run away from life as a banker because I could never ever be as good as Dad or Granddad. When the chance to model came along, I grabbed it so I'd have an excuse. And I've been running away ever since."

"So you've decided to stop running?"

"Yes. The bank is my responsibility. However, the image of sitting behind a desk bean counting for the rest of my life doesn't fill me with joy."

"I can't picture you doing that either. However, if you think about it, it's not really what your dad or uncle did, either. Gramps once told me your dad spent his life helping make people's dreams come true. He said a bank like yours is there to help businesses and families." Kate looked over at Agnes who sat staring off into space as though remembering the two men who'd run the family bank.

"Remember, when the bottom fell out of the market people lost everything? However, the ones, who had their investments at Forester's guided by Paul, didn't. He was careful with their money and they ended up doing fine. What about the housing crisis? Forester's got noticed by the *Wall Street Journal* for not serving any foreclosures. The people who had loans with Forester's, those in financial straits, Paul adjusted their payments and extended their loans."

"You're right. That made me proud."

"Think of the programs you've already set up with the bank. You use the money you've earned modeling to help inner city girls get a good education. I remember you and Paul sitting at the Christmas table, while everyone else watched football in the other room, going over the financial details so sufficient capital was available to have the yearly grants paid out of the earned interest. I watched your face while you did it. Agnes, the happiness on your face reminded me of your father's when he helped a company no one had ever heard of get started."

"I'd forgotten. You're right. I loved doing that."

"I don't know where your relationship with Sean is. It's not my business. But if you marry and have kids, don't you think they'd enjoy coming into your office to spin around in your big leather chair?"

"Kate, you're an idiot. This is the absolutely the most schmaltzy pep talk I've ever heard."

"Hang on a minute, George Bailey, while I pull out my DVD of *It's a Wonderful Life*." Kate peeked over and saw the beginning of a smile play on Agnes' lips. She reached out to squeeze her hand, and Agnes smiled. She didn't grin, but it sure beat the tears. "Admit it. I'm right."

Turning on the engine, Agnes pulled back onto the road. "I'll think about it."

As they drove along, the campus buildings gave way to a series of nice residential streets of mostly one- or two-family houses displaying small lawns fronted with sidewalks. Each house had a porch stretching across the front and separated itself from its neighbors by an identical narrow driveway. A mental image of the fourteen acres of lawns and woods around her home popped into Kate's head, contrasting vastly with this setting. This was the sort of neighborhood where Harry had grown up.

He and Kate had talked some this summer about the

flexibility of his business and how he would have no trouble moving it from Boston to Connecticut. She knew, though, it would be an adjustment for him to leave the urban existence when they married. But Kate couldn't do her work in the middle of downtown Boston. What space and facilities he needed to add to Kate's place became one more thing to add to the ever growing list of things they needed to talk about.

Agnes turned onto a narrow cross street that, according to their GPS, would take them back to the highway and to the hotel. They passed a crowd of parked cars and Kate suddenly sat up, putting her hand to the window, and told Agnes to slow down. The SUV they passed was like Rufus'. Up ahead appeared flashing lights. A cop kept traffic moving forward at a crawl. As they passed an ambulance, Kate spotted Harry, Rufus, Sean, and Kevin standing in the driveway of a small English cottage-style house painted charcoal-gray with lighter gray shutters and a bright-red door now being held open by one of the policemen crowded into the entrance. Everyone's attention focused on the stretcher being wheeled out by medics.

Kate's first thought was Harry's gunman had found another victim, though it wasn't likely. She watched the gurney being pushed down the sidewalk, but she couldn't tell if the victim was dead or alive.

CHAPTER TEN

Neither Agnes nor Kate spoke during the rest of the drive. The hotel seemed welcoming after this unending day. When Agnes stopped, the light from the entrance shone on her face, highlighting a vulnerability she hadn't seen since her parents' crash. Her expression brought the memories back fresh and raw. Agnes, only a young teenager at the time, had been brought to their home in the middle of the night. The car accident killed both her parents but left her with only minor injuries. That night, and for several months after, she'd shared Kate's room and taken over her life. Kate listened to her rage and cry and wallow in the heartbreaking pain of loss. She told Kate she wished she'd been killed in the car, too. Kate hadn't argued. She'd merely sat stroking Agnes' hair until exhaustion beat down the rage. She had later told people Kate had treated her as an injured puppy. She was not far off. Kate's mind would have worked in such a way. She had more experience with hurt puppies than with a cousin who'd had had her family snatched from her in a matter of seconds.

Much as Kate's siblings could annoy her, the thought of having no parents or siblings horrified her beyond belief. She started calling Agnes her big sister to include her in the family until the term had become habit. Kate told her she had more than enough brothers but had always wanted a sister. After a couple of months, Agnes went to stay with her grandparents who luckily lived only a twenty minute bike ride away in the next town.

"Answer me this, Sis." Kate's voice cut through the silence. "If you had no plan to be involved with the bank, why did you get all your degrees in math?"

Referring to her as her sister brought out her first real smile of the drive.

Her reply, so soft Kate could barely hear, seemed more question than answer. "Because I love math?"

Kate saw a bit of her despair lifting. Agnes had decided on a whim to become a model when her uncle took over running her father's bank. The fact she'd excelled in a profession as far from banking as she could get, Kate mused, made her question any thought of her following in her family tradition. She probably had convinced herself being a top model made her appear flighty rather than solid and reliable as a smart bank president should.

Kate had only found out by accident Agnes had been taking courses, first by mail and then online, to get her bachelor's and master's degrees in applied mathematics and had recently finished her PhD in statistics. Claire, Kate's mother, had let drop in passing to let Agnes know, if she spoke to her, about an upcoming online seminar in the new taxation rules for privately owned banks.

Kate, the only person in the family with a non-mathematical career, seemed also to be the only one who hadn't known her cousin/sister had been spending years getting degrees that would help her not at all with a career in modeling but were vital in the world of banking.

Kate decided to try an additional persuasion. "Agnes," she said, her tone of voice forcing Agnes to turn toward her, "has it occurred to you with your style and imagination, to say absolutely nothing of your enormous worldwide reputation, you could make this banking career into anything you want. I'll bet you within two years you'll be back on every billboard in the city as the coolest banker in New York City or even the US. Think about it. You're already the most recognizable person in the country, short of the president. You should use your reputation to put your own stamp on Forester's. You have forward thinking ideas in the works already, with what you and your uncle Paul put together. Think what you could do if you started applying some of the same creativity to the banking world in general. Forester's could be the go to bank for entrepreneurs who need a bank with imagination and a desire to make the country better.

"You should call your gram in the morning. Ask her to tell you why both your father and your grandfather loved working in the bank. She may surprise you with the answer."

She watched the Agnes she knew and loved emerge. The stress burdening her since Kate arrived seemed to drop away. Her shoulders straightened, and her head lifted. Turning, Agnes caught Kate's grin as she gave her a high-five, and she matched it.

"Damn, I'm good!" Kate whooped as she slipped from the car into the parking lot doing a little happy dance. The roar of Agnes laughing seemed louder than the engine, the thousand dollar smile everyone knew back on her face.

Letting the passenger window down, Agnes leaned over and said, "Thanks." Then she waved and pulled out of the parking lot into traffic.

Happiness for Agnes filled her. However, when she reached the hotel door, concern for their safety crept back in. She stopped and gave the parking lot a quick scan for blue sedans, but saw none.

Kate pushed open the door to the lobby, and after a minute reached the room Lily and she shared with the five puppies. Lily slept on the bed closest to the puppy pen while quiet classical music played on her iPhone to soothe them. Kate stood gazing down at the puppies and smiled, at last. The two puppy piles slept on silently. Lowering herself to the floor, she studied them, glancing from one to the next, mentally comparing each with the puppies she'd bred herself and those bred by her dad and grandpa down through the years for Shannon Samoyeds.

Normally, from the day a litter whelped, Kate would spend time sitting like this daily, watching them develop. She hadn't been able to do it this time and had to rely on photos Lily had e-mailed her and what she saw before her now. The influences of both sire and dam appeared to a certain extent in all the puppies but mostly in the boy with the blue ribbon and the girl with the red. What pleased her most was the resemblance between Blue Boy and Dillon at the same age. Maybe realizing she watched him, the puppy under scrutiny stood up, moved across the pen until he stopped right in front of her, circled once, and settled himself on top of a fluffy chenille monkey. She resisted the urge to pick him up and snuggle, which would certainly wake everyone.

Instead Kate uncrossed her legs and stood, making her way across the room and, with her suitcase, slipped into the bathroom. A few minutes later, now in pj's with clean teeth, she crawled into the second bed. For a day that had begun like a total disaster, it had ended on an upswing for her Though concerned about Harry's friend, without details, she didn't know how the evening had ended for him.

Kate's phone lay on the nightstand so she quickly sent Harry a text. *Agnes and I ended up driving by the house where you guys were tonight. It seemed like someone got hurt. Is your professor okay? I'm settled at the hotel. Take care. I'll see you at breakfast. Love, Kate.* She hit send, made sure to plug the charger in then rolled over to sleep. The phone vibrated a minute later. She took it and read. *Someone shot while at Stubbs' house. Stubbs not the victim. He's disappeared. Get some sleep. See you in morning. Love, F.*

Her mental clock, still in another time zone, came in handy since before dawn had really gotten its act together, the sound of small barks had Lily and Kate throwing jeans and sweatshirts over pj's and grabbing room keys, poop bags, and puppies. Kate grabbed the two closest puppies, snapping on leads without matching up collar colors. Lily clipped on another lead, piled a third puppy on top of the load, and opened the room door, pushing Kate out into the lobby extension. Kate thanked God the door to outside didn't require hands to open it. When she reached the grass, she lowered her load, untwisted the spaghetti of tangled leads and then started walking.

Kate watched each puppy move while her mind again went into comparison mode. It played mental videos of at least four generations of eight-week-old puppies she had bred. This was why she had traveled almost twenty-five hundred miles. She checked how they stopped, how they held their heads and necks, each puppy's rear moving away and front coming toward her. The male caught and held her eye right away. He had what her dad always called presence—the ingrained knowledge every eye should be on him and everybody else could step to the end of the line. Dillon had it, as did his father and grandfather. All of a sudden, Kate found herself crying. Death had taken both her grandfather and father from her a year ago, and she missed them so much she ached. They used to stand together each morning as the puppies went from the whelping room to their pen, not talking, simply watching. She could almost feel Gramps' hand on her shoulder as the little red bitch breezed by her purple ribbon sister, striding out beautifully when they trotted across the grass. Kate breathed in a shuddering breath and focused back on Blue Boy.

The lessons she'd learn in those "watching sessions" as she'd grown up, now played out in her head. Kate let the puppies romp and sniff while she took mental notes. Decisions shouldn't be made without at least a cup of tea in the morning, she told herself. Blue puppy set off at a brisk trot, ignoring his sisters as he explored every clump of grass or low bush in search of a perfect crap spot. When Lily emerged with the other two puppies, Kate noticed he stopped, stacked, four-square and alert, ready to be judged.

"He's like his dad," a voice behind her said. Kate glanced over her shoulder, and her heart did leap. She didn't answer since her emotions still raged. A sleep-deprived Harry stood behind her, his hair sticking up in little clumps, his clothes rumpled as though he'd slept in them, his bare feet in beaten-up loafers, and the morning shadow of his beard sharpening the planes of his face. He stepped close behind Kate, his arms circling her waist in a hug, and for a minute they stood with Harry's cheek resting against hers, while watching the puppies. "Your dad and granddad are with you right here, Kate. They're proud you're carrying on their work. They know they left Shannon Samoyeds in the best hands." Taking the third lead and giving her a quick kiss, he said, "I saw you walk by my window and had to come say good morning." They walked slowly, watching the girls tackle their brother, rolling about to draw his attention. Laughing, they unscrambled the once again tangled leads and got the pups back to focusing on peeing and pooping. Kate leaned against Harry and, feeling much better, went back to doing mental comparisons.

When the last puppy had taken care of business and the poop bags were deposited in the garbage, they began the challenge of convincing the puppies to climb the two steps to the hotel door. Each step matched the height of the puppy's shoulders so, as far as they were concerned, they needed to climb mountains. Now they had to train them to be mountaineers. The girls each mastered the first step. Blue boy sat and thought about it, got up, and tried to find another way. Then he sat again. Harry finally bent and placed the pup's front paws on the step then boosted his rear into place before he could think. At step two, the pup put his own front paws up then looked over his shoulder at Harry, waiting for a boost. Harry laughed and scooped him into his arms as Kate lifted the girls and headed toward the hotel room.

Lily had beaten them back and replaced all the piddle pads covering the tarp in the puppy pen. Food bowls came next and the puppies were happy. Kate gave Harry a quick kiss and told him she'd meet him for breakfast after she'd had a shower and changed into something she hadn't slept in. He left to do the same. As Kate stood in the shower, she realized she hadn't seen any blue sedans in the parking lot, but then she hadn't really been looking. She'd have to be more careful.

Wrapped in a towel, she went through her suitcase, pulling out a flattering T-shirt with a scoop neck, her favorite jeans and the comfortable soft half boots. She made quick work of the shower then simply fluffed her hair and put on lipstick and a little blush. Then she slipped on the beautiful silver hoop earrings Harry had given her, smiled down at her engagement ring, a one-of-a-kind with Samoyeds carved into it, and decided she was ready to take on the world, or, at least, her part of it. Moving all her things out of the way to give Lily room, she headed out to find some breakfast and take on a day without danger and threats, she hoped.

CHAPTER ELEVEN

Lily had selected the hotel with the puppies in mind and gotten two rooms next to each other on the ground floor, opening onto the lobby extension, near an exit so they could shuffle puppies in and out. Rufus had managed to book the last room facing the parking lot on the same floor. Kate didn't ask how he pulled it off. After again checking to be sure the puppies, bellies full and content, had sorted themselves into two sleeping piles, Kate went in search of food and tea. It turned out this extension of the lobby became a cafeteria/ lounge for the hotel during the breakfast period. The area measured about forty feet wide and the length of four hotel rooms.

It had been empty when Kate took the puppies out and back at daybreak, but now a hum of conversation announced breakfast was served. The smell of fresh-baked muffins, coffee, and bacon filled the air and set her in motion. Grabbing a tray, Kate put a plate, bowl, and cup on it and began checking out the offerings. She filled a bowl with hot oatmeal covered with blueberries, Craisens, walnuts, a little brown sugar, and milk. Next came a cup of tea and a raisin bagel. She could now take on the world, which arrived five minutes later in the form of Agnes and Sean, followed by Harry, Rufus, and a still half-asleep Jordy, carrying breakfast trays filled from the buffet. Kate had finished her oatmeal and tea and started on her bagel when a second cup of tea appeared at her elbow and Harry slid into the chair next to hers. She leaned her shoulder against his for a minute in thanks. The sound of eating, the only noise at their table for about a minute, was broken when Kate asked, "Are you going to share details about last night?"

Sean looked at Harry and Rufus. "Um, we couldn't talk to the professor last night so we'll have to leave you girls on your own and go back today."

Kate focused first on Agnes and then on the men. "I thought the injured person wasn't the professor. Isn't he missing?"

Sean turned to Harry. "You told her?"

"Agnes and Kate saw us at Stubbs' last night."

Sean turned to Agnes, who munched on a piece of bagel she'd snatched from Kate's plate and stared at the ceiling. "You saw us."

Agnes lowered her gaze to his. "Yes, we did. Kate and I had some family business to discuss. We turned down a street and saw you standing in a driveway watching paramedics wheeling out a gurney and putting someone in an ambulance. The police kept cars from stopping, so we continued on to the hotel. Was it your professor who got hurt?"

"Who was hurt? What ambulance?" Joyce put her tray

on the table. She, Lily, and Cathy waited as Rufus and Jordy pulled a second table over so as to seat everyone in the group. Rufus made room for Cathy between him and Jordy while Cathy nudged an extra muffin onto Jordy's plate and set chocolate milk in front of him then unloaded her coffee. She winked at Jordy as Rufus pushed in her chair.

Harry answered. "We don't know. Last night there was some kind of attack at the professor's house. Someone got hurt, and the professor is missing. Other than the fact there was blood in the kitchen, we didn't find out anything. As outsiders, the cops weren't inclined to share."

Joyce scanned the group. "Let me see what I can do." She pulled out her phone and dialed. "Billy?" she asked someone on the other end of the call. "Some friends of mine flew all the way across the country to speak with Professor Stubbs at the college, but when they got there last night, it seemed all hell had broken out and nobody would tell them anything. Yeah, I can vouch for them. One's a Connecticut State Trooper and one's former FBI who now has his own security business. They're good people. What can you tell me without getting in trouble with your guys? Okay. Yeah, okay. Got it. Thanks, Billy. Say hello to Sharon and the kids for me, and I'll tell the guys in Denver you're still alive."

Joyce reached for her coffee and finished her eggs and bacon before turning to the waiting crowd. "Sorry, I saw no sense in letting my food get cold. Billy is someone who grew up near my family's ranch not far from here. When he got out of the service, they weren't hiring on the force here so he ended up becoming a Denver sheriff's deputy. He married a girl from Lubbock and, when the kids started coming and a job opened up, he moved here so they could be closer to their families. Anyhow, Billy told me they got an anonymous call of a disturbance at your professor's home last night and, when they got there, blood covered much of the kitchen floor, the professor was missing, and another math professor seemed to be bleeding from a bullet wound. Someone saw a blue sedan parked in the driveway earlier in the day. There's an APB out for your professor. The other man is in the hospital, under guard, but the doctors say he should recover. Oh, and it seems your professor is already in trouble with the SEC and the FBI over theft of funds from the college's retirement fund as well as funds of several other colleges. Busy man!"

Kate stared at Harry. He sat in silence, not contributing to the speculation flying around the table. She rested her hand next to his, barely touching. He glanced her way and smiled. After a minute, Kate leaned in and spoke softly. "I'm fine here checking out the puppies. Why don't you see if you can find out more about this SEC problem? It sounds like the reason he needed you. If you can figure out what's going on, it might give a clue as to what caused the mess you witnessed. Kevin might be able to fill you in."

As if conjured up by her magic powers, Kevin Connelly walked into the lobby, accompanied by a bunch of people who appeared, from their outfits, to be Texas Poly students and faculty.

"Hi, guys," Kevin said approaching the table. "I brought this crowd with me because they've all had Stubbs as a prof and they're worried about what's happening. It's all over campus Professor McNatt got shot at Professor Stubbs' house. They want to help. Of course, the actual reason they're here is to meet the genuine Harry Foyle."

Harry's face turned a lovely shade of crimson as he focused on the remains of his breakfast. Kate leaned over to whisper in his ear again while grinning and nudging his shoulder. "You're a wizard, Harry," she quoted. His dimples flashed as he glanced her way.

Kevin's manners burst forth with the help of the kick under the table from his brother's foot. "You know Harry." Harry stood politely and nodded. "This hot lady is Kate Killoy, who I've known all my life. She raises Samoyeds, Arctic dogs for those who don't know, and brings killers to justice in her spare time. Next to her is my brother Sean who's a Connecticut State Trooper. And this, of course"—Kevin bowed low—"is the supermodel Agnes Forester whom everybody who doesn't live in a cave must know. She's Kate's cousin and she and her gram raise Greyhounds. She also owns a bank, Henry, so make nice with her. Next to her is Jordy Blackburn who is trying to out-Harry Harry. He's at MIT in math, even though he's only eleven. Next to him is Cathy Harrison who is a nurse, a Samoyed breeder, and a dog show judge. Then you've got Jordy's dad Rufus who's a professor in the math department at U. C. Denver. Next is Joyce Marks, who I found out is with the Denver Sheriff's Department, a Samoyed breeder, and a dog show judge, and Lily Peters who's a district attorney and has a litter of unbelievably cute puppies somewhere around here. Everybody, meet Andy, Mac, Henry, Burt, and Cleon better known as Statistics, Cryptography, Finance, Chaos Theory and Probability. Oh, yeah and this is Toni Dunn, Stubbs' TA, as well as Dr. Kimbel, and Mayleen Ke from the math department. What you see is the Stubbs' posse."

Kate focused on the teaching assistant, Toni Dunn, whom she had thought to be male when Rufus mentioned the name. Though about her own age, she dressed like the students but with a quite serious face peering out from under her brunette bangs. Not very tall, she appeared shorter by standing next to Kevin. Though she smiled up at Rufus, her total focus was on Harry. Rufus reached over to pat her shoulder. "Toni is one of my former students."

Sean pulled his brother aside, speaking in a low growl, and Kate could see some friction between them. Agnes watched the angry, shoving byplay with a frown for a few minutes then turned to Harry. "Much as I'm used to Killoys bickering all the time, they, at least, have the grace not to do it in public. Sean is playing the big brother ticket, and it's not working. I hate to ask, Foyle, but could you bring some civility to this sideshow?"

Harry glanced at Kate and then, cocking his head for

Rufus to join him, headed into the battle.

Kate decided to distract the group eagerly watching the battle. She asked what year each was in and what they planned doing after graduation. Some answered, but they focused on the men still holding center stage so Kate nudged Jordy's foot under the table. He started discussing the paper he'd had to finish this weekend, and slowly the group turned back toward their table. Kate knew his charm would distract, and soon everyone's attention hung on the pint-sized mathematician. Everyone except Miss Toni Dunn, who still had her gaze locked on Harry with an expression like Dillon's when he got a new chewie.

Kate turned her chair to face Toni and asked, "Have you been Professor Stubbs' TA for long?"

Dunn turned, her scowl showing her annoyance at being distracted from her quarry. "What? Oh, I've been with the department for two years." She gazed back toward the men across the room. "I've completed my masters and am working on my PhD."

"What's your field?" Kate asked politely.

"Oh, you wouldn't understand it." Her response made it clear exactly what she thought of Kate.

Agnes barked out a laugh, but Kate smiled and quietly said, "I know something about math, and I'd be interested."

Toni Dunn stared at her with contempt, as though she were about to lecture a two-year-old.

As she opened her mouth, Agnes leaned over and tapped her on the arm. "Be careful, princess. Before you start tramping through cow shit, wrap your calculating little brain around these factors. One, her last name is Killoy, and two, she's engaged to Foyle."

Kate kept her expression interested and merely raised her eyebrows. She watched the woman's brain processing what Agnes had told her and saw exactly when the penny dropped. She turned to Kate and asked, "Claire Killoy?"

"My mother." Kate informed her, not letting the woman know her mother was her biggest critic and still hadn't accepted the fact she'd chosen a career other than math.

"Oh."

Jordy smiled at the TA. "Hi, Toni. Wait 'til you see the cool puppies here. They are so much fun." He jumped down from his seat and took his dishes to the cleanup area.

Kate turned to Dr. Kimbel and Mayleen Ke. "Kevin mentioned your names but he didn't say your fields. What are your areas of interests in the department?"

Dr. Kimbel answered, "I'm in statistics. I have heard of Harry and, of course, know of your mother because of her books but I didn't know there were other Killoys."

"Well, brace yourself, because I am only one of five, and the others are far more intense when it comes to the world of mathematics than I. When my father and grandfather died last year, my brother Tom took over the family business, and

Will is set to join him when he graduates next year. I don't know what fields the twins will end up in since they've got this year of high school to finish." Kate laughed.

Mayleen Ke broke in. "I am planning to hear your mother at a symposium in November. I shall keep my eye out for talks by you and your brothers as well."

"Will is the only one who enjoys getting up and speaking to crowds, so he's the only one you need to watch for now—"

Dr. Kimbel interrupted. "Is Foyle here to investigate the theft? Is he trying to get this professor's name cleared? He'll have a hard time. Baxter, Kline and Baxter have been working with the university for almost twenty years. They insist there is no possibility of wrongdoing on their part. Harry is not going to have an easy time of it."

"Well, I have found over the years what appears factual often is an interpretation that upon further analysis could be disproved. Harry will find the person behind the problem and, if it's the professor, he won't let friendship color his findings," Kate said loyally. "He spent five years with the FBI and is very talented at uncovering even the most cleverly hidden crimes."

Before the conversation could continue, the men returned. Kevin turned to his friends. "Let's go, everybody. We're going to head back to campus and see what information we can pick up. My brother and the others are going to go deal with the cops, the SEC, and FBI. I'll pass what we learn to my brother, and they'll let us know what they learn." They all scraped back their chairs.

"And we," Lily said, "are going to take the puppies to the park and socialize them. A morning spent romping with children and exploring play equipment will be exactly what they need."

Kate noticed the towheaded beanpole she thought Kevin had called Henry now in deep conversation with Agnes. Somewhat red in the face and hesitant, he spoke softly to her then asked a question. She answered equally quietly, but whatever she said brought a smile to his face and Kate watched him shower her with thanks. Agnes reached into her purse and handed him her card, making a note on the back. As he walked toward his friends already at the exit, his feet seemed to dance.

Kate looped her arm through Agnes' and said, "Normally, I'd say from the young man's expression, he'd asked you out and you'd said yes, but considering what we talked about last night and the fact his major is finance, I'd say Agnes the banker, not Agnes the supermodel, made his day."

"I told him to contact me when he finishes his master's degree. Banks always need people with good backgrounds in finance.

Kate reached out and gave Agnes a hug that she surprisingly returned. Agnes said, "I talked to Gram this morning. It helped." Then she turned to Lily, asking to see the puppies.

They had all headed toward the room when Harry, Sean, and Rufus met them. Harry pulled Kate aside. He rested his hand on her cheek and leaned in to rest his head on hers. "I hate leaving you with Soucek still on the loose. I don't know if what's going on with Stubbs has anything to do with him, but there's been violence and what could have been Soucek's car spotted there earlier. I wish you were safe with me."

"I haven't seen any sign of the blue sedan since we arrived. I'll be careful. I think the plan is to take the puppies to the park, wear them out and then have Joyce and Cathy evaluate them. I plan to play with the puppies and take a few hundred photos. I'll have my phone with me and call if I see Soucek or anything that might mean trouble."

"While you're relaxing with the puppies, perhaps you could spare a thought as to where and when we're going on our next date. I promised to wait for two more dates before I sic your mother on you to name a date for the wedding."

His smile warmed her heart as his words reminded her of what she had promised. Her grandparents had gone on five dates before they got married. Grandma Ann said she knew she'd marry him five minutes into the first date, but since she almost never had a chance to eat out, she made gramps take her out five times before she named the date. She'd told Harry this story and he'd decided five dates would work and then Kate could name the day for their wedding. Unfortunately, with the schedules they both carried, the pair had only managed three dates thus far. Their talking every night and texting constantly didn't count. Harry knew, due to her inexperience, Kate had needed time.

Kate nodded then leaned in as she walked him to the door. "Let me know if there's anything I can do." She kissed him as he joined the others, including his fan club that seemed reluctant to leave. The men got into their cars, as did the students, and they all headed out. Kate checked to see if there were any sign of the blue sedan. There wasn't but she did see the TA, Toni Dunn, climbing into a fancy car parked at the curb. As it pulled away, Kate got a glimpse of the driver—a man with silver hair.

CHAPTER TWELVE

Kate reached the room in time to be mowed down by the charge of exiting women holding puppies and heading the other way. She suddenly held a male puppy as well as poop bags, treats, her purse, and the room key. Someone placed the cowboy hat she'd bought in the airport on her head and she found herself doing a one-eighty to get her moving back the way she'd come.

"We're heading for the park to socialize these little buggers," Agnes said, sounding more cheerful than she had in months.

The crowd quickly divided itself. Agnes and Jordy joined Joyce and Cathy in Joyce's SUV, along with Lexi, and Kate got in with Lily. The puppies had been settled into the back of the white Ford Flex and the curtains drawn to keep the air conditioning and the breeze from the battery powered fans focused on the puppies. They'd needed all this effort to stay comfortable since the heat climbed as the early morning cool disappeared. They had only pulled out of the parking lot when it occurred to Kate she hadn't had a chance to fill Lily in on the situation with Soucek. She pulled out her phone and brought up the photos as they headed out of the metropolitan area of Lubbock into a more suburban section.

"Harry and I ran into a problem on the way here, which is something you should know about since the problem seems to be on hold but not solved. There is a man named Anton Soucek who…."

Lily's eyes widened and she sat bolt upright, glanced in Kate's direction then focused firmly on the road. Kate found the photo and, since they'd stopped at a traffic light, held it for her to see. Lily nodded but still didn't speak.

Finally, Kate asked, "Okay, how do you know Soucek?"

"I didn't say I know him."

"No, but your reaction seemed excessive for someone hearing a name for the first time. This man followed us onto the plane yesterday, and we spotted him on the way to Lubbock. I've been told he's been in prison and therefore considered dangerous but had recently gotten out."

Lily sighed. "I doubt very much he'd be dangerous. I suppose I can tell you how I know of him, since the case is closed, and anyway it took place in a different jurisdiction from mine and is a matter of public record. A couple of years ago, a friend from law school asked me to glance at a case he'd lost and see if could have done anything to change the verdict. He had defended Soucek on the charge of grand larceny. The actual charge had involved stealing over a hundred thousand dollars from the company where Soucek worked as an accountant.

"My friend Jimmy felt the district attorney had been influenced by the company to close the case quickly, without sufficient investigation. Jim took me out to dinner and brought me copies of the trial transcript and a list of all the evidence in the case. There wasn't much. I never would have gone to court with so little. The money hadn't been found. No paper trail led to Soucek. He had money in his bank accounts, but their records proved he'd been saving part of his paycheck every week for years, and the deposit records matched the balance.

"Jimmy knew this company had made a very large donation to the Republican Party's election fund in the past and felt since both the prosecutor and the judge were up for reelection on the Republican ticket, this financial history might have influenced their decision to ram the case through on circumstantial evidence.

Jimmy filed an appeal, but within a week, his witnesses had all disappeared. When his family started getting threats through the mail and over the phone, he finally gave up and closed his practice. He and his wife moved to

Pennsylvania where his uncle practiced law and welcomed him into the firm."

"Did they call in a forensic accountant?"

"No, Jimmy didn't. I never would have taken the case to a judge. Nowhere near enough evidence existed for a conviction. He should have also insisted on a jury trial. After I read the case files, I felt that faults existed on both sides. The prosecution proceeded with too thin a case, and Jimmy didn't do enough to defend his client. He wrote to me later asking what I'd thought of the case, but I never answered. I still have the files tucked away."

"And now Soucek is out of jail and trying to find Harry. I'd better send the photo to Agnes and tell her to watch for him. With all the family stuff she and I dealt with last night and then the mess at the professor's place, I forgot all about it." Her fingers flew over the keys of her phone, texting Agnes the details and then sending her Soucek's photo. Kate's phone buzzed a few seconds later with her response. *Joyce and Cathy already filled me in. Good thing you've got friends who are on the ball. A*

Kate's mind still focused on what Lily had said about Soucek's case. She picked up her phone again and texted Harry. *Have information on Soucek. Not pressing. Will tell you when you get some time. K*

A minute later, they reached a large park located on the outskirts of the city. This early in the day, they managed to park both cars together though the lot was filling up fast. To the right stood a large area with a tower, swings, slides, climbing bars, and all sorts of challenges. This was swarming with children. Next to it sat a bouncing platform big enough to hold about ten kids plus a bunch of other kid-friendly pieces of equipment. Alongside these activities stood tables and benches where parents could sit. Trees gave some shade, but it was for the most part an open area.

To the left, a manmade lake held a collection of both domestic and wild ducks and geese. Having dealt with geese on more than one of their search and rescue training sessions, Kate decided to give them a wide berth. The puppy might think it cool to chase one of these noisy birds, but in a battle of goose versus eight-week-old puppy, goose would win every time.

Kate checked the parking lot for blue sedans, but the only blue car was a station wagon from which a pregnant woman unloaded a stroller, holding her toddler on her hip. The woman, in a single motion, flipped open the stroller into locking position, deposited the kid into it, and kicked the bumper to close the hatch. Before the puppy wranglers were half done, the woman strode across the park toward a group of mothers and fathers and a pack of about twenty preschoolers running around.

Kate lifted Blue Boy out of the pile of puppies, eager to get with the action. She clipped on the blue lead and checked her pocket for poop bags then left the others matching leads to collar colors and dividing up the pups and stepped back only to bump into Joyce.

Joyce declared she and Lexi would be hiking around the lake, needing the exercise after all the driving yesterday. She commanded heel, and the beautiful bitch moved smoothly at her side. Kate watched them, go pleased with Lexi's rear action. She would probably see her in the ring at the National Specialty in October. She thought the bitch had qualities she'd like to see in her line. Kate needed to get Joyce to send her a pedigree.

Her phone buzzed. Harry. She walked a little way away from the others as she answered. "Hi. What have you been able to find out?"

His voice sounded frustrated and distracted. "We're running into a brick wall here. No one knows where the professor is. The agents involved in the financial investigation are not sharing any details. I've got Sadie working on it, but I'll tell you, sweetheart, there's something definitely off about this whole thing. The person in the hospital is the professor's best friend who is also under investigation because he's on the same committee as Stubbs. Where are you now?"

"I'm at the park with the girls and the puppies. There's no sign of Soucek, but from what I learned from Lily, I'm sure his goal was to get to you for your help rather than to hurt you. It turns out she knew something about his case and his defense could have used you or K and K. A friend of hers presented the defense, and he discussed the case with her after he lost.

"We all need to sit and talk about this stuff. Why don't you guys come over to the park and play with the puppies? Joyce might have gotten some more information from her contact, and you could talk to Lily. If nothing else maybe you and I can spend an hour together without someone with a gun chasing us."

"Unique idea. I'd like to try it. Rufus wants to spend time with your friend Cathy. I think he's smitten."

"Does anyone say smitten anymore?" Kate laughed.

"I do. I know I'm smitten with you and have been from the first minute I saw you."

"In my case, I fell like a ton of bricks and was scared witless at the same time."

"You know you never have to be scared of me." Harry's soft voice seemed to reach out and hold her.

"I know. It's the concept of falling in love that used to scare me. But you're the reason I'm not frightened anymore. I really do love you, Harry Foyle."

"And I love you, Kate Killoy. I'll see you in about ten minutes."

Kate tucked her phone back into her jeans and strolled over to where the girls had gathered by the bouncy

-board. Agnes and Lily sat on it with the puppies, and Jordy went over to teach the kids everything about the puppies, as though he'd been studying them all his life instead of for the last twenty-four hours. Kate sat in an open slot on the piece of equipment that had now become a puppy jungle gym and told the others they'd be having company in about ten minutes. She leaned over the little bitch puppy with the red ribbon and asked Lily how she could obtain a copy of the case they'd discussed. Lily said since it was in public do-main, she'd have her assistant send the link. A few minutes later, her phone beeped with the link.

Next to her she saw Cathy had used a hairbrush, which was now in the blue puppy's mouth, and was putting on fresh lipstick and checking herself in a small mirror. Kate lifted the puppy and Cathy retrieved the "toy," shoving it back into her purse. Kate walked over to watch Agnes and Jordy who sat on the ground surrounded by kids. Jordy was giving petting lessons. One of the fathers told another the woman had to be Agnes Forester. He saw her daily as he'd passed a billboard with her smiling and wearing shorts and a T-shirt as she was now. She chuckled as they got one of the kids to go ask her if she really was Agnes Forester. Agnes smiled at the kid, ignoring the dads. She seemed so much more relaxed than even twenty-four hours ago.

A pull on the lead told Kate Blue Boy had a need for adventure. She saw there was time to take him for a walk and told Lily to let Harry know the way she headed. She paused to take a few photos including a shot of Agnes and

Jordy, side by side, buried under a pile of puppies, definitely a keeper. Kate stepped away and lifted the camera when Jordy said something that made Agnes laugh. Agnes leaned over and kissed his cheek as Kate clicked the shutter. He'd get major bragging rights at MIT when she mailed him the shot. Changing to video, she panned the whole scene of friends, puppies, and kids in this beautiful setting.

As they approached the path around the lake, Kate filmed Blue Boy's movement coming, going and from the side. She pressed the button to send the camera back to stills and snapped some shots of him challenging the geese from a safe distance. Kate felt herself relax for the first time since she'd gotten the text from Harry. He was safe. She took in a deep breath and let it out slowly, allowing each muscle in her body to unwind and let her mind wander. Life was good.

She needed to come up with a name for the puppy. She couldn't keep calling him Blue Boy. Kate had playing with ideas for names over the last few months and had come up with Quinn, Finnegan, and Devyn. She watched the puppy walk and began trying out some names. They entered an area with a hedge on one side and a row of benches on the other. The puppy romped from bench to bench, attacking the legs and leaping over the bars connecting them. Kate laughed as she tried to keep up with him and to untangle the lead as he worked from one to the other. "Devyn," she called. He ignored her and continued his game.

"Finnegan." No response. He ignored her completely. The lead tangled again. Undoing it, they walked on until the pup spun around toward the hedge, froze stacked four square, and growled. Kate's first thought was of the similarity to his dad, Dillon, her second to focus on his reaction.

Without thinking, she called, "Quinn." The puppy turned back to her but then returned to growling. Kate had never seen hackles stand up on a puppy. She slid her hand down the lead until it rested above the collar. She followed his gaze. The puppy focused on the hedge, but she couldn't see anything. "Quinn." He glanced over his shoulder again, and Kate reached down to stroke his back. Tension seemed to be running through his entire body, and he resisted her distraction.

Finally, Kate stood, turning to go back along the path the way they'd come. "Quinn, let's go," she said giving a slight tug on the lead, and began walking down the path. He didn't move. "Quinn, come," she said with authority this time. He stared hard at the hedge then, giving her a look that said she was an idiot, began trotting at her side. After a few steps, he whirled again and began barking frantically. Kate turned back toward the hedge, saw the gun, and heard, "Don't make a sound, Miss Killoy, or I'll shoot your little puppy."

CHAPTER THIRTEEN

Something felt wrong. Harry sat in the passenger seat of Rufus' car, willing him to drive faster. Traffic moved at a snail's pace, and it took all his restraint not to hop from the car and run. He didn't know what had set this feeling off, but he knew Kate was in trouble. He'd been uneasy since breakfast. He checked his phone hoping for more texts from her but nothing. The light finally changed, and they began to move.

"Four more blocks." Rufus said glancing at Harry with a worried frown on his face. His concern, though probably well meant, annoyed Harry. He didn't want sympathy, he wanted speed.

"I'll begin on the printouts when we get back from the park," Harry said to hide his impatience. "I think the answer to what's going on is in them but I've not had time to give them more than a glance. With the professor in hiding, there's no choice but to find the source of the original problem. I'm sure last night's shooting was meant for Stubbs. What McNatt was doing there, I have no idea."

"I think I know the answer." Sean piped in from the back seat where he chatted on his phone. They had dropped Kevin at the campus. "The contact Joyce gave me in the department said McNatt stayed at Stubbs' place while his mother-in-law and her two cats visited his wife. It seems McNatt is highly allergic to the cats."

"So his presence is explained. The fact none of the students knew about it meant anyone who saw a man moving around the kitchen, at night with the shade down, probably thought it was Stubbs." Harry mused for a couple of minutes. "He wasn't shot by a professional. In spite of the amount of blood, the bullet hit him high in the shoulder and almost missed him completely."

"Do you think it was a move to draw attention away from the theft from the retirement account?" Sean asked.

"Absolutely. I think the answer lies somewhere in the paperwork. I'll spend an hour at the park with the girls, but then I've got to start picking apart the program."

Rufus pulled into the parking lot as a car backed out. They got out and headed toward the crowd of people near a castle-like structure of play equipment. Sean told them wherever there was a crowd, they'd find Agnes.

Kate stared at the gun for a second and then, with a

sweep of her hand, scooped the puppy into her arms and turned to keep him out of the line of fire. In front of her, Anton Soucek stood, holding a gun, seriously threatening. She kicked herself for feeling any pity for this jerk after hearing Lily's story. Anyone who could threaten to kill an innocent puppy didn't deserve a nanosecond of her concern. Kate narrowed her eyes, trying to sum him up. "What do you want, Soucek? Why did you follow me from Connecticut to Texas? I've never done anything to you."

"Move if you don't want the dog hurt." He grabbed her arm, only to let go fast when the puppy bit his hand. Puppy teeth were sharp as needles, so his hand had to hurt. He grabbed her shoulder, keeping out of puppy reach, and shoved her toward the blue sedan sitting at the edge of the lot, its engine running. He yanked the back door open and shoved her inside. Then, sliding into the passenger seat, he yelled to the older man behind the wheel, "Go, go."

"A gun, Anton? Are you insane? Why do you have a gun? Who is this lady? You said you wanted to talk to Foyle, not kidnap a woman. What is going on?"

"Lyndon, drive please, while I think. Foyle wasn't here, but he'll come if he wants to save his fiancée."

The older man put the car in park. "No." He stared at Soucek. "You will not do this. Harry Foyle will not help a man who threatens him." He turned in his seat, and Kate got her first look at the getaway driver. He must have been about Sal's age, wearing a short-sleeved dress shirt and bow tie. His had sharp blue eyes, but his white hair was askew, and he seemed exhausted. He didn't appear to be a kidnapper. He looked more like a school teacher or—Lyndon? She'd heard that name. It was like the former president from Texas. Lyndon... Lyndon... Stubbs. The missing professor was working with an escaped prisoner? She stared for a second and then, shifting the puppy, who still quietly growled at Soucek, held out her hand to the other man.

"You must be Professor Stubbs." Kate smiled slightly, feeling as though she'd landed at the Mad Hatter's Tea Party. "I'm Kate Killoy, Harry's fiancée. I'm told you tell a story about Harry to your students every year."

He smiled. "Yes, I do. He glanced down at the puppy in her lap. "And who is your little Samoyed friend?"

"You know the breed?" Kate asked in both surprise and delight. "This is Quinn. He's eight weeks old and showing remarkable good taste by not liking your nasty friend, Mr. Soucek, here."

"Anton. Put the gun away. You're frightening the young lady."

"It's not loaded." He sulked.

"You're an idiot," Kate told him. "If a cop had spotted you pointing a gun at me, he would have shot first and asked questions later. Why are you trying to kidnap me, anyway?"

"I need someone to prove I didn't do the crime for which I was sent to prison." His shoulders slumped. "Lyndon thought this friend of his could figure out who stole the money and could tell the cops."

"So, rather than pick up the phone and call Harry and ask him to help you, you break into his condo, threaten us on the flight to Denver, track us to Lubbock, and kidnap me? Brilliant, absolutely brilliant."

"I did not break into any condo. It is against the law," Soucek protested.

"I'm in the hands of the gang who couldn't shoot straight." Kate sighed. "Luckily for you, Soucek, I've already arranged to have your case notes sent to Harry, though you don't deserve it." Kate turned to the professor. "Now, you are another problem. Why are you hiding from the police? Why was there blood all over your kitchen? And did you shoot Rohon McNatt?"

"Shoot Rohon? Don't be ridiculous. Wait. Blood on my kitchen floor? Has something happened to Rohon? He's house sitting for me while I'm helping Anton. His mother-in-law is visiting his wife and bringing her cats. Rohon is allergic. I told him he could stay at my place until Wednesday when she leaves. Why would anyone shoot Rohon? His field is chaos theory. Most people don't understand what he says, but it's certainly not a reason to shoot him. He's a professor emeritus who only teaches a few seminars now and serves on a few committees."

"I hate to be the one to tell you this, but your friend Rohon was shot at your home last night. It may have been someone who thought they were shooting you. I know you're in trouble with the SEC and FBI right now. Tell me. Is there anyone who wants to kill you?"

"The retirement fund problem is all an error. I called Rufus. He said Harry would come and explain to these people I have done nothing wrong. They are accusing me of stealing huge amounts of money. See this car, my clothes? Do I look as though I have money? It is all a mistake on the part of the company, and I'm being wrongly accused."

"I'm sure Harry will do his best to help you but, in the meantime, you two need to get your acts together. Professor, the police need to talk to you. They'll want to know where you were last night instead of at home. You should talk to them sooner rather than later and then speak to your friend Rohon who is in the hospital."

Quinn, who had been sleeping in her lap, chose that minute to wake up, slide to the floor of the car, and begin sniffing. "This puppy needs to get out. Quinn is about to pee and poop all over your car." Kate opened the door and quickly lowered the puppy to the ground where he proceeded to pee immediately. She followed him out, reaching into her pocket for a poop bag as he settled into sniffing the ground, getting ready to take care of the rest of his business.

Kate turned to the men and told them where they were staying and that they'd be back at the hotel after they finish socializing a litter of puppies in the park. "Anton, if Harry can't help you, I can talk to my brother. Killoy and Killoy might be able to help. I'm surprised your lawyer didn't request a forensic accountant check the records, when you went to trial."

"My lawyer didn't believe the prosecutor had a case. It astonished him when I ended up in prison. He was going to appeal, but he ended up only going away."

Kate saw Quinn had finished and bent down to clean up after him. As she did so, she heard a ping as something hit the top of the car. Kate knew that sound. Then the glass in the car window next to her head smashed. She reached out, grabbed Quinn, left the poop bag on the ground, and, pulling open the door, dove back into the car yelling, "Shots, go, go, drive."

The professor had serious skills at getaways. He peeled rubber and shot forward, only clipping the curb slightly with his back tire as he turned onto the street. He drove straight for a block then turned right then left. Kate clutched the puppy as she balanced against the seat corner then grabbed a box of tissues to push the glass from the seat. She slid across to the cleared area on the far side, managed to put on the seat belt then grabbed the armrest to steady herself.

Kate didn't ask where they were going. Holding

Quinn's lead tight in her left hand to keep him away from the broken glass, she rested her head against the seat back and reached for her phone. Hitting the number Harry had put there yesterday, she held her breath while it rang. If it went to voice mail, Kate swore she'd kill him.

"Hey, love. We're at the park, and I don't see you." His cheerful voice focused her thoughts.

"Don't talk, just listen. I found your professor and Soucek, who's a friend of his. While we talked, someone took a couple of shots at me. I'm not hit, and we escaped. We're driving somewhere on Martha Sharp Freeway, and I don't think we're being followed. Tell Lily Quinn is safe."

"Shots, Kate? Who's shooting at you? Who's Quinn? Who are we?"

"Quinn is blue puppy boy. We are the professor, Soucek, and me. Harry, it sounded like New York. The gun must have had a silencer. The ping was the same. Someone wants me dead, and it's not Soucek. Get everybody out of the park and back to the hotel. Tell the police to look over by the end of the walk with the hedge. They'll see the spot. Tell them to watch for broken glass and a purple poop bag. Get everybody safely back to the hotel. Harry, if whoever this is wants me dead, they may want to kill you, too. Be careful, please. Call the cops then let me know when everyone's safe." Kate ended the call and slipped the phone back into her pocket. Then she closed her eyes and held the puppy against her cheek. His raspy tongue washed her face but she pulled back when he switched from tongue to sharp puppy teeth, wanting to play with her nose. She noticed they'd left the freeway and had turned into the huge parking lot of a strip mall. The professor pulled the car into a space facing out. He turned to her.

"If you want to hide, the best place to do it is in the middle of a large crowd." He sighed, closed his eyes, and leaned back.

Harry ran toward the group of women and puppies. "There's a gunman in the park who shot at Kate."

Sean went into cop mode with the 911 operator, and gave the information. Next, with an authoritative but calm voice, he told the parents shots had been fired in another part of the park so they needed to get their children out of here as quickly as possible.

"I thought I heard a backfire," one father said as he dashed toward them from the goose pond. He picked up his daughter in one arm and son in the other. Panic traveled through the crowd, and both children and adults screamed as people ran to their cars.

Cathy shouted to Rufus, "Joyce is walking Lexi around the pond." He took off at high speed to find her.

Lily, Agnes, Cathy, and Jordy gathered up the four remaining puppies and ran for Lily's car. "Kate said Quinn is fine," Harry told Lily.

"She's calling him Quinn? She's decided." Lily smiled slightly as she inserted the puppies into the back of the car then slipped into the front seat to turn on the engine and air conditioning.

Sirens filled the air, and a minute later squad cars and cops filled the parking lot. Sean and Harry raced toward them, and Agnes turned to greet her returning friends as they ran past ducks and geese into the parking lot.

The police asked who had seen the shooting and where had it happened. Harry explained his fiancée had called telling him she'd been shot at while walking her puppy on the sidewalk near the hedge. She had escaped in a car with friends unhurt. No, he told them, he didn't know where they were now. He and Sean accompanied the officer who took off along the path. Harry spotted the purple poop bag lying on the grass next to the edge of the parking lot, surrounded by window glass. A second cop found a spent bullet with blue paint on it lying in the parking lot nearby.

"She said the sound was a ping like the gun had a silencer." Harry informed the officer in charge.

"Your fiancée knows guns?" he asked.

"No," Harry answered reluctantly, seeing where this might be going. "She was shot at last winter in New York by a gun with silencer. She said it sounded the same."

Both Sean and the cops stared at Harry for a second.

Defensively, he told them, "A killer chasing her cousin, shot at her in a case of mistaken identity. The police have a record of the incident. Speak to Sgt. Sanchez in the Fourteenth Precinct."

Harry and Sean moved to join the girls in the now almost empty parking lot as the questions continued.

"You didn't say whose car she escaped in or where she is now."

Harry winced. He'd hoped to duck this question. Finally he admitted she was in a car driven by Professor Lyndon Stubbs and he had no idea of their location.

"Stubbs?" Rufus reacted to the name. "How did Kate find Stubbs?"

"Did this Professor Stubbs shoot at your fiancée?" the officer asked.

"No," Harry explained. "They were talking as he sat in his car when the shots came from behind. She grabbed her puppy, jumped into the car, and they left in a hurry."

"And you have no idea where they are?"

Harry winced. This guy wouldn't give up. "No. Her phone goes to voice mail." Harry lied. He didn't want the cops talking to Kate or the professor before he did.

Lily stepped forward and introduced herself, including her title as District Attorney of a county two hours south of Lubbock. She said she had a litter of eight-week-old puppies in the back of her car they'd been socializing and now needed to return to the hotel for food and rest. Her controlled tone brooked no argument. Harry bet she didn't lose many cases.

Five minutes later, the discussion moved to the hotel. The police hadn't finished asking questions, but they headed for a place where everyone could be safe while a team searched the park for any sign of the shooter. After thirty more minutes of questioning, the police left, saying they'd be back with more questions later and for Harry to notify them if he heard from his fiancée.

Kate leaned back against the seat, stroking Quinn and fighting the shaking that took hold of her as soon as they were safe. Her mind flashed back to last February. She'd been in New York to show Dillon as well as Harry's sister's German Shepherd and to have the first fashion show of her designs. Then, thanks to Agnes, she had a killer trying to murder her. Kate had met Harry when Sal, who knew him well, decided he would make a perfect bodyguard for her. It pissed Kate off at first to be thought helpless, but after Harry saved her life a second time, she agreed. They'd been walking the dogs on West Thirty-Second Street late one evening when Dillon whirled around and growled. When Kate bent to check him, a bullet barely missed her head. Harry had pulled her to safety, but in the process had taken a bullet himself. The ping sound without a bang, the police later told her, indicated a shot from a gun using a silencer.

Kate had helped catch the murderer, and he was locked up in prison. So, now, who wants her dead?

CHAPTER FOURTEEN

Kate's phone buzzed. It was Harry. She went to answer then let it go to voice mail. She needed to talk to him—but alone. Kate keyed in Sadie's number.

"Hey, Kate girl, how's the trip going? Did the guy in the airport give you any trouble? He's a convict who got out."

"Sadie, I need a favor. I need you to call Harry and tell him to get away from everyone and then call me. I need to talk to him without people finding out I'm calling."

"Katie, what's going on? You're not pulling a New York again are you?" Kate was trying to think of what to say when Sadie yelled, "You are! Is someone shooting at my boy?"

"No, Sadie. Harry's fine."

"So someone's shooting at you. Sal will go ballistic."

"Please, don't call him. I don't want him worried.

There's nothing he can do. Harry's with a bunch of people, most of whom I know and trust. But, someone shot at me who knew where I was, information only known by the people he's with. I need him to get away from them so we can talk. Can you help? It's one o'clock, here. Tell Harry I'll call him at one twenty but I'm turning off my phone 'til then."

"Okay, Katie. I'll take care of it. I'll text him now. Keep me posted." She hung up.

Kate let out a breath and turned off her phone. She could see why Harry loved his assistant so much.

Quinn, who had been dozing in her lap, woke and began sniffing. Kate threw open the door and moved him to the ground, where he quickly took care of business. She spotted a Petco at the corner of the mall. Quinn would need food and water and a few other things if they couldn't go right back to the hotel. Kate needed to get his feet off the hot asphalt, too. Picking him up, she leaned into the car and suggested the professor stay where he was because law enforcement was looking for him. Kate saw his face turned ashen, and she reached in and squeezed his hand. She suggested Anton go over to the McDonald's at the other end of the mall and get them some lunch and some extra water. She reached into her pocket for money, but he waved her hand away. They agreed to meet back there for lunch in fifteen minutes so they'd all be together when she called Harry.

Kate stepped away from the car and headed across the parking lot. An empty Petco cart sat abandoned beside a car, so she put the puppy in it. She expected him to try to jump out but, instead, he sat quietly, not fazed in the least by the new experience.

Once inside, Kate found the dog food area and located a small bag of the food Lily has been using and a measuring cup. She also got some piddle pads, two dog dishes, and some extra poop bags. On the way to the register, she stopped in the toy aisle and let Quinn check out some squeaky toys. He loved the roaring blue dinosaur almost as big as he and the small Kong. He was already chewing on the Kong when they reached the checkout. Kate paid and then headed back to the car with a contented puppy.

While they'd been gone, the professor had cleaned all the glass from the back seat and found a bullet lodged in the back door on the driver side right below the window. Kate saw Anton approaching with a bunch of takeout bags. Checking her phone, she noted she still had four minutes. Getting to work, she set out the piddle pads on the car floor, put down the dishes, measured food into one and added water to the other then set Quinn on the floor. He dug right in. One minute left. Kate reached into the bag Anton had put on the seat next to her and bit into the cheeseburger. Kate hadn't thought she'd be hungry after what happened, but the bite she took was heaven. As she ate, she used her other hand to wake up the phone. She checked the time and dialed Harry's number.

"Kate, damn it, where the hell are you?" His yell attracted Quinn's attention, but after a few seconds, the puppy went back to the food again.

"Are you alone?" Her voice was quiet and controlled. Kate didn't like being yelled at.

"Yes, I'm alone," he said with exasperation. "I'm in the parking lot of a pizza place. Kate, why are you hiding from me?"

"I'm not hiding from you. I'm hiding from whoever shot at me."

"Soucek?"

"No, I was standing five inches away from him at the time. Harry, whoever shot at me knew I'd be at the park and watched me go down the path. They also recognized the professor's car. I think their plan was to blame him or Anton for my death. If I hadn't bent over to pick up puppy poop, I'd be lying in the park with a bullet in my brain. The only people who knew I'd be there today were at breakfast with us this morning. So, unless Lubbock has people wandering city parks killing for no reason, someone from this morning's breakfast targeted me.

The silence at the other end of the call stretched out. "Kate, this is entirely my fault. Whenever I'm around you, people start shooting."

"Sadie thinks it's the other way around. She feels I'm a disaster magnet, so don't start beating yourself up." Kate turned to the professor and asked the street address of the mall. "Harry, put this address into your GPS. Also, check your car to be sure there are no tracking devices, and when you get to the parking lot, call. We'll be waiting for you."

"We, who's we?"

"I'm here with Professor Stubbs, Anton Soucek, and Quinn. Come as fast as you can, but be careful you're not followed."

Kate turned to the two men in the front seat polishing off the last of their lunches and asked, "Professor, where have you've been for the last forty-eight hours?"

He exchanged a glance with Soucek and then sighed. "I've been at Allen and Josie's, trying to figure a way to help Anton."

"Who are Allen and Josie, and where do they live?"

Soucek spoke. "Josie is my niece. She's married to Lyndon's son Allen. They live in Brownfield. Josie and Allen are cotton farmers. I'd never met her children. We had a wonderful visit, but I couldn't stay because I need to have someone help keep me from having to go back to prison."

"How did you know I'd be at the park?"

"I emailed my assistant, and she told me you and Harry would be at the park."

"I see." Kate sat for a few minutes then turned to the professor. "Professor, why did you need Harry to come to Texas?"

The old man squirmed. "I am in trouble. You see, I am one of three faculty members on a committee to oversee the investment of the faculty retirement fund at the university. I'm accused of a crime. The printouts of the deposits from the investment house don't match our printouts. The investment house said I falsified records. Our records come directly from the school's accountant, so they couldn't be wrong. An investigation began. At first, I thought it might involve a hundred dollar error but they're claiming it's millions. I have kept track of Harry's work since he left school, both with the FBI and in his own business. I thought if anyone could figure out how this is happening, he could. Anton tells me I wouldn't do well in prison."

"Who are the other two faculty members on the committee?"

"Rohon McNatt and Annabel Marchant. Annabel had an accident last week when coming down the stairs in the mathematics and computer science building. She fell. Luckily some painters had left a pile of tarps and cans of paint at the bottom of the stairs and she landed on the tarps. She's in the hospital saying she didn't trip but was pushed. I hated leaving Rohon to deal with the administration, but he has been staying at my place while his mother-in-law visits. I tried calling him yesterday when the newspaper published the article accusing me of this theft, but it went to voice mail, and now you tell me he's been shot."

"So what you are saying is both of you are on the run

from the law because you've been falsely accused of a crime."

They looked at each other then nodded. The professor shrugged and said, "Anton says you are a clothing designer who does something with dogs."

"Yes, I raise and train show dogs. Samoyeds, like this puppy. I also train other people's dogs in obedience, show handling, agility, tracking, search and rescue, and this year we've added police dog training, plus I design sweaters to be worn by dog lovers that have pictures of dog breeds worked into the pattern.

"How did you get to know Harry?"

"While doing a fashion show and exhibiting my dog and one belonging to Harry's sister last February in New York, I was mistaken for someone being hunted by a killer and a mutual friend drafted Harry to protect me. He got shot when some thugs hired by the killer came after us. They used silencers on their guns as well, which is how I knew what the sound was."

Kate sat thinking about why someone would take a shot at her in the park. They didn't target either of the men, only her. What had she done to make herself a target? She didn't think she'd been here long enough to piss anyone off. So maybe it had something to do with her being with these men. Kate could feel the thought-gerbils running around their wheel in her head. She slowly stroked Quinn who, full of food, slept peacefully.

The heat of the day made the car feel like an oven, and

her clothes stuck to her body. She wished she'd worn shorts in spite of the problem of getting scratched with puppy claws. Kate reached for her water bottle and found it near empty though she didn't remember drinking it. She drank the lukewarm water and was screwing the top on when her phone vibrated. Agnes. She let it go to voice mail. Then it vibrated again.

Kate answered. "Where are you now, Harry?"

"I'm in front of Petco."

"Drive forward until you're in front of the restaurant, turn left and go to the third row of cars then turn right. We're about thirty cars down. You'll recognize the blue sedan." Kate lowered the sleeping puppy to the floor and quietly opened the car door. Without waking the puppy, she slid out, eased the door shut, and moved forward to see the approaching SUV.

Harry pulled into an empty spot three cars farther along the row on the other side, jumped out, and ran to her. Harry, equally disheveled with his hair mussed from too much handling, his shirt partially tucked in, and his glasses slipping down to the end of his nose, reached her and put his shaking hand on her cheek. Kate didn't hesitate or speak but pulled him against her body, holding on for dear life. He let out a ragged breath and wrapped his arms around her, kissing first the top of her head and then her mouth. A car hooted its horn and some guy yelled "Get a room." Kate pulled them to the side of the aisle and, without letting go, over to the car where the professor and Anton Soucek stood.

"You have grown, Harry." The professor stared up at him and Kate saw a smile play across his lips.

"Yes, sir, I have. I understand you wanted some help on a serious matter. Perhaps we might talk about it." He turned to Soucek. "You chased Kate through the Denver airport, but she seems to think I should help you in spite of this."

"I would appreciate it if you could, sir, but Miss Kate said I broke into your condo. I didn't. I have never been to Boston. Lyndon's friend said you would be at the Connecticut airport, so I went to find you there. I did no wrong and should never have been sent to prison.

Harry said, "No, you aren't the man who broke into my condo.

"Miss Kate tells me things should have been done to keep me from going to prison. I too need your help. I am sorry for frightening her, but I didn't think she would pay attention to me if I didn't force her. I can see she is smart and kind and I should simply have asked."

Quinn woke up and joined the party. Kate opened the car door, attaching his lead, and took him out. He took care of business then bounced from one set of legs to another, seeking attention. Kate handed him to Harry and gathered up the supplies, including the dinosaur and the Kong, and they headed to Harry's air conditioned

SUV.

Spreading pee pads on the floor of the passenger seat, Kate slipped in, handing Quinn the dinosaur while still holding the toy's neck until he settled. When he jumped up again, she put the Kong on the floor and covered it with the dinosaur. He immediately went after the Kong, but she frustrated him by hiding it under the other toy until he finally pounced on the dinosaur to hold it still and at the same time dug out the Kong. Pleased with himself, he gave her a smug grin and settled to chew on the Kong. Mission accomplished. Kate glanced up to see Harry smiling at her.

"What?"

"You're going to be a great mom." She felt her cheeks heat and glanced down at her hands but he reached across to cover them with his.

She searched his face and saw all the pain and guilt she'd put him through in the last few hours. They needed to figure out what was going on and do it quickly. Kate turned to the men in the back seat, clearly enjoying the air conditioning and the cold soda Harry handed each of them, and asked, "Professor, who knew you would not be in your house for the last forty-eight hours?"

"Only Rohon knew. I didn't want anyone to know I was going to talk to Anton or where I'd be. I needed time to think about these charges they wanted to bring against me."

Harry turned a suspicious gaze on her. "What are you up

to, Kate? You are not, I repeat not, going to get involved in this. I'm going to get you to safety before anything else happens."

Kate reached out and took his hand. "Exactly. I've been thinking while I waited for you, and I've worked out a way to keep us all safe for a while. There have been two crimes attributed to people in this car. Neither crime committed by the accused. However, both crimes involved virtual money being stolen."

"What is virtual money?" Soucek asked.

"Money moved from place to place using the Internet. In both cases, money was stolen not by people with guns and bags for cash but by computer savvy thieves who not only could steal the money but also leave a trail of breadcrumbs leading to someone else. To do this, they had to both know you and know how you might access the money. They then used the information to set you up. I think my being shot at happened because the criminal thought your talking to me would expose the crime and I would catch the culprit.

"As far as the shooting at your home, Professor, they're busily setting up a scenario in which you have been working with a known felon, Anton, and it's therefore a classic case of a falling out among thieves resulting in an attempt on your life. The fact Dr. McNatt was wounded instead will be chalked up to a mistake. However, since McNatt is on the committee, I'm sure the person setting up this drama will have no problem saying either you're partners in crime or he's ratting you out. Either way, they could make a case for your shooting him.

"What I think really happened, was the person who committed these crimes is not an expert with a gun. First, they missed trying to shoot you through the window. So, next, they must get rid of the people who had been brought in to save the professor and catch the guilty party, ergo eliminate the math experts who had arrived to find who's really behind the thefts."

"Sorry, darling, but as we all know you are a designer who shows dogs. I don't think anybody would think of you as the math whiz brought in to break this case."

Kate bristled slightly but explained. "Most people wouldn't, but when you gentlemen stepped aside to argue at breakfast this morning, Agnes introduced me as Claire Killoy's daughter, engaged to you, and Kevin added I specialize in catching criminals. If you heard that introduction, what would you think?"

Harry stared and his face turned slightly gray. The professor stated the obvious. "I'd think you were my secret weapon for proving I didn't do it. By the way, I'd like to meet your mother sometime. I've been using her overview book as a text with my freshmen for a number of years, and there is a section that could use some changes I'd like to discuss with her."

Kate stared at the two men in the back seat for a minute

and then grinned. "What an excellent idea, Professor. I'm sure she'd like nothing better than to spend time discussing it with you and, really, there's no better time than the present."

"No, Kate, absolutely not. You can't get involved. I absolutely forbid it. You're here to get your puppy and then go back to your life. You're not trained for this. Sal wouldn't even be there."

"Forbid it?" Kate sat there, shocked Harry would go all dictatorial on her. She crossed her arms and stared at him, waiting for the dust to settle.

The professor stared at Harry with a frown. "Mr. Foyle. You once criticized me for coming to a conclusion without all the correct information. I did not expect you to do the same. I think Kate has more to say and I think it is very important you should listen to her. She is a very intelligent lady. Miss Kate, how do you plan to make this work?"

Ignoring Harry, Kate turned to the professor. "You two need to get to the Albuquerque Airport and then fly to Bradley Airport in Connecticut. I'll arrange to have you met. Professor, you can stay with my brother Tom in my grandparents' home and visit with my mother. Anton, you can lie low in the kennel, working with me. I often take on temporary help. There are two bedrooms in the kennel loft, so you can stay in one of them. Sal will be notified I've taken on some kennel help as a favor to a friend and he'll feel better not leaving me with all the work to do while he's away. Harry, you will let people know you are worried about me and will be escorting me home."

"Which is exactly what I am going to do and then I'm going to set armed guards around you."

"I've got that covered. The dogs won't let any strangers on the property without setting barking in alarm. I'll have Dillon with me twenty-four seven, and my brothers are all home since the twins are still on vacation through Labor Day.

"This way, you can work with the professor and find out what's going on with him, and I can have Tom check into Anton's problem. If the person doing this tries anything else, we can give these guys alibis. You tell everyone you'll contact the professor when he turns up."

Kate listened as Anton suggested he should buy a burner phone to stay in touch while they would be on the road. She watched him become more animated since it appeared something might be done to keep him out of prison. She enjoyed his enthusiasm as he told Lyndon Connecticut is a very pretty state, very green and it would be nice to visit since he didn't have time when he was there on Thursday to visit any sights.

Kate reached for Harry's hand. He stared at her. "Kate, someone shot at you. They wanted you dead. If anything happened to you…"

"Harry, you're right and I'm scared. I'm not Wonder

Woman. I've had the chills since it happened. When I think of going back into the hotel and calmly eating dinner with someone who might have tried to murder me, I want to throw up. They hate us, but more importantly, they fear us. They think we'll find them, stop them, and they will be punished." She stopped to take his face in her hands. "And you know what? They're right on every point. The police will want to talk to me. I'll need a cover story as close to the truth as possible. One of the bullets is lodged in the door of the car so they may be able to trace the gun. I need to see Lily and sign the paperwork for Quinn so he can be registered, but more than anything, I need you to take me home."

Harry leaned over and kissed her gently on the mouth. "We'll go home." He pulled out his phone and called Sadie. Within fifteen minutes, the two other men had left in a rental car with instructions to fly out of Albuquerque to Hartford and stay in the hotel by the airport until Kate and Harry arrived on Monday night. They'd meet them at the hotel and take them to stay with the Killoys.

Harry let out a long breath and stared across at Kate. "What's bothering you now?"

"Harry, Anton followed us from Connecticut then chased me through the Denver airport, but he did not break into your condo. My question is, who did?"

CHAPTER FIFTEEN

Harry called the cop who had been in charge of the shooting at the park to let him know he'd found Kate. Quinn had woken up, so Kate stepped out of the car and walked him up and down in a small grassy area at the end of the row. Harry stood watching over her but also scanning the parking lot for trouble. She picked Quinn up when he finished, and headed back to the car. Harry took Quinn from her and snuggled him as she climbed in. Then he reached out and pulled Kate to him, holding both of them without talking.

When a police vehicle pulled up behind the SUV, two men got out. Exiting the passenger side was a man built like a tank. His struggle in the heat to get into his lightweight sports coat accentuated his ruddy complexion against his buzz-cut gray hair. The other man was young and slim with features speaking of an ancestry both black and Asian, and who displayed an aura, of self-confidence. He slipped into a suit jacket that screamed upward mobility. Kate guessed Mr. Up-wardly Mobile would be the first to speak, and she was right. "Miss Killoy, I'm Detective Quan Steele and this is my partner Detective James Butler. We heard you had some trouble earlier today. Could you please tell us what happened?"

Kate organized her thoughts as she turned to face them, her feet now on the running board. She began telling them about the trip to the park, meeting up with the professor, getting shot at when she was letting her puppy poop, escaping through the city in the professor's car, calling Harry to tell him about the shooting and warn him to call the police and get everyone to safety. We ended up here and I ran into Petco to get something for the puppy, found my charger and plugged it into a plug in the store and called Harry to come get me. When I got back, the men who saved me were gone.

"They had swept up the glass in the back seat and put it in a McDonald's bag. However, there's still a bullet on the inside of the far door post.

"I fed the puppy while I waited for Harry and then when he got here, he called you. He told me everybody is safe. I don't know if it's some crazy person or a pissed-off kid who shot at me but I'm glad whoever did it missed." She snuggled the puppy that Harry had returned to her lap. "I will never, ever complain about having to clean up your poop, my little Quinn."

"Quinn?" Detective Steele asked.

"I decided, he's my pick puppy, and I've named him Quinn. He'll be registered as Whimsy's Quinn the Valiant of Shannon since he saved me." She smiled down at the sleeping puppy.

Steele went over the facts again, asking questions first from one direction and then from another, trying to shake more information out of her head. He wanted to know if she'd seen the shooter. No. Did she have any idea why someone would shoot at her? No. Had she headed down the path for a special reason? No, the puppy went where he wanted so long as he stayed out of reach of the geese. Did she think the person was trying to kill the professor? She didn't know, but the position would have been wrong to make that shot. The questions continued while the crime scene people came and took photos of the professor's car and then towed it away.

Suddenly, Harry's phone rang. Sal's bellow came through loud and clear since Harry, in an attempt to save his hearing, had removed the phone from his ear.

"Where is she, and why is her phone off in the middle of the day?"

She reached out a hand and Harry passed the phone to her with a shrug. "Hi, Sal. Got all your packing done for your trip to the Cape?"

"Don't give me that. A friend called me from Texas to tell me my boss had been shot at. What the hell is going on, and where are the cops if someone's using you for target practice?"

"The cops are right here, Sal. I'm safe. I'll tell you all about it when I get home."

"Hand them the phone, Katie, and don't mess with me." She handed the phone to Detective Steele and went back to petting Quinn Glancing at Harry, she saw a slight smile flicker on his lips. Kate had a feeling he liked to watch Sal in full cop mode, provided he wasn't on the receiving end. Sal's years as president of the National Association of Chiefs of Police meant he knew cops everywhere. Detective Butler's phone had buzzed, and he turned away to answer then glanced back in time to signal Steele not to get abrasive. She listened as the detective repeated what she had told him and then moved away. Kate was sure Sal was telling him what to do and how to do it. She felt sorry for the detective who had been polite and hadn't really had a chance to get into the case. Finally, he turned back and handed the phone to Harry, who quickly ended the call.

"According to your friend Sal, Miss Killoy, you seem to make a habit of getting shot at. You've been lucky, and you seem to have friends with clout," Steele said. "Do you know where the professor and his friend are now? We'd like to talk to them?"

"No, Detective, I honestly don't. I wish they'd stayed so I could let them know how grateful I am for their quick action in saving me. If they hadn't driven away so quickly, the shooter might have had time for a third shot and not missed. I am very glad to be alive."

Harry intervened, saying he'd like to get her back to her friends. They both left their contact information. Kate told Steele he could call her anytime if he had questions, once she got her phone charged again. It took a few more minutes and a promise to stop at the station and sign a statement before they left town before the police would let them leave.

Once on the road back to the hotel, Kate leaned back and closed her eyes to relax. It had the opposite result. She heard the pings. Over and over, the pings and the smashing glass. She smelled the grass, heat, car seat, puppy poop, and fear. She breathed in to a count of four and out to a count of four, trying to calm her growing anxiety. It didn't work. Then she began shaking and gasping for air. Kate knew she was in the car, but she was also in the park. *Ping, ping, smash, ping, ping, smash. Pain! Ouch!* Kate lifted her hand. There was blood. Quinn barked, jumped down to the floor of the car, and bit at her jeans, grabbing the cuff and growling. Kate realized the car had stopped and Harry had his hands on her arms, shaking her. "Harry, Quinn, stop," she yelled.

Harry and Quinn both froze. Kate gasped and leaned back. "I'm fine. Quinn, no bite."

"Kate, God, every time you're near me you're in danger. I brought this on you. It's my fault. I should stay away from you, but I can't. I can't lose you, do you understand? I can't lose you." Harry's fingers clamped on her arms.

"Harry, I'm okay." Kate reached out barely able to touch his face with him pinning her upper arms in his grip. Not enough, he wasn't focusing. She needed to get his attention.

She leaned in and said, "Harry, I'll marry you in December." He blinked twice and focused on Kate's face. It seemed she'd found the right way to bring him out of shock. He slid his arms around her and kissed her hard. When he stopped, Kate reached up to check him out. Harry slowly released her and started the car. Kate realized they were near the hotel, so her tension kicked in again, but this time she handled it. She counted her breaths and stroked the puppy.

They pulled into the hotel parking lot and stopped. Harry jumped out and came around to open Kate's door. He reached in and took Quinn then reached back to help her out of the high seat. As they moved toward the hotel door, he leaned in and asked, "What day in December?"

CHAPTER SIXTEEN

"Kate!" Agnes' scream rang out over all the noise in the lobby. She sprinted past everyone and gathered Kate in a hug that threatened to cut off her breathing.

Kate croaked, "I'm okay." But it took Sean pulling Agnes off for Kate to get her breathing working normally again or it would have been if everyone hadn't gathered around her asking questions. Kate gazed at the group with a weak smile pasted on her face. All the people from this morning were there. Knowing one of them probably shot at her had Kate shaking again. As questions came at her from all sides, she turned to Harry for help. He held up his hand and silenced them.

"Kate's been through a very traumatic experience today and she needs rest. I'm going to get her settled and then explain the details of what happened."

Harry gently took her arm and led her to her room. Lily had already taken Quinn and put him in the pen with his sisters.

He closed the curtains, darkening the room, had her lie on the bed then removed her shoes. He gently massaged her feet until she felt herself turn into a relaxed blob then he pulled the covers over her and, without saying a single word, left. Kate knew tension wouldn't let her sleep.

She woke when Lily came into the room to get a puppy and told her she'd been sleeping for two hours. She said Joyce was doing her evaluations in her room and Cathy was doing hers in the room shared by Rufus, Jordy, and Harry. Jordy's role was puppy transport.

"Will they write down their results?" Kate asked, still bleary eyed from the deep sleep she hadn't expected.

"I've got forms for them to fill out."

"Good, I'll want to keep Quinn's to match with his father's at the same age."

"You're calling him Quinn?"

"Whimsy's Quinn the Valiant of Shannon will be his registered name. There is no way I'm going to be separated from a puppy who saved my life. When you finish the evaluations, we can finish up the paperwork. Which one are you keeping?"

"Red girl."

"Good choice. She's absolutely lovely."

She opened the door and handed a puppy to Jordy

and then took another and quietly closed the door. The room returned to darkness. The puppies barked for a minute and then settled back to playing and eventually to sleep. Kate closed her eyes, but this time sleep didn't come. Instead, she called up the faces of everyone who'd been in the lobby when she and Harry returned. It matched the group that had been there at breakfast. Kate hadn't been able to study their expressions, but they didn't have the look of killers, and nobody said, "Oh darn, I missed." They all seem perfectly normal.

Someone thought she and probably Harry could bring their game to a crashing halt. Kate knew this attack would, in the end, be tied to the thefts of which the professor and Anton were accused. It must have been the introductions. Kevin had told them she caught criminals, and Agnes had told them not to underestimate her mathematical abilities. Though everyone had heard, only one felt threatened.

Kate needed to get back home and do some digging. Everyone was online today. People had few secrets that could be hidden from someone with the ability to ferret them out. The twins could help her find any dirt on them. But, more than wanting to stop this person, Kate wanted to be home in her tiny house with Harry and her dogs, especially Dillon. She didn't feel safe without Dillon.

Kate got out of bed and stared at herself in the mirror, which showed one side of her hair flat and the other standing straight up. She looked as though someone had barfed all over her. She unzipped her suitcase, skipped the T-shirt and instead grabbed the long-sleeved silk shirt that matched her eyes. They'd be going out to dinner, and she had no intention of dressing like a victim—again. As she undressed, she found tiny pieces of glass from the car window embedded in the waistband and back pockets of her jeans. She placed the pants in a plastic bag to keep the glass contained and then hopped into the shower and gave herself up to the hot water as it eased her tension. She stood there until her fingers began to pucker then dried off and dressed. The "unsinkable" style she achieved with skinny jeans, the high boots and a long sleeved, floaty, blue top. Then she put on the pin she'd bought yesterday.

Yesterday? It seemed as though years had passed since she'd left home. Kate quickly finished fluffing up her curls into what might be considered a style and not a rat's nest and used extra care with her makeup to hide any signs of shock or fear. How had the old commercial phrased it? "Never let them see you sweat." Kate smiled, also remembering a Donna Karan ad that said, "Feeling tense is understandable. Looking tense is unfashionable." Kate smiled. Karan had always been a designer she admired.

When she stepped out of the bathroom, she found Lily at her computer. She'd pulled up the AKC registration program and completed registering the little red girl in her name. Kate sat on the end of the bed and gave her the information to register Quinn. Lily had had all the puppies micro-chipped when they had their last physical, so they transferred the chip for Quinn to Kate's name and filled in his registered name instead of the listing of blue boy puppy. Having a breed where the puppies are all the same color meant putting ribbons on them as they are born so you could tell them apart and keep their records straight. When they got older, Lily had exchanged the ribbons for collar colors. When they finished online, Lily handed Kate the packet she prepared for each puppy owner with his pedigree, puppy photos, portraits of parents and grandparents, vaccination and physical records, and the diet he'd been on. Her packet also included copies of the evaluations Joyce and Cathy had done on him while Kate was sleeping. She'd read those later. The packet also included information from the AKC on raising puppies for the benefit of those buyers who hadn't owned a purebred puppy before.

Kate tucked the packet into her suitcase and fished out the small, soft-sided travel crate in which Quinn would travel under the seat on the plane. At eight weeks and twelve pounds, he'd just fit. Kate knew at the rate Samoyed puppies grow, in another week he wouldn't, and she didn't like flying puppies in with the luggage. She set the travel crate on the bed and opened both the top and side entrances so he could get used to it. Then she went and pulled him out of the pen and put him into the bag. He shot back out in a nanosecond sniffing the outside but not happy with the thought of being inside. She pulled some puppy treats out of a bag she'd brought and quietly slid them deep into the crate with a trail of them leading to the opening. It didn't take him long to discover the treats, but he knew they were up to something. Lily and Kate both sat and watched, telling him what a good boy he was. After going in and backing out several times, he finally decided it couldn't be a trap and went all the way to the back to polish off the pile of treats then scooted back out. Kate praised him, snuggled him, and put him back into the pen with his siblings. She calculated in about three more sessions he'd know going into this thing couldn't hurt him. He'd only have to be in it for a few hours on the plane, and then he'd be done. Her twelve-year-old Chartreux cat, who teased all the dogs for the exercise of being chased, had already informed her when she brought this "cat abode" back, it was hers. She'd slept in it the night before Kate left. Quinn may have smelled her scent inside as well as the treats, which would be all to the good.

Lily ducked into the bathroom to shower and change while Kate pulled out her phone and snapped more photos of the puppies, both Quinn and his siblings. She wished her dad and granddad could see them. Watching puppies had been more fun than watching the Memorial Day Parade and Fourth of July fireworks together. Gram would find them sitting on the folding chairs they kept in the whelping room, not talking but just watching the puppies. Occasionally, one of them would make a comment, but mostly they simply watched. Gram told Kate once if it hadn't been for the yips from the puppies, she'd have thought she'd walked into a silent movie. When both men died last year, Kate fell apart. It took Agnes, with her steamroller approach to any problem, to get her back on track and in doing so changed her life. Kate suddenly felt the presence of her dad and gramps with her, watching the puppies, a hand each on her shoulder. Their approval washed over her and brought peace.

Kate's phone buzzed with a text as Lily emerged from the bathroom. Everybody else waited in the lobby. Lily reached into the pile of puppies and handed her Quinn. Kate opened the room door to find Jordy, Cathy, and Rufus standing there waiting to carry puppies out to the car. The puppies would sack out in the back of the station wagon while the rest of them ate.

Harry met her in the lobby and reached for Quinn, snuggling him in one arm as he reached for Kate's hand. He peered into her eyes, examining her for any sign of trauma, then, satisfied, smiled and kissed her quickly on the lips. "You're beautiful. Did you have a good rest?"

"Yes. But what I want most right now is to be home in Connecticut with you and Quinn. We still have to get to Denver and then take the flight on Monday."

"You're going to be staying at the Blackburn's with me tomorrow night. It's all arranged. Rufus will take us to the airport with Jordy on Monday. We're going to caravan with Joyce and Cathy. Rufus will be with them on the way north so whoever went after you doesn't decide to take a shot at one of your friends."

"They're not in danger. They don't pose the threat I do to this person." Kate walked quickly to the exit and to Lily's car. The back lay open with Jordy supervising loading each puppy inside.

"This is the puppy you're keeping, Kate?" Jordy asked. "What are you going to call him?"

"His name is Quinn." When Kate said his name, she was startled to see the puppy stop playing with his sibling and turn toward her. It seemed they had bonded quickly.

Jordy bent down and petted him. "Here, Quinn," he said and held out a toy. Then he moved the toy to the other side of the pen. "Come get it, Quinn." The puppy immediately left off chewing on his sister's ear and trotted across to the toy. Jordy smiled and petted him. Fantastic! Quinn may end up smarter than his dad, a feat damn near impossible. It would be so much fun to train them together. Dillon would enjoy teaching his son all his little tricks. Joyce stepped up next to her. "You're happy with the boy? He fell second in the evaluation. His smile could be tighter and his tail naturally falls to the side away from the judge."

"What he's got going for him in brains and instinct more than outweighs those minor flaws. He's going to be like his father, if not a little better. I can't wait to do a tracking aptitude test on him. I'll bet he'll nail it first try. To tell the truth, Joyce, I'm thrilled with him."

"Good. That's what counts. Your grandfather would really have liked his rear and his neck carriage. He's going to be a striking puppy in the ring. If he has even some of Dillon's ring presence, he'll be fun to show."

She moved toward her car as Rufus and Cathy came out. Kate had to smile. This pairing seemed to be working out nicely. She liked how Cathy related to Jordy as well as Rufus. This might be a good thing for all of them. But they didn't need her butting in. Her own relationship was complex enough with Harry chomping at the bit to get married. Kate still didn't see why he loved her but she was glad he did. They need to figure out this mess so she could wrap her brain around the thought of a wedding. Then there was the fact, Harry still owed her two real get dressed up and go out dates.

Lily followed them, placing red girl in with her siblings. She closed up the back of the car as Jordy ran to get into the front seat so he could watch the puppies. Cathy and Rufus joined Joyce and Harry and she went to Rufus' car. Kate had no idea of the restaurant's location, but they all followed Lily. Apparently she'd worked there during graduate school. She had told Kate they would have steak unlike any a New Englander had ever eaten. Kate really preferred seafood over red meat, but if someone recommended a steak dinner this highly, she'd try it. A chance to relax with these friends and not worry about shooters was what she needed.

When they got to the restaurant, Kate saw a long table with more place settings than needed by the seven of them. She'd turned to ask Lily about it when her eye caught sight of

Agnes and Sean moving across the restaurant followed by Kevin Donnelly, Toni Dunn, Dr. Kimbel, and Mayleen Ke.

CHAPTER SEVENTEEN

Agnes seemed embarrassed as she took her seat across from her. She whispered, "Not my idea," shrugging. Kate felt Harry's hand on hers under the table. He squeezed it and reached for a drinks menu. "Hang in there."

"Well isn't this nice?" Dr. Kimbel greeted the group with an overly loud, forced bon ami. "We know your visit ends in the morning, but we really haven't had much time to chat with you. When Kevin mentioned you'd be here this evening, I called the restaurant and added extras to your reservation. We've all been anticipating Harry's visit since the professor mentioned it, but didn't know he was bringing a Killoy with him."

Toni Dunn pasted on a smile and said with feigned interest, "We would absolutely love to have your views about the possible loss of funds from the retirement account Miss Killoy."

Kate studied her and the rest of the crew who had pushed themselves uninvited into their party. "I'm so sorry but I must disappoint you Miss Dunn. I came to Lubbock to pick up my show puppy and to have a restful weekend talking dog breeding with my friends Lily, Joyce, and Cathy. Instead, I've been both distracted by other people's problems and shot at. While I do sympathize with the professor's problem, this evening is the first time since I arrived I've had had a chance to sit and talk about a hobby my friends and I share. I hope you can understand, what with the stress of the last twenty-four hours, the only topic I'll be discussing at dinner tonight is dogs. Also, not having been thoroughly briefed about the problem, I'm sure any contribution I might make would pale in comparison to those of Harry or Rufus."

"I would think a Killoy…" she pushed.

"A Killoy would want to bring work into every social gathering? I'm sorry, but no. As Agnes will tell you, my father and grandfather shared my passion for discussing dog breeding. It is considered the Killoy vice, and I make a practice of indulging in it as often as I can. So please excuse me from your discussion. I'll leave you to solve the professor's problems while my friends and I tackle the varied problems of the dog world. Enjoy your meal. I'm sure Harry, Rufus, and Agnes would be happy to converse about math with you."

Kate glanced sideways for a second and thought she caught the glimmer of a smile from Harry. She was sure the party crashers considered her a perfect bitch, but she'd take it as a compliment. Something about Toni Dunn got her back up. Kate forced herself to smile at the foursome from the college, realizing one of them considered her dangerous and since she wouldn't give them her take on the problem, the danger would remain. One of them had shot at her. Whoever it was had come to dinner wanting her to reveal whether they were safe. Well, tough. She'd left them spinning in the wind. A foot nudged hers under the table, and she glanced up. Agnes smiled and nodded.

At the end of the table, Lily was talking about her trip to New York City. Kate's ears pricked when she said, "Did I ever tell you girls about how Kate took apart the Saint Bernard handler at the Garden in February? She almost got him thrown out of the group. According to my friend Diane, who had her Rottie in the group, it was fantastic. First she practically throws the Saint over her shoulder in the benching area so he wouldn't get into a fight and hurt anyone. Then she almost does the same to the handler who had been off drinking when he should have been taking care of the dog. Finally, when he tries to get revenge against Kate during the group judging, she steps in front of her dog, almost getting bitten by the Saint, and the judge reprimands the handler on national television."

"I saw it happen when I watched the group on TV," Joyce said. "But I had no idea he did it on purpose. It seemed like lousy handling. I've only watched him in the ring a few times but have been unimpressed by his skill. He seems to depend on bravado over technical skill."

Kate leaned back shivering slightly, remembering the night in question. It was an evening she'd never forget, for more reasons than an obnoxious handler. It happened to be the last time someone tried to kill her—until today. She could hear Kevin and Rufus discussing the charges against Stubbs.

Toni Dunn, who sat on Rufus' right with Cathy on his left, leaned in, letting her ample breasts rest on his arm to improve his view of her low-cut V-neck dress. She was all sympathy but let things like the professor's absent-mindedness slip into the conversation without stating it outright. She laughed at everything Rufus said while flashing slightly pitying smiles in Harry's direction, implying he was stuck with a fiancée who didn't care about his friend. Kate's focus remained as the conversation at her end of the table moved from bad handlers to the difference in judging style between UKC and AKC dog shows.

Kate now watched the byplay as Toni reeled in both Rufus and Sean like prize-winning bass then decided to cut her line. Harry leaned into the conversation and asked Toni who had been brought in as an independent forensic accountant to give the unbiased assessment of the problem.

Toni asked, "Forensic accountants? Baxter, Kline and Baxter had the accountancy firm they'd always used to check the university's accounts examine their figures. The firm declared they were correct."

"You do realize, though," Harry argued, "that if the professor goes to trial, the accountant's work would be the first thing an independent forensic accountant would call into question due to their history with the firm. In fact, since the accountancy firm had been handling the account for years, they might be considered a much better suspect than the professor. After all, they had access to the money on both ends of the transaction. The defense, if not the court itself, may require an independent audit to examine all the figures on both sides. They'll probably require a complete audit of the company's fiscal behavior with all its major accounts for the last few years.

"Since Baxter, Kline and Baxter is bringing the charges, I suspect the defense has the right to choose the forensic firm and the court may order the expense to be split between both parties. Such has been my experience when I've been asked to testify in cases such as these. So, for them to accuse randomly a member of an oversight committee who, as I far as I can see, had little to do with the actual transfer of funds, is a case that is not only weak, but would probably never see the inside of a courtroom. I'd be interested to know who at the auditing firm actually inspected the transfers."

Most of the party crashers now nodded but Mayleen Ke said, "I think the name I heard was Jarel Dunnett."

Toni Dunn jumped at the name and said she'd met Mr. Dunnett and had thought his reasoning was sound. Kate thought it interesting someone who purported to be on Stubbs' side, seemed so quick to defend his accuser. Another argument was about to break out when, thank goodness, the food arrived.

Kate had ordered the smallest steak dinner on the menu since she didn't have much of an appetite after being shot at. Sitting at a table with people, one of whom hated her enough to want her dead, tended to curb her appetite. The plate put before her still had too much food, but she took a bite of the steak and sighed. Talk about melt in your mouth—a steak so tender the knife floated through it. Lily credited the meat being raised probably less than fifty miles from where they sat eating.

Jordy had ordered the chicken fried steak. Kate was horrified they'd coat such a wonderful piece of beef with breading and fry it. Lily agreed. "If you want the bread flavor, grab a chunk of bread." They all laughed.

When barely halfway through her meal, Kate knew she'd run out of steam. "I can't eat another bite," she announced.

Jordy and Kevin chose up to see who'd finish the other half of her steak. Kevin won so Jordy began studying the dessert menu. Watching that small boy polish off every bite of his pie with ice cream made Kate wonder where he put it all. His metabolism must not be high but off the charts.

As the meal wound down, she noticed Toni Dunn had turned on the charm with Harry. She leaned forward, displaying her wares by reaching across the table to touch his arm every time she wanted to make a point. She laughed at his jokes and stared into his eyes, sending clear messages. Harry sat passively watching the show. Kate couldn't blame the girl for wanting Harry. He had it all, handsome, smart, charming, and engaged. For some reason, this didn't feel like a simple attempt to seduce away another girl's guy. No, she felt sure more was going on with the play Toni made. Kate was curious to ask Harry what he'd been talking about to Toni Dunn.

As the party broke up, Joyce took Kate aside to talk about the breeding. On paper, Dillon and Lexi's pedigrees worked well together, and she'd gone over Dillon at his last National, but Joyce told her Lexi was due in season during the National and wanted to know if she could stay an extra day or two to do the breeding rather than having Joyce drive all the way to Connecticut. Kate said it shouldn't be a problem so long as she kept Lexi away from him prior to all the judging. She and Joyce had been walking toward the front of the parking lot where Joyce, Cathy, and Rufus had parked. Kate patted Lexi on the head, admiring her beautiful expression.

As they left, Kate headed back around the restaurant toward the far corner of the parking lot where Harry had left the car, waving to Jordy and Lily as they drove past her. Turning the final corner, she reached into her purse to be sure she hadn't missed any calls while she'd had phone off at dinner. She'd almost crossed the parking lot when she looked up and stopped. The parking lot was empty. No Harry. No car

Kate reached for her phone and dialed his number as the lights in the parking lot went out. She walked back to the restaurant entrance to see if she could wait inside, but the door was locked. She banged on it, but the lights inside were dim and nobody came.

Kate listened to her call ring but then go to voice mail. Frustrated, she stood and thought. Finally, she dialed Jordy since Lily was driving. He answered, and she asked if Lily could come back to the restaurant and get her because she'd been stranded.

"Where is Harry?" he shouted over the sound of yipping puppies and the car's engine.

"I don't know. But please get back here quickly because I'm alone in a dark parking lot."

She disconnected the call and then heard the sound of a car engine moving slowly toward the restaurant. She began walking toward the street but then instinct had her instead step back into the shadows of the bushes surrounding the parking lot. A dark SUV like Rufus' pulled into the lot, deliberately sweeping the headlights into every corner. She took a breath to yell at Harry for leaving her when she spotted the shape of the person behind the wheel. It wasn't Harry. This person was both shorter and a woman. Kate slid deeper into the bushes and waited.

The car, which had been circling slowly, stopped. Kate watched as its high beams came on, flooding the lot with light, and waited. Then Kate heard the sound of a second car. Lily! Suddenly Rufus' SUV pulled into a tight turn and peeled onto the street. It shot past Lily's car causing her to swerve. Lily stopped and Jordy opened the door, flooding the cab with light. Kate ran toward them, shouting, "Call 911."

Kate made Lily turn in the direction the SUV had gone. She thought she saw the taillights of the car ahead until it turned. By the time they reached that intersection, it was gone. Meanwhile, Jordy got the police on his phone, set to speaker. Kate took it and told the dispatcher her fiancé's car had been stolen. He asked what kind of car it, where had she had last seen it, and did she know the license plate number. Kate stared at Jordy, drawing a blank, but he broke in, "It's a dark-blue Cadillac Escalade, four door." He recited the plate number.

"Last seen heading north on Avenue Q toward Martha Sharp Freeway with a woman at the wheel and no sign of my fiancé," Kate interrupted, her mind spinning. Where was Harry? Was he hurt? Was he in the car? They'd lost track of the car, so Lily took them back to the hotel. Jordy and the others began unloading puppies. Kate turned to help but stepped aside when her phone rang. Answering without even glancing at the screen, she yelled, "Harry?"

"Where's Harry?" asked Sal. "Kate, what's up? Why isn't Harry with you?"

The sound of Sal's voice caused her panic to hit full force. Her legs didn't want to hold her so Kate dropped down hard onto the hotel steps. She needed to pull it together. "He's, he's..." Kate tried to get more control over her shaking body.

"Katie." His voice softened. "Tell me what happened,"

"Sal, Harry's missing."

CHAPTER EIGHTEEN

"Sal, it's my fault for not being with him. I stopped to talk to Joyce, and when I got across the parking lot, he was gone."

"Kate." Sal's now firm voice got her to focus. "Start at the beginning and fill me in. Don't leave anything out."

"Harry came here to help a professor of his who's been accused of stealing funds from the faculty retirement fund. Sean's brother Kevin brought some friends to see Harry today. While we talked, one of them tried to brush me off as not understanding math. Agnes informed them I'm a Killoy and engaged to Harry. She passed me off as a math genius. I was so pissed with the snotty woman, I didn't correct her. The professor had disappeared, and one of his friends, house sitting for him, was shot presumably by someone mistaking him for the professor. Then, with everyone searching for the professor, I went with my friends to the park to socialize Quinn. You know how that ended up. Then, tonight, we went to dinner, and when I went to find Harry in the parking lot, he and the car were gone. I called him, but he didn't answer. Then the car came back with a woman driving and it sped off when Lily came, and Harry's missing and might be hurt."

"Who's Quinn?"

"The puppy I'm bringing home. I run to Lily's car and we try to unsuccessfully to follow it, but it gets away. We've notified the police. I'm worried. Harry hasn't turned up. I'm scared something has happened to him."

"Kate, hold on. I've got a friend on the Lubbock force on the line."

She waited. She heard talking in the background but not what was being said. Finally, Sal picked up the phone.

"Kate, they've found the car. A man was found on the ground not far from it, unconscious, smelling of booze, with no ID on him. He's being taken to University Medical Center. He fits Harry's description and, hang in there, girl, he's been shot."

"Shot!" she screamed and began running toward a car pulling into the lot. "Sal, there's Agnes' car. I'll make her bring me to the hospital. I'll call you back when I get there." Kate shoved the phone into her pocket and ran for Agnes's car, which had turned into a parking space. The passenger door was locked, and Kate began banging her fists on the window. Agnes unlocked the door and Kate jumped in, slamming it behind her.

"Killoy, what the hell are you doing?"

"University Medical Center! Now! Harry's been shot. Go. Go, now."

Agnes reversed like a race car driver and burned rubber getting on the road toward campus and the hospital. Kate pulled the seat belt partway across herself and Agnes grabbed it from her hand and shoved it into the lock, downshifting in the same motion and running through a very orange traffic light. In what felt like forever but was probably less than four minutes, they arrived at the entrance to the emergency room. Kate shoved open the car door and headed for the glass doors at a run.

"Go. I'll find you." Kate heard Agnes shout before she gunned the engine. Kate burst in and headed to the desk marked information. The person there spoke into the phone and ignored her. She opened her mouth, but the woman's hand came up like a human stop sign. Kate wanted to bite it. Then she spotted some cops talking off to one side. She headed straight for them, interrupting them.

"A man was found shot next to an SUV and brought in here. Could you tell me where he is?"

"Miss, what is your name and how do you know about this man?"

"My name is Kate Killoy. I'm visiting from Connecticut. I was on the phone with my friend Sal in Connecticut when he told me the police had found Harry's car abandoned and an unidentified man on the ground nearby, shot. He said they were bringing him here. I've got to see him." Kate could see they were trying to hide their skepticism. She'd begun to explain again when a man not in uniform but obviously a cop approached.

"Lieutenant, this woman claims a friend of hers in Connecticut sent her here about the gunshot victim—"

The lieutenant cut him off, asking, "Are you Kate Killoy?"

"Yes. Can I see Harry?"

"I'm Lieutenant Garrison. We don't know who the man is or whether it's your friend. If you don't mind coming with me, you might be able to help with his identification." Kate followed him through the doors by the stop sign lady. When they passed through a second set of doors into an area hung with a forest of colorful curtains surrounding gurneys, he headed to the fourth curtain on the right. The cubical was empty. He spun around latching onto an orderly walking by, and found out the man was in surgery.

Kate's legs didn't want to hold her. She'd been in this spot before. Harry'd lived that time, but now—how many times could a man get shot and live.

"Miss Killoy." The lieutenant made her focus. "I need a description of your fiancé to see if it matches the man in surgery."

She stared at him for a minute. Reaching into her pocket, she fished out her phone and pulled up photos Harry and she had taken of each other in front of the lions at the New York Public Library last February. They'd taken a few minutes to relax from the strain of running from a murderer. Kate found her favorite shot of Harry and passed it over to the lieutenant. He checked it out and then flipped through the other photos, causing her to blush. Two photos after that, Harry had grabbed her camera to take a shot of them together and, as he pushed the button, kissed her. The lieutenant smiled. "He's a lucky man. Now let's hope he comes through surgery with no problems."

He handed Kate back her phone, which buzzed. Agnes. Kate put her on hold and turned to the lieutenant, telling him her cousin was in the waiting room.

He suggested she join her. "I'll let them know at the desk to notify you as soon as your fiancé is out of surgery." He walked her back to the waiting room, and Agnes rushed up to hug her. Kate could see the somewhat stunned expression on his face as recognition set in. The Agnes effect. Agnes pulled Kate over to a couple of chairs she moved slightly apart from the others.

"Kate, tell me what's going on with Harry."

"He's in surgery. He's lost a lot of blood. I've got to call Sal."

"I'll let the others know where we are and what's going on." She turned away and spoke softly into her phone while Kate stared at her phone for a minute and then hit Sal speed dial.

He answered almost before Kate could get the phone to her ear. "Kate, talk to me."

"Sal, he's in surgery. They say he's lost a lot of blood. Agnes is here, and so are the police."

"Let me talk to the cop in charge, now."

Kate scanned the room and saw Lieutenant Garrison talking to a group of officers in a corner of the room. She stood up, amazed her legs could carry her, and walked toward them. Garrison spotted her and came forward. She held out my phone. "My friend Sal needs to talk to you."

He looked at her and then the phone. Deciding to humor the hysterical lady, he took the phone while Kate returned to Agnes' side. Agnes reached for her hand then pulled her into a hug as Kate felt her tears splash into her lap. She took a gasp of air, and Agnes handed her a handkerchief. No tissues for Agnes Forester. Kate wiped her eyes and forced herself under control. She glanced up to see Garrison.

"Sal wants to talk to you. I'll go check and see if your Harry is out of surgery yet." He turned away.

Kate lifted the phone to her ear and said, "Sal."

"Katie, I know this is going to be twice as hard because of what happened last February but I need you to tell me what you remember, who's involved, any possible motives. I want you to talk to me as if sitting together here in your office with our feet on your desk. Talk to me, missy, just talk, no order, no deciding what's important, just tell me everything again, even your guesses, and we'll figure it out together. Begin when you got the text you said wasn't from Harry."

Kate took a deep breath and began back at home on Thursday morning. It seemed like a month ago instead of two days. She again described what had happened at the airport, on the plane, in the Denver airport—leaving out the kiss—what happened on the drive to Lubbock, the party and finding out the professor was missing and his friend shot. She repeated about this morning meeting Kevin's friends and the people from the college, the trip to the park, meeting Soucek and the professor, getting shot at, Harry bringing her back to the hotel, going out to dinner and having all the strangers from the morning show up, what happened in the parking lot, Harry's car going missing and then returning for her only to have it disappear again when Lily arrived, and finally returning to the hotel to find he'd been shot. Kate turned and gasped, "Oh shit." Everyone from the dinner was walking into the waiting room. She leaned into Agnes and said, "Run interference for a second." She stood, pretending she hadn't seen them, and stepped over to Garrison's side. "Everyone who was there in the parking lot just walked in."

He peered over her shoulder then back at her and grinned. "Perfect timing."

He glanced back at the nurse he'd been talking to. "Why don't you go with Nurse Rodriquez? Your fiancé is being brought into recovery, and she'll take you to him. We'll go chat with these nice folks." He nodded to the other cops and they all moved to greet the people filing into the waiting room.

Kate followed the nurse who led her to a bed behind more curtains where she saw another nurse hooking up the bags with drip lines running into Harry's arm. He had an oxygen mask over his face, and his eyes were closed. Kate stared at his chest, holding her breath until she saw it rise and fall a few times, indicating he was breathing. She sat by the bed and gently reached through the bars pulled up on the sides to keep him from falling. She took his hand, gently lacing her fingers through his. Kate didn't know if he was asleep or still unconscious. She sat watching him breathe and remembered the last time he'd been shot.

She loved this man, but it seemed as though they were cursed. Every time they got together, bad things happened. Kate let go of his hand and reached for the lever to lower the railing. She pulled her chair up tight against the bed and studied his face, counting his breaths. She felt movement and looked down to see his hand brush hers and then grab it. Kate couldn't stop the tears now. They fell, soaking the sheet beside her, Agnes' handkerchief no longer up to the job. A wave of exhaustion swept over her, and all she wanted to do was sleep and wake up to find it was all a nightmare. Kate laid her head on him and felt Harry's hand stroking her hair and she looked up to see his beautiful green eyes.

"Harry, I am so sorry. I should have been with you. I'm so sorry."

"Marry me." Kate barely made out the words. "Marry me soon. I know what you're thinking, Kate. Don't run away." He lay back and closed his eyes, his strength used up.

She heard the curtain pull back. A doctor checked Harry's vitals, adjusted the drips, and then turned to her. "You must be the fiancée, Kate. He mentioned you before he went under. I take it from the previous damage to his body you've been down this path before. Well he must be part cat because he seems to have nine lives. The bullet nicked an artery, and he should be dead now, but he was lucky. When he fell, he landed in an area with rocks. One of them caught his body right on the wound. His body weight put pressure on the bleeding. It stopped until the paramedics rolled him over. Luckily, they could stop it again, and we've performed an arterial repair, which should heal up nicely. He'll need new clothes because we had to cut what he was wearing off him, but it's a small price. He'll wake up again soon. Stay with him." He turned to leave then, smiling, stopped. "And I should tell you, miss, before he went under, he told me to let you know he'd heal much faster if he were getting ready for a wedding."

CHAPTER NINETEEN

"A wedding?" Kate whispered, not noticing Harry had woken while the doctor was talking, and pulled off the oxygen tube.

"It's a good idea, love. I know I'd recover much quicker if I could hold my bride in my arms each night." He stared at her and tightened his hold on her hand. "Katie, I know this brings the terrors of New York back. But life is full of dangers. You could have been killed by that St. Bernard, for heaven's sake. There are no guarantees. All I know is from the day I fell for you, my love has only grown. Will we argue? Hell yes. Will we be put into situations to test our love for each other? Probably, but I know you are the best thing in my life and I only hope I can be a good enough husband for you." He reached for Kate's head and hooking her neck pulled her face down so her eyes were only inches from his. "Plus," he whispered, his dimples suddenly on full display, "I really want to get into your pants." Kate went to pull back, but he moved the extra inch and kissed her until she melted into him.

When she sat up, she whispered, "I thought the plan was to get to know each other better?"

"Kate, we know each other better than 90 percent of couples getting married. We've lived 'better and worse' already, and we're still together. It's us against the world."

Kate knew he was right. She wanted nothing more than to wake up every morning in his arms. She couldn't let stupid and fear get in the way. Only last week Gram had told her she'd married Gramps after only being engaged for two months. She told her when it was right, it was right, and time didn't change a thing. Kate knew she feared she wouldn't be a good enough wife. Then she remembered how scared she'd been when she launched her design business, and again when she had to do her first solo fashion show. All it took was a ton of work to find success.

Compared to that, marrying Harry seemed a no-brainer. She smiled at him. "You're right. Getting married is an excellent idea. Where else will I find someone who puts up with all my dogs and who loves them as much as I do? We'll talk to Father Joe as soon as we get home.

"Oh God, where is my brain. Here we are talking about a wedding, and you're lying in bed after being shot. You're injured, Harry. How soon can you travel? Will it hurt your recovery? Will the police let you go back home? Harry, someone is trying to kill us. I know it's cowardly not to stay and fight back, but I want to get out of here."

"Glad to hear it," Lieutenant Garrison said from the doorway. "You two are killing my violent crime statistics for the year, if you don't mind my saying so. Since you arrived in town, we've had three shootings, and the weekend isn't over. I hate to interrupt wedding plans, but, Foyle, I need to know what you can remember from the time you left the restaurant until we found you."

Harry, still holding Kate's hand, turned to Garrison. "Everyone exited the restaurant. I was standing next to Kate when Joyce asked to speak to her. As they walked toward Joyce's car, the group from the college surrounded me, asking questions about how I planned to help Stubbs and did I have any idea of where he was. I moved toward my car as I fended off the questions. I told them I didn't have enough information and I hadn't a clue where the professor was at the moment.

"When I reached the car, they all moved off in a crowd still discussing the problem. I unlocked the door and turned to see if Kate was ready to leave when my eye caught a movement to the side and something hit me over the head. I heard a man swear and a woman squeal and then felt a gun barrel pressed into my right side. I remember turning left, away from the barrel. When it went off, there was instant pain, then nothing. The next thing I remember, I awoke on the ground with a mouth full of dirt and an EMT asking me who I was. I must have passed out again. I remember talking to the doctor for a minute before surgery, and the next thing I woke up here with Kate agreeing to set the date for our wedding." He smiled at her.

"So you didn't see your attacker?"

"No, but I remember the gun sounded unusual. I suspect it had a silencer.'

"Well, since nobody heard it, I'd agree. The person or people who shot you must have been strong enough to push you into the back of the SUV. It's where we found the most blood. The car had been wiped down, and our people haven't found any prints on the car or your wallet, which was turned in by a woman whose dog found it under a bush in her front yard. It's a little chewed up. Someone took the cash but left the license and one credit card."

"I only brought one with me tonight and two hundred in cash. Everything else is at the hotel."

The doctor walked back in and asked, "Did you collect your other gunshot wounds while working for the FBI?"

"Some of them, but my job tends to bring me into contact with people you wouldn't want to invite to dinner."

"And yet, strangely enough, it's beginning to look as though one of the people at that dinner shot you," Garrison put in. "I've been filled in by Detective Steele about the attempt on Miss Killoy this morning. I think you two are making someone very nervous."

Kate broke in and asked the doctor whose name strangely enough was also Quinn, how soon she could get Harry out of there.

"I would advise rest, but I've been informed you two are traveling with a surgical nurse so you may leave once your paperwork is complete. I would advise staying out of the line of fire and, when you get home, have your own physician check you out."

Harry agreed and Garrison said he'd have an officer posted at their hotel and would make sure everybody gets on the road safely tomorrow."

As Garrison left, Agnes and Sean pushed their way in, Agnes displaying her usual take-no-prisoners mode.

"It's all arranged," she announced. "Rufus, Joyce, Cathy, and Jordy are on their way back to the hotel. They're getting on the road right away and will drive through what's left of the night to Denver in Joyce's car. Kevin will bring Rufus' car to Denver next week. They're taking your puppy, Quinn, with them. They'll all go to Rufus' place and, except for Joyce who has to be at work on Monday, they will meet you there. Lily has already packed both Harry's and your luggage, Kate, and Marco, the driver, picked it up on the way."

"On the way where?" Kate asked cautiously, remembering Agnes never did anything by halves.

"On the way" Agnes said, "here to the hospital. Then he'll drive you to the airport. Maddox was so upset to hear all this happened while visiting his city, he arranged to fly you to Denver in his plane. It will be much more comfortable for Harry, and he can rest up at Blackburn's place for a whole day before your flight across the country. I suggested you take the puppy, but Joyce seemed to think he'd travel better with Lexi for the journey north before having to be stuffed under the seat for the flight. I'll go talk to your doctor, Harry." She disappeared, leaving only the light scent of lavender behind.

Sean shook his head, smiled, and followed.

Harry opened his mouth to say something but I held up my hand like the stop sign nurse. "Don't waste your breath arguing. She will win. She always wins. The only thing you can do when Hurricane Agnes blows into town is hold on tight and hope you survive."

A few minutes later, the doctor returned, and Kate was told to wait outside. She saw Lieutenant Garrison and asked about Dr. McNatt's condition following the shooting in the professor's kitchen. Garrison said, "He's hanging in there. He's old and apparently the strain of being shot and the blood loss aggravated his already weakened heart to kick up a little, but the fact he's still alive is because he's such a tough old codger."

"Could the shooter have thought he was shooting the professor?"

"It's one theory. The fact the professor has vanished is suspicious. We haven't found a trace of him." Keeping what she knew to herself, Kate nodded then walked over toward Agnes but stopped because of the crowd around her. Women were asking about life being a famous model, and men stared. Kate changed direction and took a seat next to Sean. He had stretched out, his feet about four miles from his chair, and tipped his hat over his face. Kate knew he wasn't asleep.

"Aren't there times when you want to reach into a crowd and yank Agnes out, throw her over your shoulder, and run off?"

"Not anymore. I merely sit here and let them all look."

Kate stared at him. "When did that change?"

"Friday night." He pushed up his hat and studied her. "I heard you two went off after the party to talk. Well, I don't know what you said to her, but she was waiting when I got back. She walked up to me, said yes, and then went to bed."

Kate stared at Agnes. She glowed with happiness. Considering what had been going on, this wasn't normal. Kate turned back to Sean who watched her, a slight smile on his face, and the penny dropped. "I guess congratulations are in order." She returned her stare to Agnes. "Did she tell you what we talked about?"

"Nope, but I don't care. I only want to marry her, and I'll take it any way I can. If I have to put up with all this"—he nodded at the crowd—"I will."

"You're a good man, Connelly. Take my word, it's all going to work out well. Hang in there."

"I've loved her since we were kids, Kate. Patience is my middle name where Agnes is concerned."

A movement off to the right caught Kate's attention. Lieutenant Garrison approached, pushing Harry in a wheelchair. She flew across the room before her brain fully took in the sight. Harry reached for her hand and held it hard, his head leaning against her arm. An officer I'd seen earlier stepped to the other side of the chair. Agnes broke free of her audience, and Sean took her arm as the group moved through the corridor to the emergency room exit. When they got outside, a man stepped out of a stretch limousine in front of them and opened the wide back door.

Agnes reached out and hugged her, saying she and Sean planned to leave tomorrow and drive straight through so they would be home in a few days. Kate then stepped into the big car and Harry was gently lifted onto the seat next her.

The officer slid into the seat facing them, and Garrison leaned in and spoke to Harry. "You have a safe trip now. I'll let you know how the investigation goes here.

You've got my number if you think of anything that might help, and it goes for you, too, Miss Killoy." He stepped back, closed the door, tapped the roof, and they were on their way home.

Harry winced slightly as they gently eased over the speed bumps in the hospital driveway, but his head finally settled onto her shoulder, and his eyes closed once they got on the highway. Kate eased him so he lay across her lap, his head on a pillow that had been on the seat. He sighed, the effort of holding his body upright no longer needed. "You make a great bed, Killoy," he muttered, settling against her a little more.

"I have my uses," Kate told him, smiling.

He glanced across at the officer, whose name tag read Ramirez. "Your boss is probably happy to see the back of us"

"He only wants to get you out of Lubbock before someone shoots at you again. He mentioned major crime statistics." His face broke into a grin.

"Well, I can tell you one thing about this shooter. He or she is not familiar with guns. Neither Kate nor I would be here if this person were a pro. But you're right. I'd like to get away before whoever it is has time to practice."

With that thought firmly planted, conversation died. Kate watched as Harry closed his eyes and seemed to be working on keeping his breathing even. Kate's hand lay in his, and he kept her aroused with the gentle stroking of his thumb. She leaned her head back and tried to concentrate on the others driving north and how Quinn was doing. She knew he'd be fine. Joyce and Jordy would see to it. Her phone buzzed. She removed her hand from Harry's and reached into pocket. The screen showed Sal even though it was three in the morning in Connecticut.

"Hey, Sal, I've good news. Harry's going to be okay, and we're heading for the Lubbock airport so we can fly to Denver tonight and he won't have to sit in a car for ten hours."

"Good going, Katie. I only now got off the phone with Garrison, who updated me on the boy's condition. Traveling by private jet? Not bad."

"Thanks to Agnes' friend Maddox Fox. This will give Harry a chance for a good rest before he has to be shoehorned into the tiny seat for the commercial flight home. It's going to be enough of a zoo for us to fly with the puppy."

"I'm glad you'll be home tomorrow night. I can put off the trip to the Cape if you need help."

"No way, Sal. You need time with your granddaughter. Anyway, I'll be swamped with help. All the boys are home right now, and I've arranged for a kennel helper to free me up from the grunt work so I can take care of Harry. Don't change your plans at all. I've got everything under control."

"If you say so, kid, but remember, I'm only a phone

call and a three hour drive away."

"You go get some sleep. We've arrived at the airport. I'll call you tomorrow when we're leaving for Connecticut."

Kate texted her mother to expect a visit from Professor Lyndon Stubbs a friend of Harry's who would be in the area on Monday. He wanted to talk to her about one of her books. Harry and she said it would be okay for him to visit with details to follow. Kate sent the text knowing her mother always checked her texts with her breakfast coffee even if she ignored them the rest of the day. She'd fill Harry in on the plane. Then she sent a quick text to Lily saying she'd call from Denver. Kate hoped she was asleep since she had the other puppy buyers showing up in the morning—correction, later this morning—to get their puppies before she and the pretty red girl puppy headed home. Kate remembered Lily's excitement over all the chaos in New York. She was pretty sure she might have gotten a lifetime's worth of excitement with this visit.

CHAPTER TWENTY

Kate's arm had fallen asleep, and she needed to move Harry to get some circulation back. Luckily, as she started to ease him up, they arrived at the airport. The limousine drove right by the terminal and up to the steps of the private jet. The driver and Officer Ramirez eased Harry gently out of the wide door and walked him to the plane. Harry's height being about six inches above that of his helpers made their progress an interesting sight as the three of them progressed slowly up the steps into the plane. Kate grabbed her purse and turned toward the trunk. The driver, glancing back over his shoulder, told her he'd take care of the bags as soon as they had Harry settled.

"Just come up here and be with him, miss." Kate thought he recognized she felt lost and out of step. Tossing the strap of her purse over her head, she ran up the steps. The pilot had joined the men in settling Harry in a soft leather seat, and his seat belt had already been fastened.

Kate slid into the seat next to him, strapped herself in, then peered into Harry's eyes, half-closed to hide the pain, she thought. What pressure had been put on the doctor to okay him to fly in this condition was beyond her. His chest rose in tiny ragged breaths, as though drawing a deep breath would tear him apart. His shoulders were hunched and his body clenched as though the smallest movement would bring him to his knees.

Kate put one hand on top of his as the men moved away to get the luggage on board. The other she slowly eased behind his neck. Without thinking but working on instinct, she felt for the muscles knotted at the base of his neck. She rested her hand against them, applying warmth. Then, without moving her hand but only flexing her fingers, she pressed each then released it. Kate had done this for years with injured dogs or those suffering the problems of age. Those tiny pressures always seemed to relax them and ease their pain.

After a minute, Harry returned from wherever he'd gone in his head so he could get through this. He let out a long breath, which Kate suspected he'd been holding since he'd left the hospital. His eyes opened and moving his head, he stared at her, His hand under hers turned over to intertwine fingers and, with a sigh, he relaxed into sleep.

The panic and fear Kate associated with flying hadn't come with this takeoff. She allowed herself to relax. The plane's air conditioning felt chilly, which couldn't be good for someone recovering from shock after being shot. Kate found a soft blanket, which she spread over Harry. Since he still dozed, she let her eyes explore the plane. The cabin felt like a living room, only with small round windows. Maddox Fox's influence extended from the earth tone palette of colors reflecting his Texas home, to the richness of the fabric, leather, and carpet. The blanket covering Harry was cashmere, the seats soft camel-colored leather, and the teak tables and wall accents glowed with a high polish. He'd created an extension of his home on wings. The night sky kept her from seeing the city, except for the taller buildings, as they took off. Kate turned back to Harry now facing her direction, watching. His body seemed more relaxed and she realized without thinking, she'd instinctively returned her hand to his neck. Kate slowly eased it out and dropped it in her lap.

"What did you do to me?" His voice sounded quiet but strong.

"You mean the hand thing? It's nothing medical. It's something I do to the dogs when they're in pain. For some reason, putting my hand on their necks at the top of the spine and applying a slight pressure seems to cause muscles throughout their systems to relax. I don't press hard; only moving my fingers enough to make the body aware of tension easing. Dogs can't tell us where they hurt so I don't really know whether I'm doing any good. It's something I've done all my life. I did it to you automatically."

"It helps." He smiled, sighed and then closing his eyes, allowing himself to sleep. Kate leaned back and let her own eyes drift shut following his example.

A change in the sound of the plane's engine woke her. Kate hadn't realized how tired she'd been until now, dragging herself from a deep sleep. A bounce came as the wheels touched the runway in Denver. Kate glanced at Harry and saw his eyes open, watching her. He smiled a real smile, dimples and all.

"What?" she asked, embarrassed at his scrutiny. "Do I snore? Drool? What?"

His smile deepened. "I love watching you sleep. I want to be able see you beside me when I wake for the rest of my life. I—"

The disembodied voice of the pilot interrupted. "Please stay seated with your seat belts on until the plane comes to a complete stop. The car to take you to your destination is waiting on the runway. We'll be in position in two minutes. I hope your flight was comfortable."

Kate peered out the window into the dark. Rufus, Joyce, Cathy and Jordy would still be on the road with Quinn and Lexi. They had hours of driving left to do. She slipped out of her seat the instant they stopped and gently lifted the blanket off Harry.

In far less time than it had taken to get into the plane, they disembarked into another stretch limousine and soon found themselves on the highway heading toward the Blackburn's home. It felt noticeably cooler at this elevation so Kate took from her backpack and slipped on a sweater she'd knit from a lightweight merino yarn warm enough to take the chill off without adding weight. Three puppy faces with their Sammy smiles were knit into the front yoke. Kate found a blanket by the side armrest in the limo and laid it over Harry, who once again stretched out half-lying across the seat, his head resting on her shoulder. The lack of traffic due to the wee small hours made the drive much quicker than the last time, and they soon reached Rufus' home. The gate opened as they pulled up showing they were expected. The circular driveway in front of the house lit up and the front door opened as they pulled to a stop. A burly cowboy approached and opened the car door.

"Hey Raymond," Harry said. "I'm back and I've brought company."

"I heard you were dumb enough to get yourself shot. Do you know who did it?" Raymond managed to ease Harry from the car and, with the driver holding his other side, up the front steps and into the house. Kate followed.

The room to the right off the entrance hall reminded Kate of her Aunt Maeve's home in New York City. It was a library in the classical sense, with oak bookcases lining all four walls, each rising up to the twelve foot high ceilings. A massive desk sat in the center of the room now, occupied by the old man Jordy had said was his grandfather. Two leather sofas faced each other on either side of a massive fireplace that elbowed itself into the mass of books. Next to these an assortment of comfortable chairs, good reading lamps, and side tables littered with books, notepads, and a laptop resided. This formed the obvious nerve-center of the home. As they entered, the old man pushed back from the desk, and Kate noticed the wheelchair she'd spotted when they'd dropped off Jordy. He quickly rounded the desk, telling Raymond to put Harry on the sofa. A woman about the same age as Raymond, her face and long dark hair a testament to her either Italian or Spanish ancestry, dressed in jeans and a white Western shirt, pushed by them into the room with an armload of pillows and blankets that she dumped on the opposite sofa. "Be gentle getting his boots off," she told Raymond. "I don't want you to jostle the wound and have Mr. Harry bleeding all over my sofa." She bent over Harry. "You never could stay out of trouble. I shouldn't have let either of you or the boy out the door. You and your adventures. First the FBI and now this. What will come of you?"

"Thank you, Antonia. Just patch up my skinned knee and feed me." Harry was losing his fight to stay awake for another second.

"I think we should let him sleep." Kate said. They all moved toward the door. As they passed out of the room, she heard him say, "Kate, meet Antonia, who manages the running of this all-male household and Antonia, this is Kate, the woman I love and my fiancée."

The woman, Antonia, closed the door after Mr. Blackburn's wheelchair cleared the room, then she whirled around and grabbed Kate's wrists so tightly she bent in pain. "I've heard about you. Mr. Rufus said Harry was shot because of you last winter. Now, because of you, Harry is bleeding all over the sofa. You bring him much pain. You're evil. You may have a pretty face to tempt my boy, but you are a she-devil. You are bad luck. Harry should stay away from you and you should stay away from him. Go away, go from this house, go far away from us and take your evil with you." She pushed Kate back, released her then spat at her and, with the swiftness of a snake, struck out and slapped her hard in the face. Kate gasped. Shaking her head to ward off the dizzy feeling of being used as a punching bag, she opened her mouth to speak, but nothing came out. She felt blood and pain when she lifted her hand to her cheek. Kate saw both men moving toward them and glanced back at her attacker, who now had both hands raised, ready to strangle her.

Kate's brain screamed *no*, and she slipped into auto-matic pilot mode. Instead of running from her, she stepped forward, her hands shooting up. Grabbing the woman's arms and hooking her foot around her knee, she threw her completely off balance and sent her, butt first, to the floor. Kate then flipped her and pinned both hands high behind her back before her attacker could move. Kate gaped at the man in the wheelchair who sat not speaking and said, "If this is your idea of a welcome to Colorado greeting, it sucks!"

Raymond grabbed the woman as Kate released her and jumped back. He held her fast since she shook with anger and struggled to continue her attack. He dragged her, still screaming curses, down the hall to the back of the house. Kate turned to scowl at Rufus's father and demanded,

"What in God's blue Earth is going on here?"

"You don't understand, what a shock this is to see Harry like this. This is his home. You are a stranger. But you're a stranger we know about. You have a history of hurting someone we love. You have been responsible for getting him shot before. Now you bring him here bloody and seriously injured. Don't you think it would upset his family?"

"I understand several things, Mr. Blackburn. First, this is not Harry's home. Your family is the one with whom he stayed when he studied at Caltech. Harry's home is more than two thousand miles away, as is the family who loves him. Second, I did not cause Harry to be injured in February or now. The person who shot Harry also shot at me, twice. I ducked and he or she missed. And third, the fact you allow someone working for you to assault me in your home while you sat and watched is criminal. If my contact with the Denver Sheriff's Department weren't in a car with your son and grandson, I'd have called her and had deputies here before you could blink. If Harry weren't lying on your sofa recovering from surgery, he and I would be in a cab heading across the city. However, I love the man on that sofa, so, against my better judgment, we're going to stay. But if that crazy woman comes anywhere near us, I'll have her arrested. Do I make myself clear?"

"Kate?" She heard Harry's voice and dashed to the door, finding it locked. Kate whirled around. "Where is the key? I need it now."

"Raymond!" Blackburn bellowed and footsteps came

running from the back. He had the key in his hand. Without a word, he unlocked and opened the door.

Kate ignored him and raced to Harry's side. "Harry, are you okay?"

"I heard you in the hall and wanted you with me. I'm going to need Raymond's help to use the restroom. Don't disappear while I'm gone. You and I need to talk to Ewen."

Kate helped him move his legs off the sofa, and Raymond easily got him to his feet and down the hall. Rather than standing and glaring at Blackburn, Kate redid the blankets on the couch and put Harry's boots out of the way. She grabbed her tote, which held her ways of connecting with the outside world, as well as Harry's briefcase and brought them into the room, setting them by the coffee table. Her fiancé now had himself a roommate.

Harry moved slowly back to the sofa. Raymond helped settle him comfortably, and Kate pulled up the blankets, tucking them around him. She moved the extra blankets to the other sofa. She was not leaving Harry again until they reached Connecticut. Kate heard Blackburn speaking quietly to Raymond in the hall and by the time she'd gotten everything arranged to Harry's comfort, Blackburn had finished and come in to position himself by Harry's head.

"What was the shouting I heard in the hallway?" Harry asked.

She waited to see what Blackburn would say. He cleared his throat, staring at her with a scowl. "Antonia had a disagreement with this woman. It came to blows. Antonia is in the kitchen."

Harry turned to her in shock. Kate reached for him, and he grasped he wrist. Wincing, she cried out. Harry lifted her arm then reached for the other and finally touched her face where a greenish-purple bruise grew. "Antonia assaulted you? God, Kate."

She focused and raised her chin. "I stopped her."

"Ewen, why did you let Antonia hurt Kate? I know she can get excitable, but she was so gentle with Helen when she was dying. What could have made her do this?"

"Antonia said this woman caused you to be hurt."

Both Harry and Kate stared at him. Then Harry closed his eyes and leaned back against the pillows. "This is insane. Perhaps we should begin again. Kate, this is Ewen Blackburn, Rufus's father and Jordy's grandfather. He and his wife Helen were the ones I told you who took me in while I studied at Caltech. Ewen, Kate and I have been engaged since February. She came on this trip to get a puppy that was fathered by her grand champion Samoyed, Dillon. She and two of her friends got together here to drive to Lubbock. Kate was shot at by the person who shot me. However, she was smart enough to duck so the bullets missed, taking out a car window and lodging in the car door. Neither Kate nor I have any idea why this person, who had already wounded a math professor at the college, would come after us, but we intend to find out. Why didn't you welcome Kate with open arms?"

"And why would I ever do that?" The old man scowled.

Harry reached for a book on the coffee table. "Isn't this a copy of the new book on probability you co-authored? I'm told it's getting very good reviews." He paused to look the old man straight in the eyes. "Well, let me formally introduce you to my fiancée, Kate Killoy, your co-author's daughter."

CHAPTER TWENTY-ONE

"I didn't know Claire had a daughter," Ewen said after a few minutes. "She only talks about her sons."

Kate rolled her eyes and Harry smiled.

"My mother and I have issues we're trying to resolve. I chose the career I wanted rather than the one she wanted for me, but I am still Claire Killoy's daughter, though I was much closer to my father and grandfather before their deaths than to my mother because of my love for dogs."

Ewen Blackburn turned from Harry's face to hers and then shook his head. "What a mess. Miss Killoy, Kate, I am sorry your welcome was so…inappropriate. I apologize."

"It's nice to make your acquaintance, Mr. Blackburn, though, if you don't mind, I'd rather avoid your housekeeper while I'm here."

He chuckled. "It's probably an excellent idea. Harry,

since peace has been declared, perhaps I'd better leave so you can get some rest."

After he left the room, Kate got Harry settled again. Then, taking the extra blanket and pillow she made a bed for herself on the couch facing Harry across the coffee table. She shed her shoes and lay down, fatigue dragging at her as the adrenaline rush passed. She glanced at Harry, expecting him to be asleep.

Instead, he stared at her. "You ended it?"

Kate sighed then described what had happened.

"You're scary," he said, staring at her.

"You're right." Kate gazed across at him holding her breath. This hadn't been the first time this had come up. It was the one question that had threatened their relationship in February and one they'd skirted ever since. If he wanted a gentle, sweet, supportive bride who never would stick her neck out to fight injustice, she knew she couldn't be that person. It would break her heart, but it would be worse to live a lie. Kate needed an answer. "Do you want me to change?"

"Never!" he said staring deep into her eyes. "You scare the hell out of me because it would kill me if something happened to you. But this self-reliant you is the one I fell in love with. Be patient with me if I go all protective." This time a smile with full dimples faced her and, with an inward sigh, she returned it.

"I don't want you to change either, not even the over

protective part. I like that you try to keep me safe. But try not to get too freaked out when I defend myself. Sal trained me. He said it was necessary for me to learn self-defense since I work with cops." Letting out a breath she hadn't realized she's been holding, Kate glanced over and saw he had fallen asleep. Deciding the crisis was over for now, she allowed herself to do the same.

Sometime while Kate slept, she felt someone snuggle onto the couch with her, but didn't come fully awake.

Later, she felt a scratchy tongue licking at her mouth. She didn't know how long it was before she became fully conscious, but she woke feeling sore, out of it, and grubby. Kate looked across to Harry only to find he wasn't there. Blinking the remaining sleep from her eyes, she scrambled off the couch and head for the library door only to have it open and have Harry, with Rufus' help, move toward the sofa. Kate noticed he had new bandages and a clean shirt. He reached for her demanding his good morning kiss.

"In all honestly, I should let you know I suspect another male slept with me, so yours is not my first kiss today."

Jordy, who'd been right behind them, broke out laughing. With a bound, Quinn shot from behind Jordy and jumped up, his paws on her legs, wanting attention. Kate scooped him up with a hug. "Have you been out to pee, my young friend?" She asked the squirming puppy.

"I took him, Kate. He likes me. But he wanted to see you. Now we're going to go play with a tennis ball." Jordy jumped up, pulling the puppy's lead from his pocket.

"Take him out the back so he doesn't crap on the front steps." Kate grinned, handing him a poop bag. The fact he'd already been out to do his business didn't mean he wouldn't need to do it again, soon, since all puppies had an unending supply of poop.

As the door closed behind him, she squatted at Harry's side to ask about the wound.

Cathy walked into the room. "Don't worry Kate. I checked the wound, which is clean and healthy, and I put on fresh dressings. He's played this game before I think. His body is like a road map of old wounds."

"I know and, in spite of what Antonia thinks, they're not my fault."

Rufus moved over to stand beside Cathy, his hand resting on her shoulder. "What's this I hear about you and Antonia having a problem?"

"Apparently Antonia is under the assumption I caused Harry's injuries," Kate said quietly. "She got overly upset by this." Harry's blanket slipped, and she reached for it only to have Cathy gasp.

"Kate, your wrists. What happened? Oh my, and your face is bruised as well." Cathy stepped forward gently examining her bruises, which now displayed an impressive shade of purple and green.

Kate shrugged.

Harry frowned at Rufus. "I don't care what Antonia thinks. She injured Kate. End of story. Rufus, you're to see she stays far away from her."

A question that had been lurking out of reach in my mind took shape. "Tell me, why would Antonia think I was a threat?" Kate asked, "As far as I know, she wasn't aware I existed before I walked into this house. Yet, less than five minutes later, she was ready to beat the crap out of me for injuring Harry. Unless she's completely insane, we're missing something here."

"Well, Antonia has always treated Harry like her pet boy," Rufus teased.

"I gathered, but this seemed over the top. She went ballistic." Kate glanced at them. "My bringing her 'pet boy' home to have his wounds nursed is not the act of someone who hurt him. No, there's something more going on. She said you'd told her I was responsible for Harry getting shot in New York," she said, focusing on Rufus.

"I never said that. I didn't even know about you until Thursday night. Don't worry, we'll get to the bottom of this." Rufus stopped speaking at the sound of the powered wheelchair. Kate wondered how long Ewen had been behind the half-open door.

Kate decided to change the subject. "Not to shift the

attention from me onto something which affects us all, but how did your trip from Lubbock go? Did you run into any problems, or is this person only targeting Harry and me?"

Rufus stole a glance at Cathy. "We were followed for part of the trip. A red Chevy Tahoe I seen parked at the hotel when we left, I spotted when we pulled off for gas in Dalhart. In Pueblo, we stopped at the Denny's because Jordy was hungry and I saw it pull into the parking lot after us. When we left, they followed right behind us. Nobody got out or came in to eat, though we were there for half an hour. I circled the lot on the way out and had Jordy check the plates. It dogged us all the way here. I checked with Joyce, but it didn't stay with her after she dropped us off."

"Do you have the plate number?" Kate asked and he fished a piece of paper from his pocket. She pulled out her phone and, flipping through her contacts, dialed. "Lieutenant Garrison? It's Kate Killoy here."

"Miss Killoy, did you make it to your stop in Denver?"

"Yes, we're safe in Colorado for now, but those driving were followed by a red Chevy Tahoe all the way from their hotel to the place where we're staying now."

"Your people didn't happen to find out who owned it, did they?"

"I've got the plate number." She read the number then gave it back to Rufus. "You might want to check it. Someone seems to be going to a lot of trouble to keep track of where we are."

"I'll do that."

"Thanks. It will help."

"How did Mr. Foyle manage the flight north?"

"Okay. He's doing some better, thanks. I look forward to your call." Kate put the phone away and glanced at her watch as her stomach let out a growl. "Sorry."

"Kate, when did you eat last?" Harry asked.

"At the dinner. I skipped eating when we arrived, and I slept through breakfast."

Rufus stood up. "Well, it's lunchtime. I'll see what's planned. I want to talk to Antonia anyway."

Cathy followed him out, a worried expression on her face.

Kate turned back to Harry, but he'd dozed off. Jordy came in with Quinn, trying to find his father. She took Quinn's lead and sent Jordy to the kitchen. She settled the puppy in her lap and he slept. Stroking him, she touched her wrists, checking the bruises. They still hurt to the touch, but she could use her hands. Kate watched Harry sleep, his color back to normal. He'd been through enough. Antonia's reaction had upset him more than he showed, but she wondered, if it was the fact Harry had been injured or the fact he'd said he loved her and they planned to be married that had set her off?

The sunlight sparkled with tiny dust particles, softening the room's masculine atmosphere. Kate watched the puppy sleeping in her lap who, in six months, would be his father's height. Life changed quickly. Puppies grew fast. People changed fast. At this time last year, she'd laid lost in mourning the deaths of her father and grandfather. She had ignored the world, burying herself in the things she had shared with those two men she loved so much. It had seemed as if giving up even the tiniest sliver of that routine would mean she didn't care. Her world had been one where she could only embrace sadness and not deal with life.

Then, last November, Kate had been wrenched into the world. Thanks to Agnes, she'd been shoved kicking and screaming into a world for which she wasn't prepared. In February, Harry had saved her life, taught her how to deal with fear, and shown her she was ready for love. When Kate saw herself now, it was no longer as a pigtailed girl whose entire world was dogs.

The room was filled with math-related books. Shakespeare, Dickens, and Dumas had all been relegated to a bottom shelf. Physically, the room resembled the library at great-aunt Maeve's, but without the warmth. Maeve's love of math probably surpassed Ewen's. But unlike this library outfitted with math and technical books up to the ceiling, the books filling Maeve Donnelly's library walls in her New York brownstone were an eclectic gathering of knowledge welcoming all who entered to partake of an esoteric feast.

"It's not much like Maeve's library is it?" Harry

asked, reading her mind.

"No. This isn't a room in which to curl up and read *Peter Pan* on a snowy afternoon."

"This was the sort of world I knew for many years of growing up. Knowledge was paramount. But I wouldn't say I loved this atmosphere. When I walked into Maeve's home, it felt different, warm. I don't know why." He said.

"Yes, you do. You know why. Think about when we sat there on a snowy evening, searching for clues to a mystery."

He frowned then smiled. You mean inclusive vs. exclusive.

Before they got too involved in the comparisons, Quinn luckily woke up. "I'd better get him outside so he doesn't pee on the carpet." She grabbed the lead and beat a quick retreat out the front door. Only when she bent to attach the puppy's lead did she realize if their stalker had a rifle and stood at the gate, she presented a perfect target. Scooping Quinn up, Kate ran for the cover of the trees ten feet to the left. Checking for any sign of a red car near the gate, she didn't spot one, but it might be somewhere nearby. Moving toward the back of the house, she kept one eye on Quinn and one eye out for possible shooters.

Quinn finished his business, and Kate pulled a poop bag from her pocket and cleaned up after him. They continued toward the rear, staying by the trees rather than on the gravel driveway. Seeing the back door, she ran across an open stretch of drive and up the back steps. As she reached the door, she heard a click. She turned the knob but found it locked. Kate knocked at the door to no response. In desperation, she called Cathy.

"Where are you we're all waiting at lunch," she said.

"I'm at the back door with the puppy. It's locked, and I can't get in."

"It's not locked. I just came in that way."

"Humor me, please." Kate ended the call. A minute later, Cathy unlocked the door and let her in. After she washed her hands, they entered the dining room.

"Kate, you must have turned the knob the wrong way. It couldn't be locked. Cathy and I came in through there only a minute ago," Rufus said.

Cathy frowned at him. "It was locked."

CHAPTER TWENTY-TWO

Thirty minutes later, everyone moved back to the library where Raymond was clearing the tray that had held Harry's meal. Kate moved a chair next to his sofa while Cathy sat on the opposite one next to a very concerned Rufus.

"When does your flight leave, Cathy ?" Kate asked.

"About eight tonight, though I should be at the airport by seven. Oh, I checked my emails, and I'll be judging in West Springfield, Massachusetts next weekend, filling in for Irma Haymann."

"Great. I'm entered in two of the four shows but not under Haymann. Hopefully, we can get together after the show."

Rufus smiled at Cathy. "I'll be bringing Jordy back to school then. You might find some time for us to get together."

"I could do that," she replied, smiling.

Kate watched the unspoken conversation between them. They had found each other, which was nice for all their sakes. Harry lifted one eyebrow and winked, smiling.

Kate hated to pour cold water on the relaxed warmth of the afternoon, but questions needed to be asked and answered. "Not to bring up unpleasant subjects, but we still have a problem with a person wanting to kill us. I'm sure it's all tied up in the professor's problems. There has to be more of a reason why the professor, who hasn't really known you since you were a child, would insist on your coming across the country to help. Rufus, did he say why it had to be Harry?"

"No. He didn't. I only figured he knew about Harry's company and it had something to do with that."

"Well, shooting at me and wounding Harry wouldn't stop the investigation into the extortion. It would only delay it."

Harry was startled. "Which may be exactly why."

Rufus asked, "What may be exactly why?"

"The person hasn't killed anyone, yet. What they have done is injure or drive into hiding the people who are working to investigate the charges against the professor. The shooter may be the thief."

"Then you agree money has really been stolen from

Baxter, Kline and Baxter?

"Oh, there's no question about that. And, as Kate pointed out, it is probably virtual money. Money that can be shifted from account to account without anyone being the wiser until an account shows a shortfall. The last paper I wrote for Stubbs talked about how to stop this kind of crime."

"Do you still have that paper?" Kate felt the start of an idea creeping in, but it floundered, vague.

"No. I never bothered to update those files, and software changes made them inaccessible pretty quickly. I gave the hard copy to the professor. I doubt he kept it. He probably threw out all that stuff when he left Caltech for Texas Poly.

Jordy burst into the room with Quinn hot on his heels. "I saw it. I couldn't see who was driving with the tinted windows, but I'm sure it's the same red car that followed us from Texas. I didn't get close enough to see the plate number, but it had exactly the same scrape on the rear wheel well."

"Where did you see it?" Rufus jumped out of his seat and pulled his phone from his pocket.

"It was outside the gate." Jordy's shoulders slumped. "Quinn couldn't run fast enough, so I didn't get there in time to check the plate."

Kate interrupted. "Do you think the person driving

might have seen you?"

"Um, I guess so. We weren't hiding. We'd explored the back yard and were bouncing a ball off the front steps and chasing it." Jordy's chin went up. "You only said to keep him from peeing on the front steps, and I did."

Rufus spoke quickly into his phone. He stared at Kate and then held it out to her." As she reached for it, he muttered, "Joyce."

Kate quickly answered her questions about Harry's condition.

Then Joyce asked if they could fly east today rather than tomorrow.

Kate turned to Harry, "Are you up to flying east tonight?"

"Absolutely."

He pulled out his phone and got busy changing their reservations. Kate filled Joyce in on their theories about the shootings.

Harry gave her a thumbs up and Kate passed on the information.

Joyce said she'd arranged for them to be taken to the airport and guarded 'til they got to security.

"I think Joyce wants to get us out of Denver before we start running up their crime statistics. We've got to be ready in half an hour. I'm going to use the restroom then get Quinn's traveling case out of my bag. I had hoped he'd have more time in it to practice before he flew, but he's going to have to bite the bullet and get into the bag."

Kate pulled it from the front pocket of her suitcase and handed it to Jordy. "Here, put some treats and his dinosaur in it. Let him come out on his own. No sense freaking him out before it's necessary."

So Quinn and Jordy set about making a game of the puppy going in and out of the soft-sided pet carrier and Kate headed for the restroom to get cleaned up before heading for the airport. As she passed their luggage, she noticed the side zipper of her suitcase partially undone and her grandmother's belt sticking out. Kate slipped into the half-bath and cleaned up then wheeled her case into the library. She hadn't touched the bag except to get the puppy carrier out of the front pouch. Kate placed the case on a table to one side of the room and started going through it. Using touch, she searched the bag, checking everything. Nothing was disturbed. As she began to slide the belt through loops on her jeans, it occurred to her to check the cash she'd placed inside before the trip. Kate pulled the belt off, sliding her fingers into its built-in pouch. She stopped. Carrying it over to the sofa where Harry chatted with Rufus, she asked, "Do you have your knife on you?"

Harry studied the belt and her face then dug into his pants for a slim but very effective multipurpose knife. Using the tip of the knife, she lifted the fabric to reveal her folded bills along with a thin piece of wire with tiny metal grips on each end. They all stared. Kate gently removed the wire and the money. She placed the wire inside a poop bag without touching the ends and put it into the jewelry pouch in the suitcase. Nobody spoke. Folding the money Kate shoved it into her pocket. Then, with a glance toward the closed door, she tucked the edges of the opening back and slipped on the belt. Harry stared at Rufus, his fury barely contained. How the wire got there was obvious, as was the desired outcome. The only thing not obvious was the why. Kate didn't say anything, only zipped the suitcase and placed it next to her purse then returned to her chair by the sofa. Harry, with some help from Rufus, walked to the restroom, and Cathy sat next to her.

"Kate, I am so sorry this weekend has been so awful for you." Cathy reached for her arm.

Kate grinned. "I'm glad it hasn't been so awful for you. I think you and Rufus hit it off. You bonded with Jordy and aren't freaked out by his smarts. You've even found someone who likes dogs, a definite requirement. But my one suggestion, if you end up living here, is get a new housekeeper." Their eyes locked, and they laughed.

Harry and Rufus returned. A buzzer went off and Raymond stepped to a control panel by the front door. He pushed a button and, two minutes later, opened the front door to a pair of sheriff's deputies. Kate pointed out their bags while Rufus and Raymond helped Harry down the steps and eased him into the sheriff's patrol car. Jordy followed with Quinn and his bag. As Harry settled, Kate dashed around to the other side and slid in. Jordy passed her both puppy and carrier bag. She slipped Quinn's dinosaur into her jacket pocket, telling Jordy they'd see him soon. As she reached to close the car door, she stopped, stepped out, and called Jordy back. She leaned close to him, quietly asking a question. Then, giving him a hug, she got back into the car.

With barely enough time for a wave, they headed for the airport. One of the deputies, who introduced himself as Burt, told them there would be a wheelchair waiting at the terminal for Harry, making it easier for him to get to the plane, and Joyce had also arranged for one to be waiting at Bradley. Kate thanked them then Burt told them Joyce wanted to remove two possible murder victims from Denver's crime statistics especially friends.

When they reached the curb, the deputies helped move Harry and sent their luggage through check-in. Kate quickly slid the puppy into his case and zipped it shut. The attendant checked his fit in the case and measured to be sure it would fit under the seat, quickly reviewing all the paperwork. In only a few minutes, they were headed for security. The deputies wished them luck. Kate pushed the wheelchair and balanced the straps of Quinn in his tote and her oversized purse displaying the head of a purple dinosaur sticking out of the zippered pouch on her shoulders. She'd barely taken a step when Harry called a stop.

"Kate, the pack mule look really isn't you. Put your purse strap over the hook on the back of the chair and give me Quinn." She did so, and he unzipped enough of the top opening so a cute white head popped out, smiling. Harry scratched his ears and chin as Kate went back to wheeling the chair toward security. When she rounded the corner and got her first view of the security area she stopped dead. Approximately the size of an airplane hangar, the area was crisscrossed with twenty different lines zigzagged back and forth through which moved virtually a thousand people. They located the correct snake heading toward the conveyor belts. Harry and Quinn held a deep discussion, mostly on Harry's side, and Kate let her gaze roam the huge, white sleek building.

Quinn's puppy growls while playing handkerchief tug -of-war with Harry drew her attention back. She watched until they reached the place with one person between them and the conveyor belt. Kate felt someone watching her from the balcony above, glanced up, and spotted someone she recognized.

Kate put her bag on the belt, slipped off her shoes, and took the few coins out of her pocket. She pulled off her watch then stopped. Glancing up, she let her gaze sweep the balcony again, this time spotting the watcher. Kate slipped the watch back on and smiled. She lifted a delighted Quinn from his bag and put it on the belt. Kate snapped a lead onto his collar. Harry went ahead and got a different style check-in then Kate moved forward with the puppy. They passed Dillon through, noting the metal latch on the lead and D-ring and buckle on the collar. Then Kate stepped forward, knowing exactly what would happen. The buzzer went off and she suddenly found herself in an examining room. At this airport, apparently she'd receive more than a quick brush with the wand. No, she was considered a possible threat. Two women played with Quinn, as Kate had to strip down to the basics and be inspected. She loudly cursed herself for being stupid and forgetting to take off her watch with the metal band. Eventually, after everyone got a chance to play with the puppy, she was allowed to dress again and met up with Harry waiting at the entrance to the shuttle trains.

"What happened?" he asked. "Did you forget to take off your watch again?"

Kate smiled at him and pointed back toward the balcony now almost out of sight. "We had an audience. I left it on for show."

CHAPTER TWENTY-THREE

Kate hooked the puppy bag next to her tote and let Quinn sit in Harry's lap as they headed for the train. The puppy happily racked up experiences by the dozen, adding both trains and elevators. They reached the gate too early to board, so Kate showed Harry how the piddle pads worked and went to get them something to eat. Returning with a cheeseburger and fries for Harry and a fish sandwich for herself, she juggled some water bottles and a bag of cashews for dessert. Quinn had settled into a deep sleep, legs extended both front and back under the wheelchair.

Kate scarfed down her food. She texted Sal they were arriving earlier than expected and needed a ride tonight. He texted her back, saying it wasn't a problem.

Then Kate dialed the anonymous number she'd been emailed earlier. Anton answered. Kate informed him they'd be getting in after midnight so they'd plan to pick them up at the hotel tomorrow morning. Next she texted her mother explaining Professor Lyndon Stubbs would be arriving tomorrow. Kate hoped it fit her schedule. Much to her amazement because of the hour, her mother responded immediately, saying it was fine. Her mother remembered Harry talking about the professor the last time he came down from Boston. Kate then sent Tom a text warning him Mom had a visiting professor coming who might need a room and she might need K and K's help with another project she'd explain tomorrow. Sighing, with all her text-ducks in a row, she sat back and reached for Harry's hand.

"You done?"

"Yup. Sal will pick us up. I'll get Anton and Lyndon tomorrow. Mom is on board, and I warned Tom's ready to help. Have I forgotten anything?"

"Yes."

"What?"

"You forgot to tell me what the hell you've been up to since we left the Blackburn house."

"Oh, that," She waved her free hand carelessly."

"Yes, that. What did you ask Jordy?"

"I asked him how he knew Toni Dunn when she showed up yesterday morning at the hotel."

"It's because she took Rufus' class at the university."

"No. I first asked him if he knew all his father's students. He didn't. He knew her because she was named after her favorite aunt. Her full name is Antonia Dunn."

Harry stared as what she'd told him sunk in. Then she continued.

"I also got a text from Garrison saying the car following Joyce's from Lubbock belongs to a professor who is on sabbatical in England. Guess who is house sitting for him and his wife?"

"Toni Dunn."

"After the gift her aunt installed in my belt, I was watching for Toni. I spotted her on the balcony right before I went through the screening. I had removed the garrote from my belt but, not wanting her to know I'd added two and two by the buzzer not going off, I arranged to become a person of interest knowing they'd only find the watch. From where she watched, she couldn't tell if I were arrested or not. Let's hope she thinks I have been so she doesn't buy a ticket and attempt to murder us on the plane."

"You're sure Toni Dunn is the shooter."

"Detective Garrison told me she was the only one who didn't park in the lot. She claimed because she parked on the street and she didn't see anything. The question is, was she alone? She's not big and probably needed assistance hefting someone your size as dead weight into an SUV. I think she had outside help."

Kate took a breath and continued. "Someone would have noticed a car left in the parking lot but not on the street. They could have hidden behind the dumpsters and, when you turned your back, one of them hit you then the other stepped out to shoot you. You said you heard two voices. I'm assuming Toni's a novice with a gun, which is why she missed me and didn't kill you. Even if she had help, I'm still sure she's the shooter. I'm also sure she thought she was killing the professor when she shot McNatt in the kitchen. The professor hadn't told her he'd be away trying to help straighten Anton's life out. As his TA, she assumed he tell her if he weren't going to be home. Stubbs told me he knew I'd be at the park because he'd texted his assistant."

"So she shoots Dr. McNatt, thinking she was killing Stubbs. McNatt doesn't have white hair; she would have noticed the difference."

"Not at night with the shade drawn in the kitchen. She saw a man's outline at the sink. She aimed at a shape, which is probably the only reason he's alive."

"But, why would a TA in the Math Department go around randomly shooting at people?"

"I'm not sure. I have an idea, but I need to talk to the professor first. I think it has something to do with a boy called Harry Foyle."

He stared at her in total confusion, but Kate continued, "In the meantime, I want you to rest up because we're going to need you working on all burners before this is over."

"Following your thought processes is like trying to solve a Rubik's Cube.

"You mean I'm twisted and colorful?" Kate asked, kissing his cheek.

She pulled a cushion from a pocket on the back of the wheelchair and eased it in behind Harry's head, placing a quick kiss on his mouth when she finished. He smiled then closed his eyes to rest. The puppy still slept under the wheelchair, and she could use a nap as well, but their flight was in forty-five minutes, so Kate pulled out her Kindle and opened the mystery she'd started on the trip out, losing herself in the plot until the loudspeaker announced all passengers needing assistance and unaccompanied minors should report to the gate.

Kate checked the other passengers who had gathered at the gate. Their assailant wasn't in sight, so she scooped up the sleeping puppy and stood him on a pee pad, which, thank goodness, he used. Then she put him into the carrier without giving him a chance to refuse. Zipping it shut, she placed the carrier in Harry's lap, hooked the straps of her bag over the hook on the back of the wheelchair, and in barely a minute they were heading for the gate. The attendant checked them in and then Kate rolled Harry down the ramp to the plane. The cabin attendants took Harry from the chair and helped him get comfortable in his seat. Kate slid in next to him, placing Quinn's carrier under the seat in front of her.

The lines of pain etched in Harry's face from all this movement had Kate praying they'd have a smooth flight home. He'd taken nothing for the pain since they left the house.

"Harry, I think you should take this to make this flight a little easier?" She held out one of the pills and a water bottle.

"No. I've spent enough time feeling out of it. I need to think, and I can't when doped up with those pills."

Kate didn't waste her breath arguing. Instead, she placed her hand behind his neck and got to work. After a couple of minutes, he sighed and, kissing her arm, closed his eyes. She eased her hand away, and he didn't move.

Kate bent down and placed her hand by the netting of the carrier. She felt a small nose sniff it. With her attention on Harry's comfort and reassuring Quinn, she barely noted the hubbub of boarding. She prayed she hadn't missed anyone dangerous.

An older woman saw the empty seat on the aisle and smiled. Kate warned her she'd be traveling with a puppy, which only made the grin grow. Their new friend explained she'd shown Dachshunds, both smooth and wire-haired, for many years.

Kate relaxed and did as all dog people do when they get together, discussed changes in the ring since they'd each been showing. The woman mentioned she'd been in long enough to remember the addition of the Herding Group in the early 1980s, the addition of agility in the nineties, and the fact the AKC, which often seemed hidebound and traditional, had been making more and more changes to enlarge the sport. They talked about the problem in agility with the smaller dogs having trouble getting the seesaw to drop quickly because of their lighter weight, and then went on to judges they knew.

Kate brought up the changes to the New York show with the addition of the Piers show site giving more space to bench dogs. How this made such an improvement over the hot and crowded lower level at the Garden.

The woman, whose name turned out to be Cora, remembered Kate had placed in a group there in February. Kate felt flattered and thanked her for the congratulations. Every few minutes, Kate checked on Harry, but he seemed to be resting, though she wondered if his sleep was feigned.

After they'd been in the air for a while, Kate unzipped the top of the carrier so she could scratch Quinn's head, and her seatmate reached over and let him sniff her hand before giving him a scratch. Eventually, the smooth motion of the plane lulled him to sleep with his fuzzy head resting on the side of the carrier. Kate quietly eased away and sat back, the stiffness of the hour bent double sending sharp pains from the base of her spine all the way into her shoulders.

Kate needed to talk to the professor. She'd suspected

something in Harry's childhood work in his class had set off red flags about the crime. The flight attendant announced over the loudspeaker there'd be a delay in arrival since they would be flying around a storm. Sal would wait but she really wanted to get the puppy home and Harry settled into a comfortable bed. Kate had bought a new bed for the guest room and had a three-quarter bath put in. He'd be comfortable there. It would save him going back and forth to Tom's as he recovered.

Kate lay back in her seat, tired of chasing questions without good answers. She opened her eyes a minute later only to see into a pair of beautiful green ones staring back and realized she'd slept. She felt a flush creep into her face and a smile begin as she thought of waking to this every day.

"You're going to need to recover quickly if we're going to get married by Christmas," she whispered.

"You really mean it? I don't want to pressure you... well, maybe I do, but you're sure you're ready to marry me?"

"I'm sure. We'll need to get to work planning a bigger house so you can have your business and for when we have kids." His hand gripped hers 'til a thump from the landing gear being lowered and the sound of the engines reversing to slow them brought Quinn wide awake and his paws working to move the zipper so he could make his great escape. Kate apologized while scratching his head as she pushed it back inside and zipped the carrier closed.

Her new friend Cora said goodbye and told her she would see Kate at the Big E shows. Kate and Harry waited until everyone deplaned before she stood and lifted the puppy carrier's strap over her head to settle it on her back, beside her purse. She stepped into the aisle then reached to help Harry only to have an attendant take over. He eased him into the aisle and gently maneuvered him to the waiting wheelchair.

Silently blessing Joyce, Kate slipped the puppy carrier off, placed it into Harry's lap, as the attendant pushed him up the tunnel and out through the concourse toward the baggage area. Unlike the cast of thousands in Denver, Bradley this close to midnight was deserted.

Coming upon a restroom, she asked them to wait and took the now bouncing carrier off Harry's lap, handed him her purse, and ducked inside. Kate unzipped the top of the bag as she reached into the side pocket for a pee pad, but Quinn decided he'd held it long enough and began peeing right on the bathroom floor.

"You couldn't wait one more second, could you?" Kate complained as she laid the pad, absorbent side down, to soak up the pee from the floor. Quinn dove to grab the pee pad in what must be a new game, but Kate was a pro and whipped it into the trash while grabbing another, waiting for him to poop. No luck. Giving up, she carried him out, hooked the carrier onto the handle of the chair, and snapped on his lead, while telling Harry how

Mr. Quick-Pee had outsmarted her in the bathroom. They started down the concourse to the sound of Harry's laughter.

Years of raising puppies had her watching Quinn's every move as they walked. After twenty feet she saw Quinn's nose start trolling the floor and, with speed surprising herself, she whipped the pee pad from her purse and got it in position without a second to spare.

A man walking by them laughed. "Damn, you're good. You sure know dogs."

They first found the trash and then the elevator down to the first floor and rolled into the almost empty baggage pickup area. Their lonely bags rode slowly around the carousel.

"What the hell!" The voice made her exhausted body jump.

"Sal, it's late, and we've had practically no sleep for two days, so could you please yell at us later. If you want to help, grab those two bags. Let's get Harry home and to bed. We'll explain along the way."

Kate checked her watch. Five minutes 'til midnight. She normally needed eight hours of sleep, so, since she'd had, at most, two hours on a couch and in a seat on the plane in the last two days, she was ready to bite anyone who crossed her.

When Sal arrived at the curb with the van, the attendant helped Harry shift into the passenger seat of the big Ford van. She loaded the luggage, Quinn, and herself into the middle and they headed south.

"Oh, by the way, Kate, a woman who didn't want to give her name called to see when you two would be getting home. I asked for her name twice, but she avoided answering. I told her the last I'd heard you were planning to spend some time in Boston before coming here. I'm sorry if I put off a friend of yours, but the fact caller ID said unknown caller, meant they'd get no information out of me."

"No, Sal, you did right. In fact, if my guess is correct, you were having a nice chat with the person who shot Harry."

"Kate, you don't know for sure," Harry grumbled.

"No, I don't. But, for now, I'd prefer not to give any strangers the advantage of knowing our exact location."

"I still think you're making too much of this."

"Says the man with the bullet hole in his chest."

Sal chuckled. "You two are squabbling like an old married couple."

Harry glanced at her and raised one eyebrow.

CHAPTER TWENTY-FOUR

Getting Harry bedded down while exhaustion had them both irritable made him growl. Kate took out her sleep-deprived grouchiness by arranging the bedclothes, making sure he took his pills, and adjusting the shades. She then dashed out and came back with a baby monitor she used in the whelping room and plugged it in. When Kate went to fluff his pillows, he grabbed her hands and held her in an iron grip.

"Stop, woman." He cast his eye around the room and then back at her. "Short of putting in a sixty-inch television and a sauna, there is nothing more to do."

"Whatever you say, sir," she answered, heading out, her shoulders square enough to use as door braces.

"Kate, I love you," he whispered.

"I know, but—"

"But what?"

"I know you love me, but I need you to listen to me. You know numbers better than anyone. But I understand people and animals. I teach both, daily, and if I can't read them, I can't help them. When I tell you I know who's behind this, I do. I may not know why or how. That's your department. But I need you to understand and respect my talent." Kate closed the door and walked into the kitchen.

It was one thirty, and she was running on adrenalin. Sal sat at the table, his oversized coffee mug in front of him, with Quinn asleep on his lap and Dillon at his feet. She knew she'd regret adding caffeine to her system but made tea and joined him. Dillon moved to rest his head on her lap and collected a scratch as a reward. After a few minutes of silence, Kate told Sal what had happened. By the time she got to the episode about going through airport security, he was laughing.

"You do realize every time we put you and Harry together, it's a recipe for chaos."

"So we should break up?" She scowled.

"Hell, no. Kate, you're too dangerous to be with anyone else. Besides, you two love each other enough to survive any chaos dogging your footsteps, pardon the pun. But, changing the subject, who are these men you're bringing here?"

"One is Harry's former professor, Lyndon Stubbs who needs his help to keep from going to jail. The other is Souchek, a falsely accused former prisoner. I'm going to get Tom to help him."

"And you want to bring these felons here?"

"Harry has got to work with Stubbs to stop the real thief. It's my theory whoever's been doing the shooting, is doing it to distract us from checking the numbers. Lily sent me the records and paperwork from Anton's trial, and I want Tom to find the truth so Anton can visit his niece in Texas without having to peer over his shoulder all the time. He's agreed to help me in the kennel while you're away. Considering how little sleep I've had in the last two days, I think I'll have you pick them up at the hotel. They're at the Quality Inn.

In fact, I'm going to bed now since I'll have to take Quinn in for his checkup with Dr. Rabani. She'd kill me if I put him with the other dogs without a checkup, despite having had one last week in Texas."

Sal stood and headed out the back door. Then he opened it again and stuck in his head. "Good to have you home, boss."

Kate locked up and made sure Harry slept soundly.

Both fuzz butts, big and small, beat her into her bedroom. Kate let them both out into the small yard beyond the sliders for a couple of minutes to take care of nature then Dillon took his favorite spot on the new rug beside her bed and Quinn, after checking the room, decided the big guy made a perfect puppy bed, crawled up onto Dillon's side, and fell sound asleep. Kate chuckled as confusion crossed Dillon's face. He lifted his head to sniff the creature settled on his back, gazed up at Kate in resignation then lowered his head to the rug and joined his son in sleep. Kate, more than ready to crawl between the sheets and collapse, fell asleep less than a minute behind them.

Waking to a collection of colorful curses coming from the monitor on her nightstand had Kate out of bed, avoiding canines, and dashing around the corner into the guest room. She found Harry sitting, half on and half off the bed, holding onto the nightstand and bent double. She was beside him in two seconds.

"I've got to pee," he growled. Supporting his good side, she walked him to the small bathroom, slipped his hand onto the safety rail she'd added in case she had older guests who needed help, and backed out, closing the door. She smoothed the tangled sheet, poured a glass of water, and laid out another pain pill. At the sound of flushing and the door opening, Kate moved to Harry's side again, pulling his good arm over her shoulder and leading him to the bed. As he sat, she handed him the water and the pill and was rewarded with a dirty look. Kate simply crossed her arms and waited, and waited.

"You know, you're a real bitch at times, Killoy," he grumbled taking the pill and washing it down. She took the glass without answering then lifted his legs onto the bed and pulled the covers over him. This last tactic got the assist of Dillon and Quinn who'd finally woken and decided to find the action. Kate turned off the light and scooped up Quinn, heading for the door with Dillon at her side. Muttering came from behind her. "This must be the worse in for better or worse."

She stopped. "You can always back out."

"The only way you're getting rid of me, Killoy, is if I'm dead, and considering how I feel at the moment, I'd recommend you check for a heartbeat before you box me up." She returned to her bedroom and the pups went out again for a minute. Four forty-five, the clock read, as Kate let the dogs in, moving like a robot not fully aware of the world around her. She used her own bathroom and then stretched out on the bed. Glancing over the edge, she watched Quinn curl up between Dillon's legs and, after a minute, they all slept again.

Sunshine filling the room and the sounds of male voices coming from her kitchen woke Kate. Finding no dogs, she checked the clock—noon! She struggled to get vertical. A shower and clean clothes was needed now. In her usual five minutes, Kate washed, dressed, and followed the delicious smells to her kitchen. This room had become a male bastion. Sal, Harry, the professor, Anton, and all four of her brothers had arranged themselves around her table, using a variety of chairs from other parts of the house. Plates littered the surface.

"The bacon is all gone. I added blueberries to your pancakes, though. The kettle is hot," Will said as he reached out and ruffled her hair.

Kate pulled the last mug from her cupboard and a teabag from the glass canister by the electric kettle. Tim, who'd been sitting by Harry, grabbed his plate and offered Kate his spot as Will placed a piece of paper in front of her. "Dr. Rabani gave Quinn a clean bill of health and said to tell you she likes the name."

She smiled at her favorite brother who, barely a year younger than she, understood her best. She knew he also thought her vet was hot, and it didn't surprise her he'd volunteered for the job of bringing the puppy this morning.

"Thanks. Where is short stuff?"

"I put him with Kelly's puppies, and he's having a ball." A scratch at the back door signaled Seamus to lean over, letting Dillon in. He trotted over to Kate and put his head in her lap to be snuggled. Will put the pancakes in front of her then dragged the butter and syrup from the other side of the table. Kate added the goodies to her pancakes and began to eat, the first bite sending her into complete bliss.

Harry leaned in and kissed her cheek. "Are we okay?" he asked quietly.

Kate stared back at him. "Are you still alive?"

He grinned. "Yeah."

"Then I guess we're still good." Kate, smiling, returned to polishing off the stack of pancakes and cup of tea.

"Miss Kate, I must apologize for dragging you into my mess…" Professor Stubbs began.

Kate waved away his words. "Do you have any idea on how she's pulling off this off?"

Harry sighed, and Tom asked, "How who's pulling what off?"

Harry broke in. "Kate doesn't like this woman, but I've told her it's no reason to suspect her of stealing millions of dollars. She hurt her feelings because Kate's not a mathematician. So she thinks the woman's a criminal. Kate, you have no proof." The condescension in Harry's tone made her want to slap him.

"How kind of you to clarify that," she replied and returned to her meal.

"You're a dead man, Foyle," Tim muttered tapping him on the shoulder as he moved away from the back of Harry's chair. Silence filled the room and didn't end as Kate stood, calling Dillon and Quinn, and then, thanking Will for breakfast, she left.

Will leaned across the table and, fixing his gaze on Harry, asked, "How well do you know my sister?"

Harry stared at him in confusion. "What do you mean?"

"Well, my supposedly smart friend, I watched you sit there with a large shovel in your hand, digging your own grave, and it made me wonder how much you really know about our resident dog nut beyond the obvious."

Harry watched Kate's siblings quickly clean her kitchen, glancing at each other and shaking their heads.

"Is someone going to clue me in on what's going on?" Harry asked in frustration.

"Ask Kate," Tom said, and they all walked out of the kitchen, leaving him behind.

At the door to the exercise yard, Kate stood, slowing her breathing, using the calm, happy scene before her to help the tension recede. All thoughts about killers and embezzlers and her problems with Harry, she pushed from her mind as she shoved the door open. Her dogs raced toward her wrapping themselves around her legs and asking for hugs, and Kate knew they were happy to see her. She worked her way through the crowd snuggling each one and for the young ones, throwing a toy. When the novelty of her return wore off, and they went back to playing with each other, Kate returned to the office to check the bookings for the next few weeks.

Then she headed out the back door to the barn, which served as her training center, equipped with the tools to teach every kind of dog from a neighborhood dog owner's pampered pet to dogs who worked as police officers. She had no classes for the next two weeks, but she needed to inspect the condition of the equipment and check on what she supplies she needed to order.

The barn's second floor housed her design studio, and Kate took the stairs two at a time, anxious to talk to her office manager, Ellen Martin, about ideas for both yarn colorways and style ideas she'd come up with on the trip. All her knitters sat at the lunch table, chatting. Kate joined them and told stories about Agnes' photo shoot and how they incorporated the puppies into the bridal shot. They wanted to hear all about Maddox Fox and his house. She described it in all its glory, especially the huge carved doors. Then she dropped the gossip bomb. Agnes was moving into her second career and would be taking over her family's bank. Ellen agreed Agnes' style could bring changes to a stuffy industry, but some of her knitters were disappointed they soon wouldn't be able to brag the country's top model often dropped in to visit them for lunch.

Ellen and Kate moved to the office where they discussed the high desert colors that had given her ideas for desert colorways in yarn selection to be incorporated in some Western-themed designs. Kate talked about modifying classic cowboy styles to build a grouping designed especially to be worn with jeans. When they finished, Kate headed back to her house. She hoped the crowd had moved the discussion to the offices of K and K in order to use the computers. She didn't hear anything when she opened the door, so Kate relaxed and headed down the hall and into the kitchen. Harry sat alone at the table, his laptop open and the stack of printouts he'd gotten from Rufus to his left. She stopped but then walked to the sink to fill the kettle and got it going. Pulling her favorite mug from the shelves where the boys had put their washed dishes, Kate took a tea bag from the canister, found a spoon in the drawer for sugar, and got the milk from the refrigerator. Neither of them spoke. She made tea then started back toward the kennel.

"Kate." Harry's voice was soft. "Could you please sit down so we can talk?" She stood for a minute, her hand on the doorknob, then sighed, returned to the table, and sat.

His words were quiet. "I am sorry for what I said this morning. I acted like an ass, so sure I was right I didn't listen to you. I didn't see how a TA could carry off this crime. She seems like a sweet girl, and she's friends with both Rufus and Kevin. For some reason, she has annoyed you. I'm sorry. You feel one of the people who came to see us Saturday has to be the shooter, and you could be right, but what I don't understand is why you have fixated on Toni Dunn."

"Have you spoken to the professor about who he thinks is behind the thefts?"

"No, we haven't had time. He did say he thought it had something to do with a program I wrote for his class when I was fourteen. Another concept I find hard to be-lieve. Technology has advanced so far. Hell, anything I wrote last year is out of date."

"Have you asked Rufus about his connection with Toni Dunn?"

"No. She was one of his former students."

"Hmmm. Tell me. Does the professor or do you have a copy of the program you wrote at fourteen?"

"Yes, he just sent it to me. Kate, this is not what I want to talk about. I'm trying to apologize for being curt with you this morning, not talk about the professor."

Kate opened her mouth to say something but stopped. After a few seconds she said, "Harry, you have been shot and then flown cross-country. You are on medication and hurting. You're now being asked to use you math skills to bail your former professor out of a jam that could send him to prison. Your dance card is full. Now is not the time for us to talk. Concentrate on the job in front of you. If you want, you could send me a copy of the program you referred to. I'd really like to see it, though I may not understand very much of it since, as you pointed out, I'm not a mathematician."

Tom walked in. "You ready to go, Harry?" He glanced over at Kate. "We're moving him to my place, so we can all work together without getting in your way."

She didn't say anything, only sat.

Tom grabbed Harry's bag from the spare room. "I've got the cart out front. I'll stow your bag then I'll be back to help you."

Harry stared across the table at her and started to say something, but Tom returned, took his good arm, and walked him to the door.

Kate heard Tom say as they went out, "I heard you called her a math dunce. Not smart, Foyle. She can get violent. I guess she must love you since you're still alive and your wound hasn't begun bleeding again."

Kate still sat staring at the door when Sal walked in a minute later. He checked around, glanced into the spare room and then sat. "I presume the math squad is off working on finding how the millions got stolen. So, answer me one question?"

She turned his way and waited.

"Do you think there will be any more attempts on the lives of you, Harry, and the professor?"

Dropping her eyes to her now cooling tea, Kate wanted to lie so Sal could relax on his vacation. But she couldn't. "Yes."

CHAPTER TWENTY-FIVE

"Kate, about my going to the Cape. I could change—"

"No, Sal. You are not calling off your vacation. End of discussion." Kate glowered at him, poised for an argument.

"I knew you'd say that, So I've already come up with a Plan B."

The bell chimed, telling her someone had turned into the driveway of the kennel. Since she'd checked the schedule and no dogs or cats were coming or going today, she stood.

Sal joined her. "Plan B has arrived."

Following him back to the kennel office, Kate saw a panel truck parked in the driveway with two men unloading gear. The older man greeted Sal like a long-lost brother. Sal introduced her to his buddy Gus and Gus's assistant, Vinnie. The plan was to install an alarm system in her cottage, the kennel, and the barn, including the studio. They swore there would be no mess left for puppies to get into and the place would be clean as a whistle when they were done. She opened her mouth to argue, but Sal handed her the accounts receivable for the last week and pointed to her office.

As she turned toward the office, Quinn's barking from there announcing danger. Sal and Kate turned to each other then shouted, "Hecate!"

She dashed in and saw Dillon lying in his favorite spot under the window, staring at his son, who was in the process of protecting them from a monster. The monster was a pure white, very large Maine Coon cat who rose from the seat of Kate's chair where she'd been sleeping, to her full height before launching her twenty-five pound self straight at Quinn. Kate had to give the puppy points for both speed and smarts, making it across the room to his father in a second. Hecate strolled like a panther over to Dillon, touched noses with her favorite dog, and then sat to contemplate the new kid who obviously needed etiquette lessons.

Settling quietly in her pre-warmed chair, Kate fired up her computer. She opened the accounts receivable spreadsheet to add this week's receipts, hoping the routine of work would help her get over her hurt feelings. She didn't intervene in the canine/feline face off. Hecate ran her own puppy training school. She'd get Quinn whipped into shape in short order so, by the time he found the other two cats, who must be in hiding somewhere in the house, he should behave better. They were Macbeth a Chartreux, stocky with a blue-gray coat that set off his yellow eyes and William McKinley, a Siamese. The three cats were named after characters in a book by E. L. Konigsburg she'd loved growing up. The author's books mostly featured girls who were clever outsiders.

Kate finished the tedious data entry. Stretching her muscles still somewhat sore from the flight, she looked over at the window and noticed a beam of sunshine now shone on the hairy white cloud of sleeping dog, puppy, and cat.

Leaving the door open, Kate slipped silently from the room and went to see how Plan B progressed. She inspected the check-in area trying to spot what the men had done. Several extra outlets with what appeared to be a color-matched button in the center blended into the walls. Kate had no idea their purpose, but she gave the guys credit for putting them out of the reach of teething puppies. Outside, she saw the men had moved on to the barn and the studio.

Harry's dismissal of her ideas this morning had hurt her. He'd treated her like a dumb blond. What she needed in order to work off her disappointment was some fresh air. Kate felt Dillon's head press against her side and glanced down to see Quinn had accompanied him. She grabbed a lead from the rack by the door for Quinn, who didn't know the rules yet, then headed out the back door of the kennel and down the path toward the woods.

She loved her home. Dad left her mom and brothers the family business, but he left Kate the kennel, the kennel manager's house, the barn that also housed her design studio, and, behind the buildings, the fourteen wooded acres crisscrossed with trails and backing up on a state park. As she moved deeper into the shady woods, the cooler temperatures felt good after the humid August sun. She breathed in the scent of warm, moist earth.

The maples, beech, birch, and oak bordering the woods began to give way to pines and hemlocks as Kate moved deeper. The bushes that thrived in the light at the edge of the woods slowly petered out as she went deeper, leaving only a carpet of pine needles covering the path. Her footsteps became silent. She stopped as a flash of color caught her eye. First a cardinal then a goldfinch flashed into sight. The rapid tapping on a tree trunk off to her left let her know a downy woodpecker now slowly worked his way around the tree trunk with the determination of growing boy at an all-you-can-eat buffet. Quinn pulled on the lead, eager to investigate every new sight and smell, but she held him to the trail to keep him from picking up ticks from the low growth of shade plants on either side. He responded well to the lead, happy to trot alongside Dillon. Kate enjoyed Quinn's enthusiasm when he tried to chase a chipmunk and then tried to drag a stick twice his size along as a new toy. These trails had been her solace for as long as she could remember. When anything bothered her, she'd head for the woods, be it winter or summer. Here, life's worries and hurts disappeared into the quiet and, if she wanted to argue with herself, only the birds and woodland creatures could hear. She walked deeper into the woods, letting the feeling of being miles from civilization and people who didn't understand her be a balm for her soul. The farther she walked, the more her resentment waned.

Kate used these trails to train dogs in the search and rescue classes and to teach tracking. When the snow got deep enough, she'd hitch up the dogs who enjoyed sled work and they'd go out on a run. The dogs worked joyously together, moving down the trails where the only sound came from their breathing.

The trail had been heading upward for a while, and it finally came to what, thanks to exposed tree roots, formed a natural staircase up to a high, flat mini plateau. Kate had built a lookout on this bluff that lay above a waterfall at the state park, and the bench she'd put in made a good place to sit while listening to cascading water. She sat, closed her eyes, and let nature take over her consciousness.

Unfortunately, even here, she couldn't shake off the need for answers. She had thought coming home would solve everything that put barriers between her and Harry. He said he wanted to marry her, but he really didn't know her at all. That was her fault. She'd thought it didn't matter. She'd been wrong. Turning her back on tradition when she chose the way she wanted to lead her life had caused problems. Kate wondered if Harry really respected what she did for a living or was like those who labeled it dabbling as opposed to working a serious career in, say, math.

Her phone's buzz shattered Kate's peace. Pulling it from her pocket, she saw a text from Tim. *Kate, where are you? We need you.* Startled, she jumped up and raced back the way she had come. Had Harry's wound acted up? What had happened? She took a shortcut, which, though narrower, was quicker making sure Quinn stayed close. She'd check his and Dillon's coats as soon as she knew what the crisis was.

Breaking from the cover of the woods, Kate upped her speed and pushed through the back door of the kennel. Everything seemed quiet. She ran on into the reception room, which was empty. She dashed down the hall to the covered walk by the puppy run and pushed open the door to her house. The whelping rooms on the left lay empty and the kitchen as well. Which only left her mother's house. The living room and porch passed in a blur as Kate raced down the walk and, ignoring the sidewalk, dashed across the lawn, past the hedge of rhododendrons and lilac and up the front steps to the porch. Opening the front door, she heard voices from the dining room, and she ran to the doorway and stopped, only to be met by a circle of staring faces.

"Can't you ever enter a room like a young lady instead of a tomboy, Kate?" Her mother's question was rhetorical since she'd long ago given up on changing her into the person she wanted as a daughter. Kate took in the startled faces, finally settling on Tim who now stared at the table.

"Tim?" She tried to slow her panting as she walked over to her younger brother. "You texted I was needed. What's the crisis? I came from the waterfall."

"God, Kate, you should have run cross country in school instead of spending your time with dogs. The team could have used you." He held his phone up to show the time.

She stared at him and waited.

He glanced around the table. "Well, sorry guys, some of us have other commitments. I wanted to get this done quickly so I could go to practice. The coach wants to go over plays with me. I don't see why we can't have her take it, give us the answer, and let us all get on with our lives."

Kate looked around the table. Her mother's glare focused on Tim. Her other siblings had developed a sudden interest in the papers before them. The professor, Anton, and Harry appeared baffled.

Kate turned back to Tim. "Are you sure it's not a date with Cynthia or Lylia?"

"No. I found out only yesterday I've made captain."

"Fine," she sighed. "Do I need anything not on your laptop?"

"No, it's all there." He unplugged the cord keeping it charged and handed everything to her. She head for the door, followed by Dillon and a very tired puppy. Behind her, she heard Harry ask if anybody would tell him what was going on. When she got back to her kitchen, she locked the doors, put on water to boil for tea, fed the puppy, and finally opened the laptop.

Time had passed, she wasn't aware how much, when Sal unlocked the door and walked in. She realized she'd missed feeding time for the dogs and jumped up and dashed into the pantry, only to find no dog dishes.

"They're fed. Seamus did it without disturbing you. Will brought this by and told me to stand over you until you eat. He says there are cream puffs in the pastry box." Kate opened the lid on the pie carrier to find a plate wrapped in aluminum foil from which came wonderful smells. She eased up the foil to find roast chicken, mashed potatoes, baked carrots, and summer squash. A heavy linen napkin wrapped two fresh-baked yeast rolls. Next to those was cranberry sauce in a small container. Kate dragged a stool up to the counter since she wouldn't find an empty inch on the table and, removing the aluminum foil, took her fork and dug in. Sighing, she stared at Sal. "Will is wasting his time with math. He could become one of the world's great chefs."

"He says he cooks for those he loves and to please

himself. It helps him relax. If he had to do it as work, all the fun would go out of it." Sal opened the pastry box and took one of the cream puffs.

"So long as he keeps cooking for us, I won't care. He's probably right not to take something he loves and put it under pressure."

"So says the lady who has spent her life competing with her dogs."

"But I love the competition. Whichever dog I'm with and I take on a challenge to work together to make something beautiful. Sometimes it's what the judge wants. Sometimes it's not. But that isn't the point. The fun is going into the ring and doing my best at something I love. So long as I know we've done our best, the results don't matter."

"Seamus said not to ask you about your work, but I confess I'm curious."

"I'm almost done. There is a very clever person behind this. It's a shame she's greedy. If she hadn't extended the program to steal on such a massive scale, she could have gotten away clean. I'd say her biggest flaw is she's young, angry, and impatient. But, thanks to those flaws, she can be stopped."

"You say she. I didn't know they'd identified the person behind it."

"They didn't."

"But you did?"

"I'm about 90 percent sure. However, I don't have enough proof to get her arrested. What I can do is stop her and recover the money. I've found most of the transfers she used to move the money offshore. With those numbers, I've been able to trace both the receiving accounts and the sending ones, including the server she's using, and have already rewritten her program to reverse the process. Over the next forty-eight hours, this should quietly retrieve the funds."

"How come Agnes says you can't figure out codes if you can do this?" He waved his hands toward the table.

"I've never been good at word codes such as those spies use, however we're talking apples and oranges here. Computer coding is logical and beautiful, like a knitting design. It's always been easy for me. Other types of math, not so much. It's like a musician who is brilliant on the piano but could never master the clarinet."

"This is what drives your mother nuts?"

"That's about the size of it. She doesn't understand I see things differently from her other children. She firmly believes I'm wasting my life by not sitting in a classroom teaching or working for K and K. Not to change the subject but, what time do you leave for the Cape tomorrow?"

"Knowing Sarah, the rest of us will be ready by seven, but we probably won't be on the road until nine. Since they're doing more construction on I-95, we're going to take the Mass Pike and then 495 south to Barnstable and then out to the end of the Cape to Provincetown. With multiple drivers, it won't be bad, and since it's not the weekend, there may be slightly less traffic."

"Good. Oh, did the men finish putting in those little button things?"

"Yeah. They also made it so when activated, a buzzer will go off here, in the kennel, and in the studio when anyone drives onto the property, but this system will let you know who, and give you eyes everywhere. I gave Ellen all the details and walked her through everything. She'll go over it with you tomorrow. Now I'm going to go home, kiss my granddaughter, pack, and get a good night's sleep before heading for fun in the sun. You will be careful, Kate. If you are even slightly suspicious about something, push one of those buttons. Don't question yourself, just do it. Now, I'm out of here. I'll see you in a month." He walked toward the door as Kate took a cream puff and her tea back to the table. He stopped at the door. "Please, be very careful. Trust your gut."

Kate nodded, and he left.

She checked at the screen before her and the program silently moving millions of dollars. A lady was going to be very pissed when she checked her offshore accounts in a couple of days. Smiling, Kate finished her tea and the cream puff.

CHAPTER TWENTY-SIX

Kate cleaned up the dishes, put Dillon and Quinn out in the side yard, took one more glance to be sure the program progressed nicely, and headed for the bedroom, only to stop when she heard a knock. She started toward the door then, remembering someone wanted her dead, stepped over to the slider and let the dogs in. They immediately rushed through the house to the door, tails wagging. Kate followed and, when she opened the door, Harry stood before her, badly in need of a shave and sleep, bandages showing through his T-shirt. He shifted when she didn't say anything.

"May I come in, Kate? I think we need to talk."

She stepped back, sighing slightly, and held open the door, at the same time trapping Quinn with her leg to keep him from darting outside. Since Kate wore sleep shorts and a tank top, she quickly scooped Quinn into her arms to keep the too-sharp puppy claws from turning her skin to hamburger. Harry followed her into the kitchen but stopped at the sight of the table covered with an ocean of yellow lined paper. Pads lay on all but one of the chairs, each filled with calculations and computer code. In the middle of all this sat Tim's laptop, the computer's black screen filled with line after line of code being written automatically.

Kate walked over to the electric kettle and turned it on, pulled two mugs out of the cupboard, and went to clear a chair and sit. Flipping Quinn onto his back so she could gently rub his belly, she held him as Dillon, pressed to her side, licked the puppy's ears. Harry walked slowly to the table, picked up one of the pads of paper, and flipped through it, then another, and another, slowly working his way through her notes. Finally, he pulled out the chair facing the laptop and stared at the program. The kettle clicked off. Kate stood, gently putting the very sleepy puppy on the floor and motioning Dillon into a down next to him. She made the tea, put a pastry on a saucer for Harry, and brought it to the table.

Kate was taking her first sip when Harry said, "But you went to a school of design and studied fashion."

"Yes, I did."

"I don't understand. This is brilliant. What you've done here is…"

"Math? Yes I know"

"But Kate, do you have any idea of what you could do with skills like this? You could have your career working anywhere you want. You'd have your pick of academic or corporate…"

"Harry, I design clothes. I enjoy designing clothes. I am happy when I create a style that complements both the wearer and the dog breeds pictured in the designs. I'm good at what I do. People like my designs and, thankfully, buy them."

"But, Kate, don't you realize how good you are at this?" He waved the sheets he held in his hand.

"Yes, I do. I turned down a four-year scholarship in math, a free ride to MIT. I wanted to follow my dream, not go into the family business. So now you know why my mother and I don't get along. If it weren't so important to protect a sweet old man, I wouldn't be doing it now." She stood, put her cup in the sink, and peered into his still astonished face. "It's been a long day, Harry, and I'm tired. I'll let you show yourself out. Good night."

She scooped up the sleeping puppy and, with Dillon at her side, went into her bedroom and closed the door. Fifteen minutes later, she heard the front door close, but it was several hours before she could stop the bouts of tears and give in to sleep.

The painful shafts of light and the throbbing of her sinuses roused her. Kate eased her head over the edge of the mattress but didn't find either her dog or puppy asleep on the floor. She could barely make out soft voices coming from the kitchen. Rolling onto her back, Kate stared at the ceiling for a minute then forced herself to stand and walk slowly into the bathroom. Five minutes later, thoroughly parboiled, she emerged clad in clean jeans, a T-shirt with the logo from the National in San Diego, and her socks and loafers.

All talking ceased when she stepped into the kitchen. By the time Kate reached the counter with the kettle, Will had poured milk into her tea. "Your cheese and mushroom omelet is coming right up, and Mary Eleanor said to tell you thanks for freeing me up to take her out last night."

"I'm happy to help with your social life."

Tim scooped the pile of papers from his spot at the table and pulled out a chair for her. "The coach and team said thanks, as well."

"Go Blue!"

Kate took a bite from the food placed in front of her: omelet, bacon, fresh-squeezed orange juice, and blueberry muffins, closed her eyes and smiled. "You could have people waiting months for reservations if you ever opened a restaurant, Will. I know you'd rather do math. So long as you keep cooking for me, I won't nag."

He leaned in and hugged her. "Any time, Katie, any time."

As Kate plowed through the glorious meal before her, she let her eyes travel around the table. The professor, Tom, and Seamus had their heads together, muttering over calculations. Tim had his laptop propped on his lap. "Eighty-five percent, Kate," he announced. She nodded and then stole a glance at Harry. He sat watching her with an expression she couldn't read. Kate stood after shoveling in the last bite, took her dishes to the sink, rinsed them, and put them in the dishwasher then walked over to Tim with a pad she'd pulled off the top of the refrigerator.

"When it reaches, 100 percent, quickly enter this." She pointed to the code. "And once it's in, change the password on her back door to this, which should solve the problem. Now, I've got runs to clean. Anton, if you could join me in about half an hour, I'll go over what I like you to do today." Kate turned and strolled out the back way into the kennel, staying in calm control until the kennel door closed. Three minutes later, with the tears gone and her breathing under control, she stepped out of the restroom, ready to get to work.

Kate flipped on the supplemental water heater as she went down the aisle, opening and closing the guillotine gates for each indoor run, letting the dogs into the outdoor runs. Then, with her boots on, she worked her way back up the rows of runs, filling the oversized pooper scooper in each and emptying it into the wheeled disposal bin. Once done, she attached the eco-friendly cleaner dispenser to the hose and turned on the power washer spray.

She worked her way down one side and then the other. At the end, she turned off the spray, shut off the water heater, pushed the wheeled crap bucket out, and emptied it into the dumpster then finally switched from boots to shoes. In the restroom, Kate combed her hair, washed her hands, and then stood for a minute staring at the person who less than a week ago had floated on a cloud of happiness and whose only worry had been a fear of flying.

"Get over yourself, idiot. You were the one who kept your math talent a secret. It's your own fault he doesn't understand." She leaned in resting her head on the mirror and missing her dad and granddad. They may not have understood why she wanted to turn her back on her math talent and go her own way, but they supported her and cheered her decision. Kate missed them so much it hurt.

A noise in the reception room pulled her from her funk. She opened the door and straightened her shoulders. Anton took in all the scrubbed runs, the reception area with its sofa, check-in desk, and sales rack with leads, collars, brushes, and treats plus the framed collage with photos of the dogs who'd stayed with them. "This is quite an operation. You run it by yourself?"

"No. Sal, my kennel manager who brought you from the hotel, begins his month's vacation at the Cape today. We also run a training facility, which I'll show you in a few minutes, and I'll introduce you to the people who work in my design studio, but first I need to know if you can operate a riding lawn mower."

"Sure. Before my wife died, I had a house on half an acre, and the only practical way to keep it up was to use the John Deere mower for the lawns."

"Good because, with last week's rain, the grass is ankle deep and needs cutting. Once you've met everyone, I'll show you where the mower is kept, and you can get started. Once the lawns are done, you can work with me on clearing some of the trails in the woods. I've got a tracking class in two weeks so I will be doing run-throughs along them with a variety of dogs. The police dog training is on hold until September because Sal and I teach those classes together."

"So, you run a boarding kennel and you train people's dogs. You're a busy woman."

Kate laughed. "That's just part of my world. You'll want to lose the sports jacket. It's hot working in the sun. There are T-shirts with the kennel logo in this closet, along with baseball caps. Grab a couple of water bottles, as well. It's hot work. You can change in the restroom. I need to check something in my office and then I'll show you around,"

A buzzer went off as she sat at her desk. Looking out the window, she saw a car pull onto the start of the driveway and stop. For a minute, it sat there and then it backed out and drove away. Her computer beeped and a new program opened itself and a message on the screen informed her that the license number of the vehicle was a CT number. Did she wish to save this information? Kate hit yes. Sal's technicians had been playing. What other little surprises had they left for her?. Picking up the mail, Kate began sorting, only to stop and look out the window again. Hum, was the car turning around or was there another reason it had turned into the drive? Could it be the shooter? She jumped when Anton walked back in dressed as though he'd been working there for years. They both grinned. He even had a red bandanna hanging out of his back pocket. They walked back through the runs and out the side door to the barn. The shed holding the larger equipment stood beside it, and Kate reached into her pocket and handed him the set of spare keys she'd taken from her desk.

"This is for the shed." Kate pointed to the silver key with a green dot on it. "The one with the red mark will open all the kennel doors. The spare keys for the mower and other work vehicles are in the lock box by the door of the shed, and that is opened by the key with the blue dot."

The bottom of the classic red barn facing them appeared traditional, with a small door in the side and the huge rolling doors on the front. The second floor, however, featured a pair of wide floor-to-ceiling windows rising, cathedral-like, toward the roof. To the left of these, a large monogram of two Ks intertwined decorated the barn. To the right rose a flight of stairs leading up to the entrance of the Kate Killoy Design Studio. She gave Anton a peek into the barn and then they ascended the stairs.

She could tell by the number of cars parked below everyone was there. Summer was a surprisingly busy time for this part of her business. The pressure would build from now until February when their next fashion show would happen. That included completing orders for the boutiques to sell as soon as cooler weather came. Staying on schedule kept things hopping now. Pushing open the door, they could see the whole space through a second set of glass doors. It saved on cooling and heating bills to have this anteroom. As Kate pushed the inner doors, they were overwhelmed by the noise of the ten knitting machines, the laughter and chatting of her knitters, and the voices of their toddlers in the nursery section on the far side of the room. Smiles and waves greeted Kate as they entered.

"I hear you've been dodging bullets again." A voice came from the office to the left. "It's a bad habit, Katie, lose it. It's upsetting my blood pressure. Who's this? Not a new knitter?" Kate's office manager stood with her hands on her hips and a scowl on her face.

Kate laughed and gave her a hug. "Ellen, meet Anton Soucek who will be helping around the kennel while Sal's away. Anton, this is Ellen Martin who keeps me sane and makes sure my studio runs like clockwork."

They shook hands, and Ellen introduced him to the crew, including their pint-sized supervisors. She explained the studio employed mostly single moms or women whose husbands were deployed with the armed services and who had small children. Their situations normally would make working difficult. However, last year they'd decided to run a staff nursery. This way, the workers could bring their preschool age kids with them. The school bus picked up and dropped off their elementary age offspring during the school year and, in summer, would take them to the camp run by the town. Salaries ran well above minimum wage so there was usually a waiting list of women who wanted to work here. On the other side of the big front windows, they'd built a sound-proofed room where the babies could nap during the day. It also offered a pair of rockers for nursing moms.

Checking the time, Kate told Ellen she was going to get Anton started and then she'd be back to go over all the security information Sal had left with her. When they got to the shed, she showed him the location of the lock box and checked the gas and oil on the big mower. Kate pointed out the areas to be done that day and what could be on tomorrow's list. She explained when he finished, he should lock everything up and then check to see how Tom was getting on with his criminal case. Lily's secretary had sent links to all the files to Tom.

Anton spoke. "Kate, please let me say I truly regret ever having frightened you with the stupid gun. I can see you're a very nice lady. You have done amazing things here. It is so impressive. I come from a traditional world. A man gets a job with a company and follows directions. If he's lucky, he is able to retire when he gets old. Never would I have dared to tell my family I want to do something different from what they expected. I have listened to the talk among your family. Your mother is unhappy you did not follow tradition. With our generation, your mother's and mine, tradition is important. But what I see here…what you've built and run even though, and pardon my sexist remark, you are a very young lady—that is remarkable. You are a wonderful, strong, smart woman, and I bless the day we met."

"Thank you, Anton," Kate said, laying a hand on his arm. "Oh, and if you want to share your thoughts with my mother," she said, laughing as she headed back to the studio, "feel free."

CHAPTER TWENTY-SEVEN

A half hour later, Kate left the studio feeling as though she were surrounded by an invisible security wall. According to the thumbnail sketch Ellen had given her, entrances to the property by car were covered with cameras recording the comings and goings and would sound warnings a car had entered. Panic buttons were all over the property. Ellen showed her the one in her office and mentioned some scattered about the studio as well. The barn and the kennel had them, as well as her house. K and K had a security system in place already, along with Tom's and your mother's houses. These now connected into this system as well. If you pushed the panic button, help would come. Kate asked her what kind of help, but Ellen didn't know. Kate wondered what if one of the dogs could reach the buttons and set it off. Tomorrow, she'd have to take the printout Ellen had given her and locate them. She could easily see Quinn calling in the Marines.

Checking her watch, she saw it was lunchtime. She needed to check the program. They wanted the thief stopped. Well, she had been. But, by halting her crime, Kate had upped the stakes. This thief wouldn't steal softly into the night. Up the hill, she saw Anton moving from the riding mower toward the main house where her mother, Tim, Seamus, and Will lived. He'd already finished the whole front of the kennel. Now he'd moved to work on the lawn linking the main house to the one belonging her grandparents where Grandma Ann and Kate's brother Tom now lived and which also housed K and K.

Pushing open the side door to the kennel, Kate saw the indoor runs had dried and were ready for the boarding dogs. Passing her office, she put the printouts on her desk and scratched Hecate's head, earning her the acknowledgment of a single eye being opened and then closed again. She smiled. At least Hecate didn't insist on sitting on her lap as the house cats did. With her size, Kate would lose the circulation in her legs in less than five minutes.

Moving into the reception room, Kate jumped. Gran sat at the main desk reading her Kindle. She glanced up, and Kate could tell there was a lecture coming, though, for the life of her, she didn't know what she'd done wrong this time.

"You are in time for luncheon, Kathleen." Gram said rising and tucking her Kindle into her tote. Kate opened her mouth to say she 'd grab a sandwich and get back to work when Gram turned and faced her. "You have been shot at, Harry injured. You traveled thousands of miles to get a puppy, which, by the way, I haven't seen yet, and someone tried to kill you."

In a play for distraction, Kate opened the door leading to the exercise yard and signaled Dillon to come, knowing Quinn would be right on his heels. Both shot through the narrow opening as she held the others back. "Here he is. This is Quinn. I'm thinking, if he lives up to his potential, I'll use him at stud to the bitch I'm keeping out of Kelly."

"He's lovely. John and Tom would have been pleased. But distracting me with an eight-week-old puppy is not going to put me off what I want to say. It has been only six months since the same thing happened in New York. Kathleen, what is going on? How do you get involved with these criminals? This is certainly not someone in the dog world."

"No, it's not. This time, if my suppositions are correct, it's someone in the math world. This has to do with Harry's friend, Professor Stubbs." Kate laughed at the irony. "I'm not even part of that world, but I became a target by association."

"I don't like someone using my granddaughter for target practice. This person has got to be caught and stopped."

"I agree. However, getting enough proof to put the person behind bars and still stay alive is not easy."

"I think you should leave it in the hands of your brothers and Harry, as well as the police. You've always been a curious child. I really think that's what gets you into these situations. I want you to tell the boys and Harry at lunch you are no longer involved. Now, come along. William is making clam chowder and lobster rolls for luncheon, and I'd rather not miss them. Who'd have thought of all the grandchildren I'd taught to cook, William would take to it and become so proficient."

There was no way to get out of this meal. However, since she loved Will's clam chowder, Kate gave in graciously, put a lead on Quinn, and headed across the newly mown lawn.

The house exuded wonderful smells when they walked in. Everyone sat at the dining room table, which could easily accommodate twelve. Will brought in the big white pottery tureen as she slipped into a chair between Seamus and Anton. Across the table, Harry talked with the professor. He had stopped for a minute when she and Gram entered but then continued.

Seamus leaned in and whispered, "Give him some time. He was embarrassed not knowing about your skills. He thought he had you all figured out and then, wham."

Kate didn't answer him but nodded. She didn't know what to think. She wanted to hide for a while and try to figure out her feelings.

They finished the chowder and moved on to the hot

lobster rolls when Anton turned her way and said, "I really liked the soundproofed room. It's a very clever idea. More companies should do it." Conversation stopped.

Then her mother asked, "What soundproofed room? Where is there a soundproofed room?"

He stared at her in surprise and said, "In Miss Kate's business. It is a wonderful place, but of course you already know that."

"Oh, you mean the knitting thing she plays at. As far as I can see, it's a complete waste of her time and her talents. With her skills, she could be well on her way to a full professorship, but she threw it all away. She didn't even get her degree."

Seamus interrupted. "Kate's got a degree in design."

"Playing with all those fashion things doesn't count. I blame it on her father and grandfather. They dragged her off to dog shows, and she never got the fashion thing out of her system by playing with dolls. Then Agnes comes along and becomes a model...talk about really wasted time. At least she got her degrees, but Kate here plays with the dogs and this fashion stuff instead of settling down and doing important work. I don't know, Harry. I had hopes you could shake some sense into her head when you got engaged."

Kate sat in silence. Old song, same tune, played over and over. She'd given up responding years ago, but she hadn't reckoned on her new champion.

"Have you ever been to her studio?" Anton asked her mother.

"Of course not. Why would I?"

"So you are—what do you call it Lyndon?— setting forth your premise without checking your facts. Excuse me, but I thought you were a scholar." Silence followed for a count of ten before he spoke again. "How many of you at this table have been to see this business your mother criticizes or do you all believe your sister"— he turned to Harry—or your fiancée is wasting her life because she does what she loves rather than what you do? Hum. So much intelligence, so little sense."

The silence went on for a while and then the professor leaned across the table and spoke. "Miss Kate. I very much impressed by the work you did to save me from prison. You have a real talent. However, listening to Anton, I get the feeling though you can do this with great skill, it does not fill your heart. It does not bring you the joy it would bring me. You saved my life in Texas, arranged this escape to safety while endangering your own life. I, for one, would like to see this work you chose that brings you so much joy. May I join you this afternoon and visit your studio?"

"I'd be honored, sir." Kate nudged a sleeping Quinn with her foot under the table, and he started frisking around. "Excuse me, everyone, but I think I'd better remove this puppy before he pees on the floor." Kate quickly made her escape with Dillon and the puppy at her side and was both surprised and impressed when Quinn made it all the way to the grass before nature took over. While she waited for him to finish, Kate stood shaking her head and wondering what had happened. She wished Dad were here to talk to, or Gramps.

Kate put the two Sams back in the exercise yard to play and then sat at her desk to check emails. A light flashed on her laptop. She clicked on it, and it told three more cars had come through the checkpoint at the end of the drive. Knowing nobody had come up to the buildings, she clicked on the link to their license plates. All three were the same. She picked up the phone and dialed Ellen's office.

"Ellen, do you have the contact information for the company Sal used for the security?"

"It's in my file. Is there a problem?"

"Yes. We have a car that has been pulling into the end of the drive, waiting, and then leaving. It's happened four times. We're being stalked. I may need more security than first planned."

"Kate, I've pulled up the page with the license plate. I've got the name of the person to call if this happens, and Sal told me what to say. I'll take care of it. Why don't you come over here and work on those new designs? I'd feel better if you weren't alone."

"Well since the alternative at the moment is updating

the books for this month, you've talked me into it. I'll be right there." She stood to leave but, instead of heading directly to the studio, went to the front door of the kennel and put up the closed sign, locking the door. She took one more look up the long, now empty driveway, and went to join Ellen and her knitters.

In spite of the fact she worked surrounded by women talking and children playing, Kate felt lonely and nervous. Ever since she and Harry had gotten together, they'd talked whenever they faced a problem. Well, almost every time. But a wall had risen up between them in the last twenty-four hours. He hadn't said a word to her at lunch, barely glanced in her direction. They'd had their differences before but always ended up talking them out. Not this time.

Even though it was warm in the room, she felt chilled. She may have lost him. Kate wanted to go hide in the woods and cry as she did when a small child. She wanted someone to tell her everything would be all right. She'd thought he'd be pleased she could take the computer problem that stole this money and reverse it. Apparently not. He had taken a hit in his male pride and was down for the count. Well, too damn bad.

Shaking her head to clear it, Kate glanced down at the sketch she'd completed, ripped it from the pad, and tossed it in the wastebasket. Garbage! She couldn't do anything right. Kate reached for her laptop and pulled up the album she'd created of shots taken on the trip to Texas. The colors flowed so subtlety, with beiges flowing into cinnamons and then into deep okras. Flipping through the photos, she slowed at the ones from the park. Cute puppies romped with Jordy and the other kids. Here the girls had all the puppies loaded on the foot powered merry-go-round. They really were adorable. She should pick some out to put up on Facebook.

Kate heard footsteps coming up to the studio entrance stairs and looked up as not only the professor, but Harry, her brothers, and her mother entered. Everyone stopped working to stare. Ellen stepped out of the office. Kate heard the professor say they'd been invited to see the studio. Ellen smiled, hugged her mother, which didn't surprise Kate since Ellen had worked for K and K for many years, and said, "It's about time you got your nose out of your dusty old books long enough to see what we're doing, Claire." She then began the grand tour. Kate stayed where she was.

Ellen introduced each of the knitters and explained how they employed women who need to bring their children to work with them. She also told about working with the state to provide benefits for the women and their children. She talked about setting up a 401K plan for each so they could learn the benefit of saving for the future and how some added to it on their own from the bonuses they were paid for special projects.

She showed the soundproofed room where the babies slept and the pair of rockers that Kate had painted with puppy designs for nursing moms to be comfortable. Then they wandered over to the play area where the kids pushed forward to show off their toys. She pointed out the special ventilation installed to keep any loose fibers or dust created while working with the yarn from causing breathing problems. She spoke of profit margins and projected income percentages from both the online pattern sales and the ready-to-wear line marketing only through select boutiques. She showed the yarn storage areas and how each woman created a complete garment rather than doing piecework, which would have been slightly cheaper but more repetitive and therefore much more boring.

Consuelo showed then a flip skirt she'd made and how the design of paw prints seemed to move, running around the hem as wearer walked, and Huong pointed out the child's sweater with a Golden Retriever puppy on it. Kate delighted in the pride they had in the work. It had been one of the goals she and Ellen discussed when they started the ready-to-wear line.

The professor and her mother both had questions about what marketing software they used, and Ellen told them Kate had written the software and had licensed the program, which now brought in another avenue of income. She mentioned how popular it had become with craft marketers across the country. Tom asked about yarn suppliers, and she told him about working with a mill over near Storrs to create their unique colorways for each year's line. February's fashion show designs would be based on the colors of the Southwest. She pointed to the wall where Kate's color work board sat with possible blends.

"You all know how amazing Kate is. To have built all this at the same time as she took over the complete running of the kennel John and Tom left her plus her work with Sal to build the new training areas, such a police dog training, is totally amazing. I don't know how she gets it all done and still has time to train and show her own dogs, but she never was a nine-to-five-sit-behind-a-desk kind of girl even when she was young."

"I never knew," Kate's mother said, staring around, annoyed. "Nobody told me this was here."

"Claire, I've known you for close to forty years and I love you dearly," Ellen said, gripping her shoulders, "but you're an idiot. You haven't pulled your nose out of your work long enough to realize you had a daughter since she was a baby and you left her to John and Tom to raise. The boys took after you. Kate was independent. It wasn't something you could deal with, so you didn't. John told me you fought him tooth and nail about her career choice. He and Tom built this facility and made it possible for her to grow her business independent of your control. They didn't want you holding purse strings over her head to force her to make your choices. I retired from K and K because I wanted to come be part of this exciting world your lovely girl was creating. Her name may not have a string of PhD's after it, nor will you find it on the title of a series of textbooks, but she has fans across the country who wait with bated breath to see the next design to come out of this studio. Claire, you have four wonderful sons. Don't you think it's about time you met your exceptional daughter?"

CHAPTER TWENTY-EIGHT

Silence fell over the group only to be broken by the ringing of the phone. Ellen ran to grab it. Her mother, for the first time in Kate's life, appeared unsure of herself. The professor gently took her arm and walked over to Kate's work table, and her brothers followed. Since she'd deep-sixed the last hour's work into the wastebasket, she had nothing to show them except the collage of scenery and puppy photos displayed on the screen over her work table. Tim shoved forward, asking to see them larger, so she clicked through those she'd shot on the drive from Denver south then on the first bunch she'd taken in the park in Lubbock, and they filled the screen.

Slowly, one-by-one, she flipped through the puppy shots, more than a little aware of Harry's hand resting on her shoulder as everyone crowded in for a better look. Fighting her awareness of him, she studied each photo as it flipped by for flaws that would need to be Photoshopped out before she could use them for publicity.

And that was how Kate found it. The program changed photos in auto-play mode, so she had to stop it and work her way back. When she reached the shot, she froze. Slowly she moved the wheel on her mouse to enlarge the background of the photo and bring the area into sharp focus. A gun with what appeared to be a tube on the barrel was held pointing down at her side, and her body, though partially hidden by a bush, was still easily recognizable.

"Kate, its Alan from the security company," Ellen shouted. "He found out the name on the car stalking the end of our driveway. It's a rental, but the name on the license of the person who rented it is Antonia Dunn."

"Antonia Dunn." Kate said at the same time. "Well, she's here. She must now know the money is gone, and I'll bet she's been practicing her marksmanship."

"I don't believe it." The professor paled. "Why would she be here? She's such a sweet girl. Why is she in the photo with a gun? I don't understand."

Harry turned Kate's swivel chair around until she faced him and took her face in his hands. "You were right. I was wrong. I should have listened."

Kate put her hands over his. "You're a stubborn man, Harry Foyle, and you hate being wrong. Give me ten or twenty years and maybe I'll be able to teach you to believe me the first time. You're lucky I love you."

"Kate, what is all this about?" the professor asked.

"Professor, I think all of us could use a cup of tea or, in your case, maybe something stronger. Let's go to my house and I'll explain what is going on." Kate turned to her knit gals and said, "Ladies, I know we're on deadline, but we have a situation developing and, in the interest of safety, I am closing the studio for the rest of the week. You'll be paid for your scheduled hours even though you won't be here, and I'll see you here next Monday. Treat this as a paid mini vacation." Kate saw shock register on Ellen's face, but she stared back at her and said, "We'll make it happen."

Ellen gazed at the crew, at the children, and back at her. "Whatever you say, boss."

They all walked down the stairs, and the professor asked to see the training barn. Kate had him step inside and gave him the ten cent tour before hurrying him out and locking up. She took everyone back through the kennel runs then, seeing the time, told them she'd catch up as soon as she'd finished feeding the boarding dogs. She grabbed her steel cart with the dishes piled on top and started scooping kibble from the galvanized can into each. She pulled up the list of supplements each dog got and from the bottles on the shelf above, added those. The red X on the list indicated which dogs preferred their food wet rather than dry, and she pulled out the pitcher to fill these. Once she finished each bowl, numbered to match the run, Kate turned to put the food into the runs only to find the group had stayed as audience. Laughing, she said,

"This part reminds me of the flight attendants on the plane serving beverages and nuts." She opened each gate, placed the food inside then closed it. When she got to the end of the aisle with each gate latched, she backed up, pulling the guillotine doors to the outside runs as she went. As each door opened, a dog would run in straight for the food. Kate parked the cart and decided to take care of picking up the bowls later and waved the group on.

As the crowd left the building, she paused at her office, grabbed Hecate's bowl, filled it, and checked her water. Then, gathering up the security paperwork from her desk, she headed out the front, making sure the door locked automatically behind her. And so, grand tour over, the visitors headed down the covered walkway to her back door.

Her Samoyeds lined up at the door to the exercise yard, waiting more or less patiently for their supper. Kate filled and turned on the kettle, pulled down her largest teapot, setting it on the counter, then grabbed her stack of dog dishes and moved to the bin by the door to start filling them. She knew by heart who got what, adding cottage cheese or yogurt depending on taste, with supplements for both the puppies and senior citizens and then, grabbing the stack of dishes, she opened the door. All the dogs flooded in, completely ignoring the room crowded with guests, focusing only on the Queen of Everything, the lady with the food.

In a quiet voice, Kate said sit. They sat in a circle with her in the center, except for the two puppies who, after peering around, also sat. Then, beginning with the youngest, she quickly placed the bowls on the floor, saying each dog's name and giving the command, "Eat." She finished the circuit and stood to wait. The room had become silent, and Kate glanced over at those sitting at the table watching in amazement as a dozen Samoyeds, aged sixteen years down to eight weeks, ate their meals without even looking at another dog. Will stood, walked to the counter, grabbed a plastic canister, and handed it to Kate. She took off the lid and slipped it underneath. After a couple of minutes, she started with the first dogs fed, picked up the highly polished dish, setting it beside her, and handed out a treat. Working quickly, she completed the circle and then, leaving the stack of dishes on the floor, stepped over to the door and said, "Out. Everybody out."

Quinn left last, taking a few extra licks at the pile of stainless steel bowls as he went. But, seeing his dad racing out into the yard, he took off like a shot after him. Closing the door, Kate saw Will had already stacked the dishes in the dishwasher, so she filled the teapot and set it on the table then grabbed a plastic bag full of chocolate chip cookies out of the freezer, spread them on a plate, and quickly defrosted them in the microwave. Telling the men the drinks cupboard was to their left and the fridge held beer, she collapsed into a chair with the folder she'd taken from her office. Will handed her a mug and then placed the rest along with spoons, milk, and napkins in the center of the table.

Kate was enjoying her first sip of tea when her mother spoke. "Kathleen, I feel it's only fair to admit I really did not understand your choice of career. Though I still feel many of your talents are being wasted, I feel bound to say after what I saw today, you seem to have built a special company. I am really impressed with what you've done to give jobs to women who might otherwise be unemployable because of their circumstances. What I'm trying to say is, I'm proud of you. I should have told you more often when John would brag of all your accomplishments growing up."

Anton had joined them, hot and slightly dusty from his work and smelling like new-mown grass. He smiled at her mother, and she actually blushed. Kate was so astounded she barely noticed her phone buzzing as it bounced across the table. A text came in, and she opened it. Agnes and Sean would be here in twenty minutes. Kate quickly let her know where they were and then flipped open the booklet that came with the alarm system to the section explaining how she could download their app and pull up everything on her phone. Kate started the download and then set the phone aside. Conversations that had been going on around her while she worked came to a halt, and all eyes turned in her direction.

"I think we have to talk about what we saw today," Kate told them. "It was the first time I'd examined those photos since I've been a little busy." She asked Harry to push her laptop over, and she linked to those files, found the showstopper, and then copied just the headshot, putting it on a white background. Turning the laptop toward Anton, she asked, "Have you ever seen this woman?".

"Of course. It's Miss Antonia, my assistant. Such a sweet girl with a lovely Southern accent."

"Did she in any way help you when you worked on the files that ended up causing you problems?"

"Yes. As I said, a lovely girl. She sent all the material to and from our department throughout the business. Such a hard worker. She would even stay late and come in on weekends when we were really rushed."

"Did your lawyer call her to testify at your trial?"

"Unfortunately, no. Right before my trial, her mother got sick, and she had to go help her. I forget where she moved, somewhere in the middle of the United States."

"You never told me about this woman," Professor Stubbs said.

"You never asked. I didn't think it important. She wasn't involved with the programs. Antonia was a secretary."

Tom smiled at me and nodded. "We've got a lot of work ahead of us if we're going to build a case but this really helps. Thanks Kate."

"Well, luckily, the cavalry is on the way. Agnes would like nothing better than to do this job," Kate said grinning.

"Let me guess," her older brother put in. "Dueling egos?"

"Absolutely, and you only get one guess as to who will win." All the boys laughed.

"And who is this Agnes?" the professor asked, his eyes searching the table and settling on my mother.

"Agnes Forester is my niece and a famous fashion model," she added, grimacing.

"Take heart, Mother. She's retiring from modeling and taking up her role as president of the bank."

"Oh, thank goodness. I know she wasn't old enough to do the job when her parents died, but—"

"She'll be here in a couple of minutes so you can congratulate her yourself." Kate kept the information about the engagement to herself. They could announce that in their own sweet time and, anyway, in her mother's world, the bank was much more important. Tom began explaining to the professor about the work she had done for K and K over the years. It would be interesting watching the older man's reaction when Hurricane Agnes blew in, whether he'd be bowled over first by her beauty or her brains.

Her phone beeped, informing her the app had loaded. She clicked it to run and saw the default page contained alarm notifications followed by the files with photos of car licenses. She noticed other sections and, as Harry peered over her shoulder, she hit the one labeled video. Instantly the screen filled with thumbnail shots of live video feeds from all over the property.

"Cool." Kate and Harry both exclaimed. She must add some cameras into the whelping rooms so she could keep track of each bitch and her puppies while she worked. As they watched, an SUV pulled into the driveway, and her phone buzzed. The license plate flashed on the screen. Kate recognized it as Sean's.

"Hang on, folks. Hurricane Agnes is about to reach landfall."

Harry groaned, and Kate elbowed him in the arm and then felt bad when he winced. She'd forgotten his pain, and guilt filled her. He leaned in and whispered, "Save me." Kate couldn't help but giggle, and her mother gave her a questioning glance. She and Harry needed to talk, but it seemed at least they were still friends.

The car door slammed and Kate pressed the code on her phone unlocking her front door. Sean opened the door letting in Twisp and Thora first and then Agnes. The greyhounds moved through the house then stopped when they saw a room full of people. Kate stood and walked to the kitchen door. "Twisp, Thora, go play puppy." Instantly, the two bitches were at her side and then pushing their way through the crowd of Sammies surrounding the door. Kate watched them take off in a breakneck run with her team in hot pursuit. Turning back, she saw Sean leaning over Harry, asking how he was doing.

"What a long drive." Agnes said. "I'm stiff all over. Harry, glad to see you're still alive. Claire, guys, good to see you. Kate, tell me, who are your visitors?" Agnes reached over to check how hot the tea in the pot was. Next, she went to the sink, filled the kettle, and put it on, then she turned so only Kate could see her face she nodded toward Kate's mother and a questioning eyebrow went up.

Kate stood and hugged her, whispering she'd explain about her mother later. "Agnes, let me introduce Professor Lyndon Stubbs and Anton Soucek. Gentlemen, this is my cousin Agnes Forester and our neighbor Sean Connelly."

The professor stared at her for a minute then said, "If I'm not mistaken, an Agnes Forester wrote a monograph on the algorithms of code breaking published last year in the *British Journal of Mathematics & Computer Science*. That would be you, I think."

Startled, Agnes answered yes, when Anton interrupted. "Only you, Lyndon, would see this beautiful woman who has been on every billboard and magazine cover in the country and associate her with a stuffy monograph in a journal not even published in this country. It is a pleasure to meet you, Miss Forester."

Agnes grinned. "And you, as well. I assume, Professor, you taught Harry when he was a boy."

"Yes, and I am happy to say he has lived up to my expectations."

Sean broke in. "You're also the professor who owned the place where Professor McNatt was shot. I presume whoever did the shooting thought it was you in the kitchen."

The professor paled. "I have brought much pain and danger to my friends."

"Well, since you didn't do the shooting, we could argue the point. Harry, has any headway been made on stopping this bastard?"

"Yes, and with an apology to the dog breeders in the room, the correct term in this case would be bitch. Kate has stopped the theft and is in the process of reclaiming the money and, minutes ago, we identified the shooter. Show them the photo, Kate."

Kate reached for her laptop and pulled up the photo, turning it so they could see.

"Well, isn't she the *sweetest little thing*," Agnes drawled.

CHAPTER TWENTY-NINE

While conversation moved around her, Kate switched her computer screen from the photo to the program that should be nearly finished reclaiming the stolen money. An attempt to breach the security wall had been made and countered, but the code involved wouldn't hold for long. The room, sounds, people all disappeared as her fingers flew over the keys, coding as quickly as she could to counteract the attempted breach. The speed at which the attack was being carried out proved more than a single computer was involved. The bitch had tapped into a powerful server, giving her more speed than Kate could produce but still she typed madly, trying to keep ahead of what Toni was doing. Suddenly, hands grabbed hers, and she found herself nose-to-nose with Harry as he screamed her name.

"What?" she asked vaguely, trying to see the screen.

"Kate." He grabbed her face and made her focus. "What is going on?"

"She's winning, and I can't type fast enough to stop her. She must be tied to a powerful server to work at this speed." The room exploded with people racing out the door toward the main house. Agnes dove for her designer tote and had her laptop open, linking her computer to Kate's.

A phone buzzed, and Harry answered then put it on speaker. "Go ahead, Sadie. You're on speaker."

"Harry, someone is trying to hack into our system. I've got bells and whistles going off all over the place."

Kate's phone buzzed. She hit speaker, and Tom yelled, "Katie, someone's trying to hack into K and K. So far, security is holding, but they've made over twenty attempts so far. Considering the time codes, there is serious speed involved."

Kate thought for a second and turned to Sean. "Get Kevin on the phone now."

"Why do you—"

"Now! Do it," she screamed.

Harry had his tablet open before him, feeding code into a program and talking quietly to Sadie at the same time. Kate told Tom what was happening with Harry. "She's causing a distraction so she can get the money back. I wouldn't put it past her to throw a large chunk of it into the professor's checking account so he gets the blame." She noticed the professor was no longer in the kitchen. Anton walked in. "Anton, get the professor to contact his bank and freeze his account, allowing no deposits or withdrawals until further notice. Tell him someone is going to hack into his account, and he needs to get the bank to stop it." He stepped into the living room to call as Sean passed his phone to Kate.

"Kevin, I need you to listen and not say a word. It's important you give me only one word answers, got it?"

"Yes."

"Good. Are you and your friends working together on a special project to help the professor?"

"Yes."

"Are you tapped into the college's high speed server?"

"Yes."

"Is Toni sending all of you code to run?"

"Yes, but how—"

"One word answers. Are there more than five people involved?"

"Yes."

"More than ten."

"Yes."

"More than twenty."

"No."

Fewer than fifteen?"

"Yes."

"Okay. Now, here's what I want you to do. I want you to let these kids know—wait, hold on a minute." Covering the phone, she whispered, "She's got a dozen kids feeding code into the server. If we have him tell them she's a crook, they won't believe us." Kate peered around the room at faces as panicked as hers. Then she spotted the business card of Lieutenant Garrison pinned to the wall.

"Kevin, the police are on the way. Toni didn't get permission to do this, and the administration is determined to make an example of any student found hacking the server tonight. You all need to shut down and get out of there fast. And, Kevin, if you want to protect them from finding Toni did this, break all your connections to her as well. Also, the FBI may be getting involved, so I'd have them turn off their phones and scatter and go silent for the next twenty-four hours. This could cost more than their degrees. It could mean jail time. Hold on." Kate handed the phone to Harry and whispered, "Tell them to do it."

He did and then gave the phone back to Sean.

Sadie's voice came from the phone at Kate's elbow. "You are seriously twisted, girl. I like that. Harry, our system is now off-line and shut down. I will run a scan to check she didn't leave any little presents behind. Keep me posted on what's happening.

"Tom? Has the threat stopped?"

"Remind me never to play cards with you. I never realized I had such a devious sister. I've got the system check doing a complete offline review. Thanks."

Kate clicked off the phone as a scream came from the other end of the table. "I've got you, bitch!" Agnes clapped her hands above her head as she did a happy dance.

She turned the screen so both Harry and Kate could watch lines of code run down the page. Agnes typed at lightning speed and saw one after another of the barrier failures disappeared until all was secure.

Kate stood up and taking the card from the wall called Lieutenant Garrison. "Lieutenant, Kate Killoy here. Yes, he's healing. I've got a favor to ask. I've found some people are trying to breach the main computer server at the university. I don't have all the details, but you might want to send someone out to check. From what I've heard, it's connected to your case." She listened for a few minutes. "We're still working on getting information on the shooter, but we're getting close. I'll keep you informed." Kate listened and smiled. "Thanks, talk to you soon."

Sean stared at her asking, "What—"

"I couldn't let Kevin lose face with his friends. He

told them the cops were about to raid the place. I set up a raid."

Anton stepped into the kitchen. "Not to interrupt, Miss Kate, but if we are done here, I noticed some wonderful smells as I passed through the kitchen at the main house. I think dinner might be ready."

Sean reached over and lifted Agnes out of her chair. "Let's go, princess, I'm starved." Kate gave one last glance at the laptop and followed them.

At the door, Harry took her arm and held her back. "Kate, I am in awe of you. You blew my mind today. I don't know which impressed me more, what you just did or what you've built with those women in your studio. How do you keep all of these things going at the same time?"

"I'm a woman. We multitask. It's part of our DNA."

"Will you accept a massive apology from a Y chromosome creature?"

"I and my sex shall gladly accept." Kate smiled and leaned in to kiss him on the cheek. He quickly moved his head, and what had started as a quick peck on the cheek became a kiss stealing all thought of codes and threats and leaving only breathless longing. Several minutes later, a shout came from Tim to hurry up. Stepping back, Harry reached out to steady her as her glazed eyes focused then opened the door, took Kate's hand, and followed the others.

"What kept you?" Agnes' voice came back to them.

"We had some things to talk about," Harry said.

"Yeah right, talking, absolutely, talking. Sean and I really enjoy talking, too." Agnes and Sean's laughter filled the evening as they linked arms and walked toward the house.

Following, Kate felt heat rise in her cheeks. This had been an insane day. Her mind slipped back to the fight ahead as adrenalin seeped out of her body and exhaustion flowed in. They may have won a skirmish today, but the larger war still lay ahead, and she didn't have a clue what the bitch would try next.

At dinner, Agnes held center stage, as usual, with stories of their visit to Texas and the photo shoot with puppies. Kate's mother wanted all the details about her taking over the bank. Agnes put her off with platitudes: "a work in progress," and "all in good time." Anton and the professor spoke warmly about visiting the studio.

"It is an interesting approach to running a business," her mother said.

Agnes turned and stared in amazement. "Did you visit Kate's studio, Claire?"

"Yes. This afternoon, we visited both the studio and the kennel. Kathleen seems to work very hard at these businesses."

"She does, and she's very successful. She is building

an excellent career."

"Perhaps." Claire turned away to speak to the professor, making the conversation officially over.

Agnes gazed at Kate and then smiled. She leaned across Harry and said quietly, "Perhaps is vastly better than anything she ever said on the subject of your business."

"It is quite a step forward for her, but she still really thinks I should devote my life to math. I'll never be able to change her mind. At least she called what I do businesses rather than hobbies." They grinned and then went back to their food.

Harry leaned in and said, "I never realized the depth of your mother's dislike for your choice of career. How long has she been like this?"

"Since I was about ten and began talking to Gram about wanting to design knits as a career."

"It's the reason your dad and granddad were so important to you."

"They backed me all the time I was growing up. Their lives revolved around math, but they loved and supported me and my freedom to choose."

Harry gazed around the table at her brothers.

Kate answered before he asked, "They don't understand what I do, but they also support me. My brothers became supportive when they learned I had a talent for writing computer code. I remember one Christmas I created them each a game and loaded it into the computer. It kept the twins busy all the way to New Year's Day. Dad thanked me and declared it the sanest Christmas we'd ever had."

"Yet you never wanted to become a gamer? You could be one of those multi-millionaire computer gamers who set up battles for the teenage set."

"No, working on the occasional program is okay, but to do it all the time—, I'd rather be out in the woods with my dogs or creating a design that will be enjoyed by someone for years. The only reason I could work with the security program you developed, which had been altered to steal, was you designed it years ago in old technology. When she altered it, she integrated in sections of newer code as a disguise rather than an integral part of the program. What was confusing you was the large sections of code that appeared be vital to the crime but, in reality, served as window dressing. The beauty of your code, for the thief, lay in its being dated and easy to hide within a seemingly more complex program so it didn't throw up a lot of red flags, which are basically set to detect more modern attacks." Kate yawned.

Good food combining with exhaustion from the stress of the last twenty-four hours was rapidly catching up with her. She still had to settle the dogs, check on everyone's water, and so on, so she stood and said her good nights and headed out. It took her a minute to realize

Harry was behind her. "You don't have to walk me to the kennel. You're tired, too."

"Let me help with the dogs and then they'll all be bedded down sooner." His long legs caught up to hers, and he slid his hand around her waist.

"Thanks." She leaned into him slightly, and they walked down the slope toward the kennel entrance. Kate reached for her phone and pulled up the app to unlock the kennel and turn on the lights. The full impact of what Sal's friends had done was impressive. Not only did the lights go on in the kennel and the runs, both inside and out, but, in addition, all three exercise yards were lit up like daylight. "Wow," she said, taking in the full effect. "I like it."

"This covers everything." Harry said, waving his hand at the display."

"Almost." Kate said. "They're coming by in the morning to finish up. We're still blind in a few areas but, after they finish, we'll have state of the art security here."

"I'll want to talk to them. Some of my clients might be interested in similar systems."

"They'll be here first thing tomorrow."

They quickly finished up, letting the boarding dogs out for one last time and giving each a dog biscuit. Then, she checked on Hecate to see if she needed anything other than a snuggle and headed for the house. In the kitchen, Kate checked the water buckets, fed the house cats and then opened the slider to let in the troops. They crossed the kitchen and each stopped at the big wash basket filled with dog toys and grabbed their favorite. Puppies who tried to grab an older dog's favorite toy soon learned to wait their turn. She next went to the biscuit bin in the kitchen and took out a double fistful of dog biscuits and, starting with the oldest, passed them out based on seniority. Quinn, as the new kid on the block, came last. His entire body quivered by the time she reached him, but she was delighted to see he knew enough to figure the system and didn't try to steal from the other dogs. He got told how good he was and earned an extra snuggle with his biscuit. Kate had turned toward the counter to put things away and wipe it down, when she felt two large hands take her shoulders turning her body toward the bedroom.

"I'll finish up. You're exhausted. Go sleep." She wanted to argue with him, but her eyes were already closing. Kate opened the door, letting Dillon and Quinn push through ahead of her, and then kept walking until she collapsed face-down onto the bed. She woke later in the dark to find herself tucked under the covers wearing only her panties and sports bra and with a warm body pressed up against her back. She felt a bandage against her shoulder and an arm draped across her. As she leaned back against him, she breathed in his scent and relaxed back into sleep with a smile on her lips.

CHAPTER THIRTY

"Rise and shine, princess. You've got workmen coming in forty-five minutes and, much as I like seeing you dressed this way, I think you might want to put on more clothes." Harry stood in the doorway wearing clean clothes, which told her he'd been up for a while. Kate jumped out of bed and headed for a shower then stopped.

"The program—?"

"It still holds."

"I wish we had more information on Toni Dunn. She obviously has skills. What we don't know is if she's working alone and why she's doing it."

"You mean other than squirreling away several million dollars?"

"Well, it's a factor, but most teaching assistants focus on adding degrees and climbing the academic ladder."

The warning buzzer said someone had entered the

driveway. Kate grabbed her phone and pulled up the app. It showed Sean's license plate. "Sean and Agnes are here. Stall them while I finish throwing clothes on." She grabbed clean clothes on the way to the bathroom. Kate didn't even bother with a shower, but dressed, pulled a brush through her curls, and put on some lipstick. Adding some color took a bit of the fatigue away. She heard Harry close the front door and walk down the steps toward the car. Dashing to the kitchen, Kate put on the kettle and pulled some pancakes from the freezer. Will had taught her to make extra pancakes every time she cooked them and to freeze them for emergencies. More than once, they'd filled in for a quick supper when she was dead on her feet. Next came a pound of bacon from the meat drawer of her refrigerator. She put the bacon tray loaded with strips into the microwave so by the time she heard the front door open, the smell of cooking bacon filled the air. Several stacks of pancakes on a plate switched places with the bacon in the microwave. "What smells so good?" Agnes asked, strolling into the kitchen.

"Bacon and blueberry pancakes. I hope you're hungry." The ding sounded on the machine, and she pulled out the now steaming pile of pancakes and put them on the table next to the bacon. Harry got out milk, glasses, and maple syrup and plates, adding them to the growing pile of goodness. The next batch of bacon began cooking, and Kate filled another platter with pancakes to be nuked.

Dillon sat quietly at her feet, doing his best imitation

of a starving dog, while Quinn ran from leg to leg, begging for all he was worth.

"Oh my God, these taste like Will's pancakes," Sean muttered between bites.

"It's his recipe, which serves ten hungry men. I like to cook them and then freeze the ones I don't use for days when I don't have time but still want to enjoy delicious food."

Harry finished his plateful and then pushed her into her chair as the ding sounded. He fished out still-bubbling bacon. She'd barely gotten the bacon on her plate when pancakes followed, and Kate settled in to enjoy the unique experience of being waited on. Tim came through the door to the kennel, laughing. Apparently Barney, the visiting Basset Hound, had somehow managed to get both his ears to rest atop his head, and the sight cracked up her brother. She saw him nod at Harry and translated their unspoken communication into the knowledge the boarding runs were done. Since no dog bowls sat on the counter, Kate realized Harry had fed the Sams. Another stack of pancakes and platter of bacon hit the table as Tim sat and Kate gazed up at Harry and smiled. They still had issues to settle, but yesterday had dispersed many of her worries.

The buzzer sounded, and she saw the workmen had arrived. Urging everyone to keep eating, she went out to tell them what she wanted. The electrician and Kate headed down the path between the kennel and the barn and out into the wooded trail toward the back of her property. Returning, she dashed through the kennel and back into the kitchen. "They'll be done in about an hour," she informed everyone as she poured tea into her cup from the still-hot pot.

"I thought they had finished," Tim said.

"The park entrance," Kate said, and both he and Sean nodded.

"Good thinking." Sean replied.

"What park?" Harry asked, having refilled his plate and added two pancakes to hers.

"My woods back up onto a state park, as does Sean's uncle's property. A path down to the park crosses both our properties. I figured what can be used to get to the park…"

"Can be used to get from there," Sean finished. "I'd forgotten about the park. I haven't been down that trail in ages."

"I only remembered because we did a search training exercise there last month. The people playing victims decided to up the degree of difficulty by going down the trail and hiding in the park. The dogs still found them, but it gave them a challenge over the usual training trails."

A knock came at the back door. One of the workmen stood waiting with an armload of boxes. Kate took him to the whelping rooms and showed him what she wanted then returned to her now clean kitchen.

"Oh, Kevin wants to thank you for the warning." Sean said. "Apparently five minutes after the kids left the building, a couple of black and whites pulled up. I reamed him out for doing anything so stupid it could cost all of them future employment if they got caught. I let him know Harry had the problem under control and they were to lie low until told differently. Agnes and I want to talk to the professor and see who else might be involved."

"Good. I'll be over as soon as the workmen leave," she told them and turned to see Harry staring at the calendar hanging by the phone.

"You have shows this weekend?" he asked and Kate stopped dead in the middle of the room.

"Shows, blast, I forgot. Not only shows, but Cathy is flying in this afternoon to spend tonight here and visit the dogs before going to the hotel where the judges will be staying tomorrow. She's got assignments for the weekend up at the Big E site in West Springfield. I expected her to text me when her flight would arrive." Kate pulled out her phone and checked but saw nothing.

"Ah," she heard Harry say. "You don't have to pick her up. Apparently, she, Rufus, and Jordy will be coming together and have arranged for a car. They should be here for supper."

"We should let Tom and Grandma Grace know

they're about to have more company. It's a good thing we have three houses available here. We're quickly becoming the Shannon Samoyeds Kennel and Hotel. Anton is going to have to move into the one of the two kennel rooms, and Jordy can have the other. They're not fancy, but the beds are good. I'm sure Jordy would love to tell his friends he slept in a kennel. We should warn Will to brace himself. He'll be cooking for fifteen. Not that he won't love it."

"Kate, I didn't ask you, but…actually I'm not sure you'll agree, considering you are expecting guests. Perhaps I'd better gather my things." Harry's face turning red and he squirmed, glancing toward the guest room. The penny dropped. Kate walked over to him and wrapped her arms around his chest.

"I need you to stay here, if you don't mind." She whispered. "I'm sure Cathy would prefer to stay with Tom, Gram, and Rufus. She'll have plenty of time to visit with the dogs."

Relief radiated from him. "Kate, tell me the truth. I know I've been an idiot, but are we good now?"

"Well we've got about forty-five thousand things still to work out between us, but we should be able to get to most of them after we're married." She kissed him lightly and then headed toward the whelping rooms to see how the camera setup progressed.

Within the hour, the new cameras and warning devices had been added into the main system and she had entered the invoices into her spreadsheet. This had not been cheap but was worth every penny if it kept them out of danger.

Restless, Kate paced her office. She was used to being busy, working at breakneck speed, so having the studio closed and no classes left her feeling out of sorts and at loose ends. What she needed to do now was talk to the professor. After first checking on the boarding dogs and her Sams, she signaled Dillon and opened the door to the exercise yard to let him in. She chuckled when Quinn dashed in under his father's body. It seemed wherever Dad went, Son followed. Kate took a lead off the rack by the door and clipped it to Quinn's collar then, with Dillon at her side, went to find Stubbs.

She found him sitting at the dining room table in the main house, staring at a computer screen with exhausted eyes. "Professor, I wonder if you'd be up for taking a walk. You've been staring at that screen 'til you're almost blind. What you need is some fresh air.

"As usual, Miss Kate, you are correct. I'd love to walk with you. My brain needs to rest and enjoy nature."

She gave the professor one of the hats hanging on the rack by the door. She had on a slouchy old Aussie canvas hat, similar to a Stetson, that had been caught in a downpour. It lacked style but molded to her head perfectly after all these years and kept the sun and bugs off her head. Kate pulled the bug stuff out of her pocket and rubbed it on and then passed some to Stubbs. "You'll find more mosquitoes and gnats here than in Texas because of the humidity."

The day seemed perfect, so far, though, on the weather station, there was a prediction of rain for later. A hurricane was moving along up the coast but they expected it to head out to sea before it could hit Connecticut. They would probably still get the outlying rain. For now, though, they had a sunny and warm day so, when they stepped into the woods, the shade felt good.

Kate and the professor walked in silence for a few minutes. Then the professor said, "What do you want to talk to me about, Miss Kate? I know we didn't come here to enjoy your beautiful forest."

"Toni Dunn." Kate let the name sit there for a minute, but it surprised her to see the professor show disappointment. It seemed he was no longer a fan of his TA.

"I assume you have learned Antonia is behind my problems. Truthfully, I'm not surprised. She is a very smart girl, but not as trustworthy as I hoped. She resents me and the fact I talk about Harry to my students every year. It would be like her to use Harry's program, the work of someone I have always admired, against me.

"Why does she dislike you?"

"It is a long story about things that happened many

years ago."

"I'm a good listener."

"When I still taught at Caltech, I had a TA by the name of Judson Dunn. He had transferred from UC Denver and brought with him his wife and daughter. He'd been with the department for about a year when I was told he was selling exams and altering grades for money. It added up to thousands of dollars. He would receive the lists of grades and change them when he entered them in our new computerized database. He didn't alter them by much, but enough to change students' eligibility for financial aid. He might have gotten away with it if his changes hadn't affected the final rankings in the department.

"Someone pointed out certain anomalies, and I went back to the original record of my grades."

"Harry?"

"Yes, Harry, but I never used his name. After being both fired and expelled, he reacted by not only leaving the college but deserting his wife and daughter. His wife filed for divorce, but he never paid child support. She got a job as a housekeeper but couldn't work full-time with the child, so she sent the girl to her sister in Colorado to be raised."

"When did this happen?"

"Soon after Harry arrived."

"And, I'm guessing, the family she went to work for

was the Blackburns."

"Yes, Rufus' mother had a stroke and wasn't able to manage on her own. Mrs. Dunn took over the household, which meant Harry could stay with them. She later married the head Caltech groundskeeper. After Mrs. Blackburn died, they stayed on with the Blackburns."

"Did Mrs. Dunn blame you for causing all her problems?"

"She never said anything to me, and from things Rufus has said over the years, I would say the answer is not really. She realized her husband had not become a thief to benefit her or her daughter."

"So moving forward to the present, the daughter now has the same type of job her father once held."

"Yes, based on recommendations from several professors, including Rufus."

"And we now know she's stealing from your department on a much larger scale than her father did at Caltech, only this time is blaming you."

The professor nodded.

"I have one more question," Kate added.

"What?"

"Where is Judson Dunn?"

CHAPTER THIRTY-ONE

Her phone rang. "Kate, you need to get out of the woods and back here now. We got an alert the hurricane has turned and is now moving fast, heading due north, straight for us. We've got to batten down and get ready." Harry sounded stressed.

"How did you know I was here?" she asked.

"Look up."

Kate lifted her gaze and spotted a small camera on the trunk of a tall beech tree. She smiled and waved. "We're heading back."

"The hurricane is coming this way," she told the professor. "I have to get everything put away or tied down and all the dogs settled inside." They hurried back toward the kennel. As they cleared the edge of the woods, her phone dinged. She checked and saw an unfamiliar car had arrived. She switched to camera mode and spotted Jordy jumping from the back of a car and running toward the exercise yard, followed by Cathy and Rufus. Kate dashed around the kennel and greeted them as Harry, Kate's brothers, and Anton came down the hill from the main house.

"Help get the luggage up to Grace's house. Cathy will tell you which bags are which," Kate suggested to the twins. "Jordy, you're bunking in the kennel. Anton, have you been able to move your things in yet?"

"Yes. It is a good room, and I will be happy to have this young man as a neighbor," the older man said as he took Jordy's suitcase and headed into the kennel.

Rufus stared as the professor followed Kate out from behind the kennel. "Lyndon, what are you doing here? Do you know the police are looking for you?"

Harry interrupted, "Rufus, we will discuss all this later. Put your car in the barn, and then help check to find anything that might become a projectile and secure it."

What had been a lovely sunny day had now turned grim with dark clouds racing across the sky. The wind seemed to grow stronger by the minute. Kate headed into the kennel, following Jordy to the second floor. She and Anton showed him his room and then, as Anton headed out to help the men, she got her young helper to start bringing the five gallon water containers down from the second floor storage closet to be filled and put by the kennel runs. Cathy came running in and helped line them up and showed Jordy how to fill each and then push it to the side and do the next. She then dragged each to a spot by a kennel run.

Since the boarding kennel was at maximum capacity, she estimated if they lost power for more than a day, they'd need at least twenty containers. Seamus pushed open the door and then shut it against the wind. He helped Cathy drag the containers to line up along the runs. This way they would be close when needed.

"Skip Tigger's run and double up farther down," Kate yelled. "That Berner can't resist lifting his leg on anything over two inches high, and I don't want to have him peeing on these."

When they finished, Seamus had Kate unlock the studio using the app on her phone so he could go close the shutters on the big windows. When they planned the studio, they'd installed the storm shutters because of the sheer size of the windows. The windows had never broken in a storm, but she couldn't take any chances. If one of the massive windows broke, the shutters would keep the storm at bay, and the machines and work would be protected.

Jordy helped Kate bring down the lanterns stored upstairs and place them in obvious spots around the kennel. She also had him put one in each bedroom. Then she checked the drawer and made sure of her stock of batteries.

The rain had begun in earnest by then, and everyone made the dash for the main house except for Harry and Kate, who went to take care of her dogs. Cathy had offered to stay, but they told her to go, they had it covered. Kate brought the Samoyeds inside, giving them their suppers early and getting everyone settled. She taped the glass of the sliding door in her bedroom and pulled the heavy curtain across. Then she repeated the routine of filling big water cans and finding lanterns. Kate hoped the backup generator, which took care of the well and some of the electricity for the kennel, would supply the basics, but she didn't want to take chances.

Kate pulled two waterproof coats out of the closet, handing her father's favorite one to Harry. An Australian drover's coat, it definitely gave him style. She slid into the yellow slicker she'd worn since she was fourteen. With its matching hat, she could pass for a Maine fisherman any day of the week. A snort behind her told her Harry had lost his battle not to laugh. She peeked over her shoulder, glad to see the sparkle back in his eyes, finally.

"Agnes is right," he said, trying to keep his laughter under control.

"Right about what?"

"You're beautiful, no matter what you wear." He reached out and folded the brim of her hat back then leaned in to kiss her. Rather than feeling awkward, she found herself pulling his head down and opening her mouth. It didn't take him two seconds to claim her mouth, and immediately she lost herself in the wonder of wanting to touch and be touched.

Kate's phone buzzed and Harry pulled his head back. "Arggg," he screamed. "Our timing really stinks."

She'd received a text asking if they had a problem, and if not to get to supper. "Supper," she whispered, leaning against Harry, trying to get her legs to hold her up.

"Right. Supper. Kate, I don't know if I can wait 'til Christmas to get married."

"How about Thanksgiving?"

"We'd need to talk to Father Joe."

"We will, but first we'd better go eat before this crowd finishes all the food."

He reached over and flipped the brim of her hat back down, pulled his Stetson lower on his head, and took her hand. Fighting the wind and horizontal rain, they ran across the lawn to the big house and up onto the porch. Harry pulled the screen door open, holding it tightly to keep it from slamming against the house as the wind grabbed it. Kate pushed the inner door open and stepped back as he made sure the screen latched tightly. Water cascaded off their coats onto the floor. Thank goodness she'd left Dillon and Quinn with the other dogs. Harry found some empty hooks on the wall and hung up his coat and hat then hers. She grabbed an old towel from the pile by the door and wiped up the mess on the floor.

Then they headed toward the dining room where a party was in full swing.

Will had made beef stew and freshly baked bread to go with it, the perfect hearty fare to fill them up during the storm. Harry and Kate sat after filling their plates. The lights went out. Flashlight apps appeared around the table giving enough light for the candelabras to be located and lit. Once done, they put away the twenty-first century technology to enjoy the gentle light of an earlier age.

Kate's plans for doing an online search for Judson Dunn would have to be put on hold as well. Oh well, she thought, hopefully the storm stopping her also kept Toni Dunn indoors and out of trouble. However, discussion raged full tilt around the table, with people sharing what they'd found out about the infamous Miss Dunn. At first Rufus refused to believe it. But when Kate mentioned she had a photo of Toni standing in the park holding a gun with a silencer, his shock changed to reluctant belief.

"How could such a sweet girl do such horrible things? Are you absolutely sure?" Rufus asked, struggling to wrap his head around the idea.

Cathy turned to him and said, "You are so gullible. All it takes is for her to bat her eyes and unbutton her blouse a little and you males rise up to defend her. It only took me a few seconds to recognize a smarmy witch. She tried treating Kate like dirt. Now we have proof she took a gun to the park, which means she shot at Kate. Considering her treatment of all the women at breakfast, any of us could all have been targets. I had a little chat with your housekeeper, Antonia, after Kate and Harry left. I asked her where she got the information Kate was responsible for Harry's injury. She told me she got it from her daughter."

"Her daughter?" Rufus asked. "Antonia hasn't got a daughter?"

The professor disagreed explaining about Judson Dunn's crimes and how they affected his family including his wife, Antonia and his daughter Toni. He made threats against me at the time because I exposed him, so I've made a habit of keeping track of where he was. Unfortunately, he fell off the radar about ten years ago. I suspect he changed his identity. I have no idea where he is now, but I suspect his daughter may know."

Jordy interrupted. "I thought Antonia was her aunt."

"No. She grew up in Denver as part of Antonia's sister's family, the DeBlasios," the professor said. "Since she kept the name of Dunn, I wonder what she was told about her parents."

"Apparently, Antonia is now very loyal to this daughter," Cathy said, "since she attacked and hurt Kate on the basis of what the girl said."

Claire suddenly demanded, "Kate, you didn't tell me you were attacked. When did this happen."

"I'm okay, Mother. It happened when I arrived at the

Blackburn's."

"Ewen Blackburn allowed my daughter to be attacked in his home?"

"I'm all right now, Mother. To be fair, Mr. Blackburn didn't know you had a daughter."

Claire blanched at the comment but then shook her head and reached for Kate's hand. "I'm so sorry."

"You guys were fooled into believing the persona she created. Toni Dunn seems to have a definite talent for lying to people in order to get what she wants." Cathy scowled at Rufus who turned to the professor.

Rufus asked, "In spite of knowing all this, you still gave her the job as your TA?"

"Well, you and several others recommended her and, I'll admit, I felt sorry for her," he replied. "It seems my pity was misplaced. Perhaps you asked the right question, Miss Kate, when we spoke earlier. Where is Judson Dunn?"

"Unfortunately, Professor," Kate replied, "it's not a question we can answer tonight. In fact, before this storm gets any worse, I think it best we find our beds. I suspect we're going to have a lot of cleanup to do tomorrow."

"But aren't you going to stay up? What if the storm gets bad?"

"This is what people do during hurricanes. Short of having a tree fall on top of the house or kennel, you batten down, get some sleep, and clean up the next day after the storm is gone."

They bundled up in their rain gear, finding Jordy one of her brother's old raincoats from when they were much smaller. In fact, the closet provided extras for all the visitors. Then, staying together, Anton, Jordy, Harry, and Kate headed for the kennel, while Rufus, Cathy, and Tom made a dash for Grandma Ann's house where she'd stayed behind, not wanting to go out in the bad weather.

Kate used her non-electronic key to open the door and Jordy and Anton said good night and went upstairs. Kate glanced at the kennel dogs, but they all slept. Hecate lay curled up on her desk chair, and everything seemed secure so she and Harry locked up and headed down the covered walkway to Kate's. They entered quietly, hanging up their wet gear in the mudroom. Then they passed through the mass of dogs who stood but soon realized nothing exciting was going on and returned to sleep. At the door to Kate's room, Harry stopped and gave her a lingering kiss before he pushed her gently through the door, followed by Dillon and Quinn, and firmly closed it.

Kate woke at daybreak and went right to cleaning the dogs' exercise yard before letting them out. The power was still off, but the kennel seemed fine. Leaves and small branches covered the outside runs, so she got to work clearing debris.

Harry appeared, followed by the twins, and Kate sent

him to see if he could find when they'd get power and told him not to do anything that would tear his stitches. Tim helped with the runs while Seamus checked the studio and opened the shutters. Ten minutes later, Cathy, wearing borrowed boots, joined them. With all the help, the outdoor runs were cleared and swept clean, holding nothing hazardous any of their boarders could swallow. Closing and locking the last of the outside run gates, Kate headed back inside.

While the twins went to get the tractor and find some chainsaws to clear the several trees that hadn't survived, Kate and Cathy gave biscuits to the boarders and then let them out to enjoy the sunshine.

Harry had Kate's portable radio playing in her office when they came in, giving them an update on Hurricane Shelly. The storm's eye had moved through an area about thirty miles east of them, playing havoc with New Haven and Hartford and causing the Connecticut River to overflow, with major damage to all the towns and cities along it. Boston and the Cape also gotten hit hard.

Kate took out her phone. "I've got to call Sal."

"Already done, and they're fine," Harry reassured her. "They have no power, and the streets are covered with debris and sand, but the winds have died down and the rain ended an hour ago. The owner of the house had a Coleman stove, so they're cooking a pancake breakfast out on the back deck. I filled Sal in on our full house and reassured him there wasn't much damage other than a few downed trees though we, too, still had no power."

Anton and a sleepy Jordy, obviously not a morning person, came down from their rooms. Kate sent them up to the main house for breakfast and promised they'd be along. Knowing Will, he probably had the both of the gas grills going on the patio at the back of the house and was cooking like mad. Harry, Cathy, and Kate headed for her house. While Harry put together the different breakfast meals, from a simple biscuit to meals for the puppies and two of the older dogs, Kate brought the ones needing meals inside and gave Cathy a double handful of biscuits to charm the herd in the exercise yard. Kate watched her first win them over with the biscuit bribes and then work her way from one to the other, going over them as if judging them in the ring. Kate peeked out to watch for a minute. Her smile grew when Cathy got to Kelly and Dillon. Kelly's two-year-old daughter, Shelagh would be making her debut at the national the following month out in Kentucky so Kate was delighted Cathy seemed to like her as well.

Releasing the puppies and older dogs back into the yard, Quinn wasted no time beating a path to someone he considered an old friend. Cathy picked him up to snuggle and commented on how much weight he'd added. Considering they didn't know if there were any wires down on the property, Kate opted to leave Dillon and Quinn with the others after their water buckets were cleaned and filled. She remember at the last minute to pick up her battery-operated cell phone charger. Finally she, Cathy, and Harry all headed for the main house to have breakfast.

Kate checked the main driveway as they crossed the sodden lawn heading up to the porch. Several small trees still blocked it, but most of the debris had been cleared leaving a stack of logs piled to one side, ready to be carted down to the woodpiles. Kate relaxed. For now, at least, there seemed to be no sign of their shooter.

CHAPTER THIRTY-TWO

Kate set her phone on the table alongside the others merrily nursing power from their battery chargers. Far be it for any of them to be out of contact with the rest of the world. She chuckled. The security system being tied into the generator meant as soon as her phone got charged, she'd could check to be sure it worked. Kate reached over the phone farm to get the butter and syrup for her pancakes. She needed to keep her non-digital body working at full capacity as well. She snagged some quickly disappearing bacon from the platter before letting her brothers take the last of it. Conversation flowed about the storm, how much more clearing must be done to get them back to normal, and, of course, when the power would return.

Cathy sat on Kate's left with Harry on her right. She and Kate had been discussing the finer points of structure Cathy had noted in her examination of Kate's dogs when she paused and leaned across her. "Harry, I assume you haven't been to a doctor since you returned."

"You're right. I haven't really had time. It's been a madhouse."

"Well, handsome, you and I have an appointment after breakfast. You can strip down, and I'll change your dressing and check to see how the wound is healing."

"How come every time you're around Foyle you're asking him to take his shirt off?" Rufus grumbled.

Cathy's dimples flashed. "Hey, he's got a great bod. Maybe I like looking at him without a shirt." She winked at Kate and Harry.

Rufus' face could have passed for a low-hanging thunder cloud, before everyone at the table burst out laughing.

Harry leaned over and grinned. "You walked into that one without even watching where you stepped, pal." Rufus' face turned a lovely shade of magenta.

Cathy took pity on him and leaned against his shoulder and then said, "Don't worry, big guy. If you get shot, I'll look at you shirtless, too."

After the second round of laughter ended, she leaned over and quietly kissed his cheek. He stared down at her and smiled, and Kate spotted him taking Cathy's hand under the table.

The relaxation broke when Kate's phone rang with a call from the cyber security company. She answered and became suddenly serious.

"Kate, someone really doesn't like you. We've had five attempts to breach your security system in the last hour. Sal told me the person who threatened you was in the area and may have seen our truck leaving your place."

He didn't need to mention the person was a hacker.

"I wanted to warn you because we're pulling your link to the program while we identify the source and track it. This way, they won't be able to lock you out of your kennel or turn off your water supply. But it means your electronic eyes and ears won't be working for you for a while. I'll let you know when you're back. So, be careful. They may have done this to get us to turn off the system."

Kate sat for a minute, thinking and, then filled everybody in on their lack of security. "This means, if she is going to come visit, she'll probably use either the front driveway or the path through the back woods from the park. The park path may have trees down. We haven't checked. If she tries to enter through areas that aren't clear, she may get in, but she'll pay with the worst case of poison ivy possible."

"Well, since breakfast is over and nobody's shooting at the moment," Cathy said, "come with me, Harry, and strip off your shirt. Kate, since you're engaged to this hunk of manhood, you can come, too. We'll get those bandages changed, and Kate can help so she'll be able to do it next time because I have dogs to go judge."

"Perhaps I'll come along and protect Harry from your advances," Rufus said, chuckling.

Kate grinned at Harry then whispered, "Rufus is going to have his hands full. I hope he can keep up with her."

"She might be the kick in the pants Rufus has needed for a long time."

Before entering the house, Kate stepped aside and told Anton and the professor she'd like a chance to talk to both of them at her place in about an hour. They agreed then Anton went off to help with the tractor moving logs and the professor and Claire disappeared into her office.

While Rufus and Harry disappeared into Kate's office to speak on the phone to Sadie, Cathy, Jordy, and Kate went about cleaning the downed branches and other debris out of the main Samoyed exercise yard. The dogs had been put in the smaller yard Kate had earlier cleaned. Cathy and Jordy gathered sticks while Kate raked debris. There was nothing like physical labor to free the mind to work on problems. In half an hour, the main exercise yard stood clear but very muddy. In spite of the fact it meant there would be a lot of baths needed, Kate gave in, and the dogs came barreling out when the gate opened.

Kate had finished checking the water for the boarding dogs when the professor and Anton arrived for their promised meeting with her. Cathy, Harry, and Rufus had arrived as well, so Kate pulled some extra chairs into her office and then displaced Hecate, who impressed both men with her massive size by stretching across Kate's desk as everyone got comfortable. Kate apologized for playing teacher but

explained she'd begun to see a pattern linking both Anton's and the professor's cases to each other and to what
was happening now. Rufus started to challenge the statement, but Cathy and Harry both asked him to listen and
wait.

"Anton," Kate asked, "can you name the person who
brought your alleged crime to light and led to your being
charged?"

"That would be Jagger Dunford, the auditor who
worked in our division. He seemed like a charming man
but insisted I had committed this theft.

"Can you describe him?"

"He was slightly taller than I, with silver white hair, a
handsome face, and appeared quite fit for a man in his mid
-fifties."

"Professor, can you identify the person at Baxter,
Kline and Baxter, who brought your crime to light?"

"Well, now strangely enough, it was also an auditor
who accused me, Jarel Dunnett, and he, too, insisted only I
had access and the math background to create such a
theft."

"Could you describe him?"

"Actually, no. I was to meet with him about the problem on Thursday, but he got called out of town, and I met
with the company's attorney instead. However, I know
some of the students, along with Miss Dunn, met with him

on my behalf."

"Rufus, could you call Kevin and see if you can get a description of this man?"

"While we're waiting, Harry, could you describe the man who paid you a visit on Thursday morning prior to your trip?"

"The description would match the one Anton gave you—" Harry said

Rufus interrupted, "Tall, silver hair, fit, good looking, in his fifties."

"Miss Kate, could you explain where all these questions are leading?" the professor asked.

"Well perhaps I should just tell you a story. Many years ago, a handsome young man who had a wife and child worked at a college. Now he had a love of nice clothes and a luxury lifestyle. Unfortunately, his salary did not support all these drains on his income so he decided to supplement his income by working a few side jobs. Those jobs meant a breach of trust with the college because he sold exams and, for a fee, changed grades. His crimes were discovered by a young student. Because of his age, the student didn't feel he'd be listened to by the administration, so he went to the one professor who had declared before an entire class he would always listen to him. When the professor heard what the boy told him, he brought the crime to the attention of the administration, keeping secret the identity of the boy. The man not only found himself fired but blackballed on other campuses so he took his ill-gotten gains and ran, leaving behind his wife and child. The professor, feeling sorry for the wife, who divorced her husband, got her a job with the family of a friend. Rather than try to cope with her new job and her child, the abandoned wife sent her child to be raised by her sister.

"Time passes. The wife remarries and when the family relocates to the city where her daughter is being raised, she and her husband go with the family. The daughter grows up, goes to college and then finds a job with an insurance company in another state. While there, she meets this charming older man who takes an interest in her and her math abilities. He recognizes her talents are even better than his. Whether through flattery or some means other than the truth, he convinces her to help him "borrow" some money from the company to invest. She agrees, and together they manage to transfer two hundred and fifty thousand dollars. They also manage to use the passwords and ID codes on the transactions belonging to the girl's boss. When the money is in the man's hands, he suggests she take a vacation and he then accuses the girl's boss with the crime. The boss is sent to prison and the money is never found.

"Fast forward a few years and the man, who has changed both job and name, is now working as an auditor at an investment firm that, by chance or plan, handles the retirement investments of the college where the professor who got him fired is now working. In fact, the professor is on a committee to transfer the funds to the investment house.

The man has kept track of the girl and now arranges for her to get a grant to study for her advanced degree in math and helps her get a job as the professor's TA.

"One day, the girl tells him about an old term paper she found, written by the professor's favorite student. It describes how to stop someone trying to steal money from an investment company. One of them suggests reversing this process would be a perfect way to steal the money. They put the plan into action with her writing the code based on the student's original work, and allowing them to steal part of each funds transfer between the college and the investment company. That money was then moved and stored in an offshore account. The beauty of the plan was it could be done with only minor supervision. The theft would be carried out by a stealth program inserted into the company's computer as part of some deposits. So it quietly worked, stealing on its own.

"Now, this theft had been going on for a while, to the tune of several million dollars, when the professor spots an inconsistency in the reports automatically issued by the company. The amounts don't match those of the college. He informs everyone he is calling in help, the very person who wrote the initial program the girl is using and someone who will easily recognize it. Seeing their game is up, they repeat the scenario they'd used successfully years earlier, and the auditor accuses the professor of the theft. The girl inserts a program that will complete the theft in six days and, at the same time, remove all trace of their involvement and lay out an obvious connection to the professor.

"Then things start to go badly for them. The man tries to eliminate the person who wrote the program, but fails. The girl panics and tries to distract people by pushing one of the members of the committee down a staircase. This isn't enough of a distraction, and the program still needs more time to finish. The girl then decides to kill the professor so he won't be able to fight back. This fails when she shoots the wrong person. Then, the man who wrote the program arrives and brings his fiancée with him, whom she's told is a math expert and crime fighter. The girl has got to get rid of them. They will be able to stop the program and may even get the professor off and put the blame on them. She tries to shoot the fiancée but fails.

"That evening, she manages to shoot the man and, with the help of her partner, take him to a deserted area and leave him for dead. Unfortunately for her, he not only lives, but then he and his fiancée, plus the professor, escape to Connecticut. She follows.

"In the meantime, she keeps track of the progress on her program and she sees someone has reversed it and is emptying their bank accounts of money and replacing it in the school's retirement accounts. Since she is now in Connecticut as well, she convinces the student friends of the professor that she's on the trail of the real criminal and to go online and upload the script she sends them, telling them it will save the professor. She almost succeeds but is caught and her trick undone. Not only that, as of yesterday, an hour before the storm hit, she found herself locked out of her own program."

"Wow," Cathy said. "She is going to be one pissed bitch."

Tom and Kate's other brothers had arrived during the tale and they quickly suggested the family compound had to be the target of this woman.

"She may no longer be working alone. She may have called her partner to help eliminate the threat. And, since all her intended victims are here in one place, she could come in shooting," Tim said.

Kate glanced around the room and at her four brothers crowded in the hall. "Where's Jordy?"

"Out in the exercise yard, practicing heeling with Liam when we came by," Will said, moving toward the door. A minute later, his shout brought them all to their feet and racing down the hall. Pushing through the door to the yard, Kate saw both Jordy and Liam were gone.

Cathy spotted the paper hitched to the chain link fence.

It was a ransom note saying, *Transfer the Three Million back into the Cayman Account or the Boy Dies.*"

CHAPTER THIRTY-THREE

"Miss Kate, you must give them the money. If I have to go to jail, I will. You must save that boy," the professor implored her.

Then everyone spoke at once. Will finally gave a piercing whistle, bringing silence.

"Professor," Kate told him, "the only thing keeping Jordy alive is the fact they don't have the money. Now, everyone listen. Nobody touch the note. The police will need it. We will get Jordy back. But we're going to do it safely so nobody gets hurt. Seamus, call Sean and have him notify the Bethany Barracks. Tim and Anton, get the driveway cleared."

Kate pulled out her phone and hit speed dial. "Alice listen, don't talk. I need the phone tree to get as many level three-trained searchers here ten minutes ago. There's been an armed kidnapping of a twelve-year-old boy from my property. We have a ransom note. Liam, who was with the boy, is gone as well. Got it?" She hung up the phone and told the rest to go to the barn and get water bottles. They'd need them as they searched.

Checking the men with tractors had tree removal in hand, she said, "As each searcher arrives, those of you who can identify Toni or Judson Dunn will buddy up with one of them. Split up, but do exactly as they say. These people are trained and know what they're doing. Don't do stupid stuff that will endanger anyone. Will, we'll need coffee, and maybe some food. Cathy, go to Jordy's room with a bunch of plastic bags you'll find inside the door to the exercise run and put any of Jordy's used clothing into the bags for the dogs to scent on, but be sure not to get your scent on them. Rufus, go with her. Harry, see if you can get Sadie to track the GPS on Toni's cell phone. The professor has the number."

Kate went back into the kennel but emerged a minute later with a tracking harness with lead and Dillon as the first cars arrived. Sean, in uniform, driving his cruiser, was first, followed by Agnes with her dogs. Next, a mixture of state police cars and search team cars came in a steady stream. Kate made sure Dillon's harness was fastened in place and the twenty foot tracking lead attached.

Claire came running up to find out what had happened. When she heard, she started ranting. "Kate, how could you endanger that child? You have always been so sure these dogs would keep everyone safe. Well, he was with a dog, and he's gone. It's entirely your fault."

"Claire, shut up," the professor said. "You have no idea what you're saying, and you're making a fool of yourself. Show your daughter the respect she deserves or go away, but don't interfere."

Kate would have liked to have the time to enjoy her mother's expression, but she didn't. She'd arrived at the barn to see the team from the barracks pulling out the tables and laying down the maps. They'd worked so many joint practice exercises together they knew where everything was. Richard, Kathy, Alice, Cora, and Lucy from her search team had all arrived with their dogs. Alice informed her the rest of the team was away on vacation.

Agnes had set up her computer and had photos of both Jordy and Toni Dunn up on the screen. Cathy and Rufus arrived with the clothing in bags. Rufus introduced himself to the sergeant in charge, and they went over the details as another officer dusted the note for prints.

Kate called the security company and told them what had happened. They said they would turn on the system fully and hold off any incursions from the hacker. She let them know the hacker was the kidnapper so she would probably be busy. Two seconds later, her phone beeped, and the system came up. Harry ran into the kennel and returned with Kate's laptop as well as his own. Putting them back to back, they could pull up cameras all over the grounds. Kate asked Richard to monitor the computers and coordinate everyone. The search team's walkie-talkies were passed out and the dogs given the clothing to sniff.

Kate had Dillon sit quietly at her side, slightly away from the others. As the search began, she said, "Find Liam."

His head came up, and he immediately headed for the woods behind the kennel. A minute later, she heard a sound behind her and saw Harry hurrying along the trail saying he had to stop for a second. "Does Dillon have Jordy's scent?"

"I told him to find Liam. His dad is probably following Jordy."

"Is Liam trained like Dillon?"

"He's had some training, and he has a tracking title, but he's on his own out there, so if he's tracking, it's pure instinct. If he bonded with Jordy, he'll follow him."

Dillon pulled to the right, and Kate saw a tree had fallen across the main path. The path he followed now became much longer, circling around before it would rejoin the main trail later on. The tree being down would slow Toni and Jordy. They moved fast over a trail tangled with debris from the hurricane.

When Dillon paused to check his direction, Kate asked Harry, "How's your wound? I can slow down if it's too much."

"I'm okay. Cathy has me trussed up like a Christmas turkey. Nothing can get at it."

Kate turned on the walkie-talkie. "Kate to base."

The response came.

"Richard, we're following the circle trail. A tree blocked the main trail. I think they're heading for the state park. We need someone to cut off exit from there. Over."

"Got it, Kate," Richard answered. "Will do."

Dillon picked up the scent so they pushed their way through an elderberry bush knocked into the trail by a fallen sapling and continued following the trail. Kate thanked God for the shade of the woods as the heat of the day had now risen to about ninety degrees. Dillon paused to check a rock and a bush. Harry handed her a water bottle and she drank and returned it. "I think these spots are where Jordy must have made her stop, and Liam must have ducked out of sight. He's prey stalking, not letting them know he's there," she told him.

They approached the place where the circle trail would meet the main trail again. Kate glanced up and spotted the tree where she'd seen the camera when she'd been with the professor. The tree had survived the storm, so hopefully the camera had as well. She waved at the camera and pointed to the direction she was headed and they moved on. Harry pulled the gun he'd gotten out of Sal's lockbox, for which he had the combination.

They had barely covered a hundred yards down the trail when Dillon lowered his head and slowed his pace. He didn't bark. Instead, he crept forward slowly. Kate and

Harry followed his lead and moved forward as quietly as they could. Then they spotted Liam crouched in a down position, ready to spring. Dillon silently moved to backup position behind him and to the side. Squatting and inching forward, Kate and Harry moved to the brush hiding the dogs.

Then they heard Jordy's voice. He warned Toni to watch out for the poisonous timber rattlesnakes and copperheads common in this area. "You also have to watch out for black bears. This time of year, they have cubs wandering around, and you might stumble across them in the trees eating the berries like those on the bush next to you. Whatever you do, don't stand between the mother and her cubs. Then there are the deer ticks," he went on, "which are so small they're like poppy seeds, but they can give you Lyme disease. It can do all sorts of nasty things to you. Old Lyme, where the disease was first identified is near here.

"You're making this up," Toni snarled and then groaned.

"No, I read it online when I knew we were coming here. I knew Kate didn't live in the city, but I didn't realize she lived out in the woods. You can't hear cars or people, but, if you listen carefully, you'll hear birds and squirrels or chipmunks and, of course, the dogs. Kate has lots of dogs, and some of them are trained like the ones police use. Kate even trains actual police dogs. My dad said I might get a puppy one day, and I'm going to have Kate train it for me. You're afraid of dogs, aren't you?"

"I don't like them."

"I love them, especially when they're little puppies like Quinn. He likes me, too. I think I want a puppy like Quinn. You know, your ankle is starting to swell up. It's probably only sprained and not broken since you can put some weight on it. You need to get it x-rayed and band-aged."

"Shut up, already. You talk too much."

The sound of feet running on the trail from the direction of the park had everyone frozen in position. A tall, silver-haired man, dressed more for a business meeting than a ramble in the woods, came into the clearing. "What's keeping you? We need to get out of here before the police block the roads."

"I've sprained my ankle. I need help getting the kid to the car."

"I don't know why you had to take the kid. You could just hack the files again."

"I told you, she's hidden the money. I've checked all the accounts at the company. There's no trace of it in the regular accounts. She's disguised it and hidden it inside another normal file like a document or a spreadsheet. Only she can get it, and she won't unless the stakes are high. We have to do it this way."

Kate heard the stress in Toni's voice. This was a

woman at the end of her tether. She leaned over to Harry after transferring Dillon's lead to his father.

She whispered to Harry, "Keep Liam here. I'm going to try to get her to move away from Jordy. If you can get a clean shot, take it."

"The police are moving into position. They won't get away. Why not wait?" Harry reached for her arm.

"She's panicked enough to shoot Jordy by accident. I'll try to distract her." She pulled loose, signaling Dillon to heel, and then casually walked down the trail into the clearing.

Toni swung the gun around and pointed it at Kate as she approached. "You, you stole my money, and you're going to give it back."

"I think you've got backwards, Toni," Kate said, "You stole the money from the retirement fund and all those hardworking people at the university. All I did was take it back. I must say, girl, you have serious skills. You almost pulled it off—almost being the operative word here. Yep, almost, but not quite. I imagine Daddy here was somewhat disappointed."

"Daddy? What are you talking about?" Toni asked, startled.

"You mean you didn't tell her, Judson? You didn't have a touching father daughter bonding moment? What a pity."

"Don't listen to anything she says. Get rid of the kid. Grab her and we'll go. We'll make her get us the money," Judson said. "I'm not staying, whether you come or not. The police will be headed this way."

"Running out on your daughter again, Judson? Toni, let me introduce you to your father Judson Dunn. It's his real name. He got caught in a crime when you were young then he ran off leaving you and your mom behind to face the fallout."

"No, my parents are dead. They died in a car crash, and I went to live with my aunt."

"Good story but not true. Your parents are alive. After your father took off, your mother couldn't cope, so she sent you to her sister and then got a job as a housekeeper. She later married again, but she's alive, and you know her well. In fact, you have her name, which is probably a tradition in her family.

"You are both named Antonia. It's how your father spotted you. You probably are the spitting image of your mother at your age, isn't that so, Judson? So, when you showed up at the insurance company with the name Antonia Dunn, he knew exactly who you were. He got you to steal for him and blame your boss. By the way, did Daddy share any of that money or did he keep it? Didn't you have any suspicions when he had a different name the second time? I'm sure he gave you a reason. You inherited your ability to lie from your father. He probably spun your head full of tales of living like a princess instead of slogging along as a TA. He made sure you got the job that not only allowed him to steal the money with your help, but also let him get revenge on the man who accused him of his first crime and got him fired."

"You're my father?" Toni gawked at the man before her. "Why didn't you tell me?"

"We've got to go. There's no more time." He turned back down the trail.

"Tell me, are you my father?" Toni screamed.

"Yeah, I'm your father. She's right. You're the spitting image of your mom. We can have a family reunion later. Let's go."

"Everything she said is true. You ran out on us? My mother gave me away? It's all true?" Her voice rose higher and higher, close to cracking. Kate watched her swing the gun toward this man who had hurt her so much as a sound came from the bushes.

Jordy yelled, "It's a bear!" as a small brown hairy creature came bounding out from under a bush heading their way.

Toni screeched, gazing wildly around, and, suddenly, the gun went off.

Judson Dunn fell to the ground, screaming and holding his shoulder.

Kate signaled Dillon, who shot forward, knocking

Toni to the ground and holding her there with his teeth at her throat. Kate dashed forward and brought her foot down on Toni's arm. Then she quickly took the gun from her hand as the woods exploded with armed troopers from the Connecticut State Police and a bunch of searchers with their dogs.

"Acquit!" Kate told Dillon, and he released Toni and moved back into hold position, daring her to move again. Sean appeared at her shoulder, and she handed him the gun. She called Dillon to heel as Sean read Tori her Miranda rights. Several other troopers worked on the wounded Judson Dunn.

Kate ran to Jordy, now as covered in mud as Quinn, the bear cub. Dillon licked his son and pawed at him, getting muddy himself. Rufus and Cathy appeared, running down the trail. Rufus scooped his son into his arms and hugged him as though he'd never let go. Cathy's arms circled them both, as she kissed their cheeks. Harry moved to stand next to Kate, with Liam at his side. Kate stared at him and saw the fear still in his eyes.

"Kate."

"I'm sorry. The only way I could think of to save Jordy was to distract her with the connection to her father. I suspected he hadn't told her."

"But she could have shot you."

"Not her. She's basically greedy. She knew I'd hidden the money where she'd never find it. She wouldn't shoot me until I showed her where. I only had to make her want to shoot her father. Once she turned away from Jordy, I used Dillon. I wasn't unarmed. Jordy's the one who saved the day by scaring her with the threat of a bear attack. Remind me to check the fence in the exercise yard. I think the soft ground allowed a puppy to go walkabout. Toni's father is lucky she's still a rotten shot."

"You're going to be the death of me," Harry muttered as he reached for her face and kissed her, hard.

"When are you two going to get married?" Agnes asked as she came up beside them, her greyhounds at her side.

Kate lifted her head but didn't let go of Harry. "Look who's talking. Let me ask you the same thing." She grinned back at Agnes.

CHAPTER THIRTY-FOUR

Kate sat with her eyes closed, vegging out in her desk chair. She'd spent the last two hours talking with every law enforcement official in two states. Lieutenant Garrison was delighted his case had wrapped up so easily. She told him she'd send him the photo of Toni Dunn with the gun, and he said he'd happily work a case with her any day. She'd talked to Lily, filling her in on how well the puppy was doing, how he saved the day and the lives of her and Jordy and then telling her about their further adventures with Toni Dunn. When Kate got to the part about her accomplice in both crimes turning out to be the father who'd deserted her as a child, Lily told her that she really couldn't make this stuff up. She rang off adding she'd see her at the National.

Hecate slept on her lap, and the recently washed and dried Sams, grandfather, father, and son, all lay asleep on the floor, in the patch of sunshine from the window. Cathy and Agnes had pitched in with the dog baths.

Kate had showered and changed, tossing everything she'd worn into the washer along with the dog towels.

Then Rufus and Cathy had left to go to the hotel where the judges would be staying. They planned on going to dinner before she checked in. This would be their first date, and Kate wished them well. She'd see Cathy tomorrow since she wasn't showing and could sit and chat. Kate hadn't entered the Friday show because she didn't like to exhibit under the originally scheduled judge. This meant she could go watch Cathy judge with no pressure. She was entered on Saturday with Shelagh to get in some ring practice before taking her to the National. She had passed on the Sunday show since the judge tended to put up only dogs shown by handlers no matter what came into the ring. Kate refused to waste her money. It gave her a chance to have a Sunday at home and maybe she and Harry could talk to Father Joe after Mass—or maybe not.

Kate sighed. She'd seen the fear in Harry's eyes after she stopped Toni. This would never be the calm marriage both her parents and grandparents had had. Maybe she should drive into the city next week. She hadn't been in New York for anything other than business since February. She remembered Aunt Maeve had handled some secret missions for MI-5 after she'd "retired" and married Padraig and lived in New York. Kate needed to find out how Maeve's marriage to Padraig lasted so many years when she put her life in danger?

She wished more than ever she still had her dad and

granddad. She'd been raised by two good men to believe she could do anything. They'd also taught her to have a strong belief in right and wrong. Every so often, though, she needed to hear their reassurances again.

Hecate's purr sounded like a motor in response to Kate's petting. The weight of the Maine Coon cat, though, was cutting off the circulation in her legs. Kate had stood to yield her chair to the big cat when she heard the kennel door open and Harry walked in. He took in at a glance the sea of white hair spread around the room and moved to the wing chair facing her desk. Kate sat again.

"Since Seamus picked up my car from the airport for me when we got back," he told her, "I'm going to take Rufus and Cathy with Jordy when I bring him back to school Sunday night. They'll fly home out of Logan."

"Okay."

"Sadie said it's going to take a while to check and make sure Miss Dunn didn't leave any surprises behind when she attacked our system."

"Right. Tom is running checks now with the K and K server."

"Um, Kate. This might take a while."

"Of course."

"So, since I'm going to Boston Sunday night, I was wondering if you'd like to go out to dinner and a movie on Saturday night."

"Go out? You mean go out on a date?"

"It's usually what they call it when you go to dinner and a movie on a Saturday night."

"A date as in one of the two dates left before we get married?"

"That's what I had in mind, leaving only one date which, if not sooner, I thought we could do while at the National."

"The Samoyed Club National? In Kentucky? You're going to the National?"

"Kate, I'm not letting you drive almost halfway across the country and stay for a week by yourself. Don't you want me to come?"

"Of course I want you to come, but I thought you were having second thoughts about marrying me."

"Never. You may scare the daylights out of me with your fearlessness, but you wouldn't be my Kate any other way. The Kate I love is the one in front of me, the intrepid, daring, venturesome, bold, audacious Kate." He smiled at her and her heart did a flip. "However, I do have some news that may scare even you. I called Father Joe a few minutes ago. He's had a cancellation. The couple scheduled for the weekend had to move their date up since they have a child on the way. So I asked him to hold it for us. If you agree, we'll be getting married at eleven o'clock in the morning on the Saturday following Thanksgiving. It doesn't leave too much time to get things ready since you're spending a week of that time at the National. Do you still want to marry me?"

Kate lifted the cat and stood, replacing her on the seat without Hecate even opening an eye. Then she walked around the desk. Harry rose from his chair to stand in front of her. She peered up into his fascinating green eyes, which now seemed somewhat worried. "Yes, Mr. Harry Foyle, I will marry you at eleven o'clock on the Saturday after Thanksgiving because I love you."

He let out his breath then smiled down at her and swept her into his arms. "I love you more," he whispered, resuming his seat and gathering her onto his lap. Then he kissed her in a way that took away any doubt.

NATIONAL SECURITY

A Kate Killoy Mystery

Book Three—Excerpt

"Kate, did you get the email from Krystyn Machnicki this morning?"

The sound of Kate's phone had interrupted her work. Though not quite eight o'clock Eastern Time, Cathy Harrison in Idaho was up even earlier. Kate hooked the handle of the pressure hose she'd been using to clean the runs in her boarding kennel on the chain link and headed for her office.

"I haven't checked my emails yet. Give me a moment to boot up my computer. Not to get off topic, but what are you doing up so early?"

"I'm bathing puppies. I've got new owners coming to pick up their puppies from my litter today."

Kate opened her emails and scanned down the list.

"Here it is. Give me a second to read it." She began to skim the email, stopped and then began again, reading more carefully.

Dear Fellow Members,

It is with regret I must state that the following members should not be elected to responsible positions on the Board of Directors of the club due to their unethical breeding practices. They are not worthy of holding positions where they might influence the decisions of the club. They are Natacha Grunsfeldt, Tracy Nikas, Cathy Harrison, and Sherman Wiel.

Krystyn Machnicki

"Is she nuts? What the hell is this? How could Krystyn accuse any of you of being unethical? It's ridiculous. Have you called her?"

"I did. She says she didn't send the email. Kate, she was crying. Apparently her phone has been ringing off the hook with people yelling at her. The email must have gone to the entire membership. Since this is the first year the club has used online voting as well as mail in ballots, many people have left it to the last minute. This email could affect the final vote. I don't understand how someone else could send an email from Krystyn, but she swears on the lives of all her puppies she didn't send it."

"Unfortunately, it's not hard for a hacker with talent to do this, and it can often be difficult to trace them. Let me talk to Harry and my brothers, and I'll call you back."

Kate quickly finished her morning routine in the

boarding kennel, checked on her dogs who were either playing or sleeping out in the exercise yard, and headed across the lawn to her grandparents' home, which also housed the offices of Killoy and Killoy Forensic Accountants. Her older brother Tom had moved into the house with Grandma Grace after their grandfather had died of cancer. When their father died of a brain aneurysm several months later, Tom assumed the responsibility of running the company.

She ran up the steps onto the porch and, instead of heading for the door to the house, she turned right toward the door for K and K. Nobody manned the reception desk yet, but Tom would already be hard at work in his office. The door lay open so she strolled right in and sat in one of the wing chairs facing his desk.

"Kate, what's up? Nothing wrong with Harry, is there? You're still getting married."

"Nope, everything's fine with us, and the wedding is still on. No, I got a call from Cathy this morning about something more in your or Harry's skill set than in mine. The membership of the Samoyed club received a nasty email casting aspersions on the ethics of four people running for board positions in the election happening now. The problem is, the person who sent the email swears she didn't do it. How hard is it to steal someone's email identity this way?"

"Not hard at all, if you have some talent as a hacker.

The problem lies in tracing it back to find who the hacker is. Sometimes you can't. It could be someone in another part of the country, or it could be her best friend who visits her home on a regular basis. I take it you haven't asked Harry about it yet?"

"No. He's in the air, flying back from Germany. He's due to land at Logan in a few hours then he's probably going to want to sleep for a while."

"After I saw what he did on this case, not only trapping the guy online but then chasing him across Europe, I'd say the guy deserves some sleep before you get him involved with this. Will can't help you since he's knee deep in classes trying to finish his degree while taking advanced work toward his Ph.D. Tim is spending every spare minute at basketball practice. Why don't you ask Seamus if he'd check into it? I'd do it, but I'm leaving in three hours for four days in Austin with a new client. Seamus might find it fun to do some searching for you. He's toying with the idea of working for Harry after college, and this might be good practice."

Kate thanked him and wished him a safe trip then went to visit her grandmother. Seamus wouldn't be home until later since he, along with his twin brother, Tim, was in his senior year in high school.

Though Kate had loved her father and grandfather dearly, she considered Grandma Grace God's gift to her sanity. Grace would sit and listen but never judge. She allowed her to talk out any problem without trying to tell her how to think. The best part was she cooked marvelously, so these discussion sessions always came accompanied by something delicious. This morning, a plate of sweet bread accompanied her cup of tea. Kate loved these long buns made from the same recipe Grace used for hot cross buns at Easter time, only without the dried fruit.

Kate asked Grace about all her activities, which included teaching knitting and crochet at the senior center. Then they discussed the wedding and the invitations, of which Grace had taken charge.

Grace, in her early seventies, appeared much younger and often seemed to have more energy than her grandchildren. She was horrified to hear about the email, especially since Cathy had been her guest last month. She warned Kate not to let Seamus get so caught up in her investigation he neglected his own life. They knew he wouldn't neglect his studies; definitely not his style. However, he didn't have an active social life. He swore his twin had gotten all the social genes of the pair when they were born. Kate knew better than to let him use working with her as an excuse to miss out on many of the activities of senior year. She had avoided all the high school activities in favor of showing dogs, and it had left her unprepared when confronting life and love. Luckily, she'd fallen for Harry, who understood and cherished her anyway.

On her way back to the kennel, Kate texted Cathy, telling her she'd have more information for her by the end of the day. Then she took Shelagh, Dillon's half-sister, a Liam daughter out of Kelly, out of the exercise yard and, slipping a show collar on her, she headed toward the barn to practice gaiting, stacking, waiting patiently, and coming to perfect four-square finishes when they moved. After a successful workout came their favorite part of the session—the games. Shelagh was lightning fast and deadly in all the games of catch and fetch. Her leaps rose even higher than Dillon's in an effort to catch the toy before it hit the floor. Ten minutes of one-on-one jumping, and racing around with toys to shake and throw up in the air, had her happy as a lark. So a smug bitch led Kate back to the exercise yard to brag to the others about how she had been spoiled.

Dillon and Quinn managed to take advantage of Shelagh going through the door to slip into the kennel. They followed Kate into her office where she had been working on the schedule for the fall search and rescue training dates. She decided to skip lunch since she'd pigged out on Grandma Grace's treats. Wrestling her chair from Hecate, her twenty-five pound Maine Coon cat, she opened her laptop.

When she clicked on mail, a flood of more than a hundred messages appeared, a complete firestorm of protest against the email from the morning. She started reading the angry replies and realized Krystyn had a serious problem. About thirty minutes into reading outraged responses, she scrolled down the list of emails until she came to some with another topic. Unfortunately, they were from her cousin Agnes.

As a former supermodel who had become a bank president, one might assume Agnes had become more staid and sober-minded. Not Agnes. She still was a lady on a mission, and her latest mission was Kate's wedding. When Harry and Kate announced they'd be getting married on the Saturday after Thanksgiving, Agnes freaked. She said one couldn't plan the catering much less a whole wedding in that amount of time.

Kate and Harry disagreed and, working around their schedules, got organized. They sat down and made of spreadsheet of those they'd invite to the wedding. Then they chose a design for the invitation, ordered rolls of stamps and, at her request, placed the invitation and reply job in the waiting hands of Grandma Grace.

Kate's brother Will had claimed the job of running the catering. He knew what they liked, happened to be a top chef himself—though his career focus fell in math—and had contacts who would make everything work smoothly.

One of the dogs Kate had trained last year belonged to the owner of the town's only florist. When Dina heard about the wedding, she insisted on doing the flowers. In five minutes, she'd discovered what Kate liked and had all the floral plans completed.

Attendants didn't pose a problem. Agnes would be

her maid of honor. Cathy and Harry's sister Sarah would be bridesmaids. Rufus, Harry's best friend, would be Harry's best man, the twins, Seamus and Tim, would be groomsmen, and Tom would give her away. Kate insisted Agnes, Cathy, and Sarah work together deciding what to wear in the way of bridesmaid dresses since she'd only be looking at Harry that day.

All that remained was the bridal gown. Kate knew the six emails from Agnes, aka Her Highness, would all contain photos of gowns from the top designers in the world, all of whom she'd modeled for over the years. Agnes had told Kate she could have her choice of any one of them. These dresses, though all gorgeous, weren't her. Kate had been resisting the suggestions and so far simply putting her off.

Kate didn't quite know what she wanted, but she thought it should be something reflecting her style. She'd had an idea flitting around in her brain the last couple of days and decided since she didn't have anything pressing at the moment, she'd steal some time to play with it. She pulled up her design program, chose her measurements from the files, and began to play with a possible design for a wedding dress.

Since the weather would be colder by Thanksgiving, she decided it should have long sleeves tapering to a point at the wrist. The fitted bodice would extend up from a natural waistline to meet a scooped yoke of knitted lace that would rise to just below the chin. In the back, the lace yoke would descend in a V to the mid-back where a knitted lace rose would attach a train to more of the knitted lace, falling gently to the floor with an additional foot and a half to create a train. The skirt would drop straight to the floor in front but the back would be divided into six gores to give fullness for dancing. Harry was a wonderful dancer. While she tweaked the hemline, her attention was jerked from her fantasy creation by the sound of her phone buzzing in her pocket. She noticed it was Harry. She quickly saved the design and answered the call.

"Hi, love. How's my bride-to-be?"

"She's probably a lot less tired than her groom-to-be. How was your flight? Did you get everything finished up in Munich?"

"It's all done. The police have the man in jail, and the client is delighted. I'm in a taxi and on my way home from the airport. I'll do laundry, take a nap, and pack for next week, so I should be on your doorstep by eight-thirty or nine."

"Wonderful, if you're not too tired to drive here. In fact, there are some questions about hacking I need to ask when you get here. A problem's come up with one of my friends. You go get some rest now and I'll see you later. I love you."

"Love you more."

The connection ended, and Kate checked her incoming emails again only to find a posting from the Samoyed club president.

Notice to all members.

It has come to our *attention an email has been sent to the membership supposedly from Krystyn Machnicki. It* was *not. This is a case of identity theft where someone purporting to be Krystyn sent out the email without her knowledge. We will be setting up an investigation. In the meantime, please do not encourage this malicious act by believing the contents or source of the email.*

Robert Bicknell, President

Kate's phone rang again. Cathy.

"Hey there. Did you see Bob's email calling off the dogs, so to speak?"

"Hopefully it works. Krystyn is a basket case. She called to say she would be taking her phone off the hook, turning off her computer, and locking herself and her dogs in the house. Her husband is away on business, and she's alone. I've got my kennel help coming here in an hour, and a couple of us from the local club are going over to her place to give her some support. I texted her so she'll know we're coming."

"Well, Harry will get here later this evening, and I'll tell him the problem. Maybe he'll know how to find this person and stop him or her."

Kate had hung up and was about to take a tea break when the intercom buzzed. Ellen wanted her in the design studio, now. Kate, knowing she could get tea up there, headed across to the barn and up the stairs to her studio on the second floor. As she entered, she saw Ellen Martin wasn't in her manager's office but rather sitting at the computer Kate usually used on the work floor. Nobody was knitting. All the women gathered around Ellen, talking in hushed tones. As Kate walked in, they all stopped and stared at her. Startled, she asked, "What's up. Is there a problem?"

"Everything is fine, Kate. In fact, everything is perfect," Ellen said, and the women all smiled.

Kate walked around so she could see what had everyone's attention, and there on the oversized monitor was the dress she'd been playing with earlier. She'd been distracted when the phone rang and saved it automatically to her design files. Ellen must have thought it something new for the upcoming fashion show and opened it to begin planning what the design would need in yardage per size and color.

"Oh," Kate said. "I was only playing around with an idea. I didn't mean to send it over here. It's rebellion against Agnes sending me so many pictures of these over the top dresses which aren't me, and I fiddled around trying to come up with an idea of what might be more my style."

"Oh my God, Kate, it's perfect," Ellen whispered. "We have to make it. I can have the yarn here by Monday, and Anna has only this week passed her test on the new lace machine. I think an ultrafine merino on the fine-gauge machine which just arrived will make a fabric which flows. You will be the most beautiful bride in the world."

"But I leave on Saturday for the National. That's in two days,"

"No problem. You'll only be gone a week. We can fit it to you when you get back. This is going to be our chance to be part of this wedding everyone else is involved in. Please, Kate, let us do this for you."

Kate felt tears filling her eyes and so choked up she couldn't say anything. She reached out to hug each of these wonderful women, nodded at Ellen, and before she started crying, quickly headed out and back to the dogs.

Kate knew she needed work to get her emotions back under control. She had just begun getting the dinner bowls filled for the boarding dogs when her phone buzzed. It was Cathy again.

"Hi," she said, "how's Krystyn?"

"Kate, Krystyn's dead."

A NOTE FROM PEGGY

I hope you enjoyed *Puppy Pursuit*. If you liked this book, the best way you can say so is to leave a review on Amazon, whether you bought it there or not. Reviews tell authors what you liked or didn't. If you want to see more of a character, put it in the review. If there is a mistake in my math, let me confess in advance I wasn't the math genius in the family and remind you this is fiction folks.

After more than forty-eight years in the world of the Samoyed, I've got lots of stories to tell. I hope you enjoy them. I look forward to bringing you *National Security* which not only will feature Dillon, his son Quinn, and his half sister Shelagh but also his father Liam, there's life in the old boy yet.

In this next book, you will join Kate and Harry when they next go off to Kentucky. They will be at the Samoyed National and will be involved in fighting not

CPSIA information can be obtained
at www.ICGtesting.com
Printed in the USA
BVHW081953310322
632889BV00007B/1939

only to stay secure themselves but to save the country.

For those who have never been to a National Dog Show for a breed, picture a family reunion with relatives you love, ones you avoid and ones you absolutely can't stand. Then imagine about six hundred of them together in one place for a week. Finally, attached a dog which looks like yours to the other end of the lead each of these people is holding and make it their goal to beat your dog.

Of course, with Kate and Harry in attendance, murder and mayhem will be added to the mix. Visit the website: www.peggygaffney.com to find when *National Security* will be coming out.

Happy reading,

Peggy Gaffney